NO BROKEN BOND

SECRETS OF STONE: BOOK SEVEN

ANGEL PAYNE & VICTORIA BLUE

NO BROKEN BOND

SECRETS OF STONE: BOOK SEVEN

ANGEL PAYNE & VICTORIA BLUE

WATERHOUSE PRESS

For the platinum bond in my life—
the glue who keeps me together

I couldn't do this without you,
my Thomas. Thank you.

Very special thanks to Victoria,
who sees me at my worst and loves me anyway!

—Angel

This one is for our dedicated readers who've
stuck with us while we walked through our
professional field of dreams. Finally!
The completion of our trio's story.

—Victoria

CHAPTER ONE

Drake

"I'll bet my money on the bobtail nag, somebody bet on the bay."

My best friend had officially lost his damn mind.

I groaned at Fletcher, who ignored me and kept bellowing the well-worn lyrics as we plodded on horseback through the tall grass of a wide Wyoming meadow. The bastard answered my agony with a wink, a grin, and more ear-piercing singing, encouraged by Talia's laughter. She threw back her head, tumbling waves of dark silky hair down her spine from under her straw cowboy hat.

Holy hell.

Who knew the woman could get sexier than she already was? But yeah, sitting astride my favorite childhood mare sure worked that magic.

Still didn't take the place of the previous night. When she'd been straddling other things. Well, one other thing. Me. While I'd caressed her perfect tits and—

"Drake!"

I snapped my head in Fletcher's direction. Judging by the look on his face, he'd called my name several times before mentally teleporting me back to the meadow. But the escape had been fun. For a few seconds, I'd been back in my adolescent bedroom at the house, during the hours from last night when the three of us had replaced innocent childhood memories with forbidden, naughty ones. What Fletch, Talia, and I had done was a hell of a lot better than jacking off to fantasies about the varsity cheerleaders from high school, that was for damn certain.

"What?" It was more a bark than an answer, but that was what Fletch got for interrupting my stroll down memory lane. Of course, neither he nor Talia missed the glazed look in my eyes, probably making me seem like the chocolate-smeared kid caught with his hand in the cookie jar. Yep. Sounded about right.

"Where do you want to have lunch?" Fletcher's eyes twinkled with mischief, matching my wider smirk. Have lunch. Ha. Read—Let's take turns making a meal of our amazing girl too. Preferably before, during, and after enjoying the picnic Mom had insisted on packing in our saddle bags.

The meadow waved softly around us, filling the air with the seductive whispers of the earth. The breeze swept through the wildflowers and wheat grass, scenting everything with a perfect combination of fresh sweetness and newly turned soil from the distant field Dad had plowed yesterday.

In that moment, it hit me.

Fuck, how I'd missed this.

Growing up in rural Wyoming, a guy took nuances like the wind in the grass for granted. Though my overprivileged eyes had been opened a lot during an infernal tour in the Middle East with the United States Marine Corps, it had taken Talia and Fletcher and the love they'd brought to my life, to make me view all of this with truly new sight. It was sheer natural beauty as far as the eye could see, and I was honored to share it with the two people I loved more with every passing day.

This. Right here.

This is what it's all about.

How was our girl always saying it? Building our foundation. I understood that now more than ever. Every proverbial brick we laid, every experience we shared, cemented our hearts—our very souls—tighter to one another.

"This should be perfect." I gently pulled on the reins, halting Sinbad under the canopy created by the full foliage of an old crab apple tree. The blossoms, dropped to the ground, had been replaced by young green bundles of leaves.

Fletcher halted his slightly taller horse, Marty, next to mine. We quickly dismounted and then turned the animals into the meadow, allowing them to graze while we had lunch.

Talia popped her feet out of the stirrups, swung her right leg over Gracie's back end, and slid down to the ground. She was already a natural with the mare, causing pride to swell in my chest. There wasn't a single thing the woman couldn't take on and master.

Including the two of us.

"Your mom really is amazing for packing all this food for us." Her voice drifted on the light wind. "So...unexpected."

Fletcher frowned. "Why unexpected?"

"Well, considering what my own mother is like—do I really need to say more?"

I scowled because she had a valid point. Too fucking valid. After she'd finally confronted her parents about our unconventional relationship, tacking on an ultimatum to them—accept us or lose her to us—they'd been anything but warm and fuzzy about things.

Not that "us" was the most conventional idea to thrust

on a family. Admittedly, I'd even worried about bringing Talia here, to meet Mom, Dad, and Lizzy. Okay, so I'd hinted to Dad for years about my tastes in the bedroom, though I was damn sure he had a strong Dominant nature like me. I'd banked on that instinct a few times, floating out the idea of sharing a woman, just to see if he'd grab the bait. More often than not, his reaction was a deep chuckle and a slow shake of his head. I guessed he'd chalked it all up to me being young, rich, and horny. A phase, passing like any other.

So...the nerves had been high about this trip.

And couldn't have been more idiotic or unfounded.

All three of them had surprised me in the best ways possible. It helped that Fletch was already a part of the family, but any strangeness around Talia simply never materialized. They embraced her with the warmth and understanding I'd dreamed they would, folding her into the fabric of our family without a second thought. I smiled a little, recalling the morning I'd watched from the breakfast nook in the kitchen as she'd helped scramble eggs and turn bacon, sandwiched between Mom and Lizzy as if she'd always belonged there. They'd chatted away about the latest episode of a mutually favorite show, oblivious to what was happening in the heart of the guy a few feet behind them. That morning, my adoration for my family had grown tenfold.

"Do you want turkey or ham?" Talia's question jerked me back once again. Perched prettily in the middle of the picnic blanket, she held up two neatly wrapped squares, weighing them in her hands.

"I'll have the ham."

I reached across the flannel blanket. Fletcher's long arm blocked my reward.

"Hey! I wanted that one."

I muscled him out of the way, grabbing the sandwich. "Unfortunate she asked me first, isn't it?"

I was being smug, fully preparing to give him the thing, but that was before a peach came flying from his side of the blanket. Talia's laughter, sweet as the birdsong from the trees, accompanied my quick defense against the fruit bomb. "Dude," I snapped, quickly flicking a wrist. "Really?"

Fletcher chuckled hard.

I narrowed a sardonic glare. "You really want to find out how cold the spring is this time of year?"

"I'd like to see you try, big man." His bright-blue eyes reflected the sun, making them look like the Caribbean instead of the usual wintery Lake Michigan. Ranch life agreed with us all, making things looser, easier. That included the brotherly bond with my best friend—as well as our tendency to rib and torture one another.

"Boys," Talia finally chided. "That's enough. Fletcher, if you really don't want the turkey, you can have my egg salad."

His wrinkled-faced reaction to that offer was priceless. Fletcher felt about egg salad the same way as I did about lima beans.

"Okaaaay." Talia giggled, assessing his grimace. "Or not."

When she laughed again, the sound started pulsing through my bloodstream...and swelling in my crotch.

"Turkey is fine, love. In fact, I was just thinking how hungry I was for a turkey sandwich."

"Oh, jeez." Her eyes sparkled in the sunlight. Her smile was barely concealed as she attempted a stern façade.

"What?" Fletch teased.

"You are so full of it, Mr. Ford."

I grunted around the bite of sandwich filling my mouth. "Don't poke the bear before he eats his lunch, Tolly."

She nodded quickly, handing over his sandwich. Fletcher was the definition of gregarious, easygoing, and lighthearted, until he was hungry. Then the world saw a whole new version of cranky—and she knew it too.

After devouring the sandwiches, along with fruit, cheese, pasta salad, and some killer brownies for dessert, we spent the afternoon being lazy under the apple tree. The horses trotted through the tall grass, entwining their long necks and enjoying their freedom from the stable. Talia lay between Fletch and me on the blanket, switching direction occasionally so we both had a chance to taste the sunlight on her lips...and caress its warmth in her skin. Fuck, she felt good—and tasted even better. Mom had also packed us some sparkling apple drink, which blended with Tolly's chemistry in some magical way, turning her lips into a damn ambrosia.

I'd sure as fuck experienced hell before—and this was its polar opposite. Heaven. Paradise. Nirvana. Elysium. Rhapsody. Dreamland. Fairyville. Who the fuck cared? I only knew I never wanted to leave. I'd never have a friend like Fletcher again—and Talia Perizkova was everything I'd ever wanted. She was my drug, my oxygen, my addiction, my strength, my weakness...anything corny I could come up with and likely a few more beyond that.

She had quickly become my everything.

No.

They had quickly become my everything.

"What is it, baby?" I issued the quiet question in response to one of her sighs, heavier than the others.

"I don't want to go home tomorrow." She lifted her head

from Fletcher's chest, reaching for the hand with which I'd been stroking her hair.

"I was just thinking the same thing." Unbelievably, Fletch's cocky grin disappeared for a moment.

His statement came as no surprise. The two of them were connected in a way I couldn't fathom—a link that would've probably freaked me out if it were any other pair. But watching them and seeing their pieces fit like that...only made my heart more full. I'd never cared for two people more in this world. Fletch's bond with Tolly made as little sense—and as much sense—as the one I shared with him.

"We can come back anytime you want, love." I stroked fingertips over her knuckles. "You've successfully wrapped every Newland you've met around your pretty little finger."

The edges of her lips twitched. "Which one?" She playfully wiggled her pinky. "This one?"

I quickly closed my hand around her wrist. "This very one." Without hesitation, I sucked that cute digit deep into my mouth and then watched intently as her eyes grew wide... then glassy. Our girl approached her feelings as honestly and fearlessly as she did everything else, making it fun as hell to seduce her. Figuring out the different ways she could get aroused was one of my new favorite pastimes.

"What about this one?" She wiggled the pinky on her other hand, calculated mischief across her face. She knew what would likely happen—and she was right—only Fletcher caught her gist and ran with it this time, grabbing her hand and repeating my gesture. Again, I sucked in her flesh too. We watched each other please our girl, turning the simple act into an erotic moment.

Or maybe it wasn't our doing at all. Maybe it was the way

Talia let her head drop back on her shoulders, chestnut hair cascading down, soon brushing her perfect ass as she circled around and straddled Fletch. I moved with her, sitting up. No way was I letting her out of my grasp.

"You're playing with fire, young lady." My voice dropped to a deeper register, teasing all the right places in her senses. I knew it as clearly as I knew I breathed.

Talia glanced back at me, gaze ignited with desire. She liked this. Very much.

So did I.

Very much.

Fletcher groaned as she circled her hips atop his. I wasn't going to confirm, but damn good chance the guy was already swollen and stiff. I was sure as hell halfway there myself.

"What else is new with this one?" he managed in a growl.

"True, brother," I murmured. "Very true."

Talia pouted. "You can't blame me. The two of you have awakened a she-monster. I lay the blame solely at your four gorgeous feet."

I let a deep sound rumble from my chest. "Baby...are you suggesting we're the ones to be punished?" I carried the snarl through in the syllables, once more knowing how she'd respond. How she craved my dominance...

"Well." She huffed. "I think it's entirely possible you need...to be...reprimanded." Now, not so much of a huff. Her strong start faded as soon as her gaze confronted my stare. Her last word was just a whisper.

I stiffened my composure. "Really?"

Her gaze dropped. "No, Sir," she rasped.

Holy. God.

My cock strained against the denim of my jeans. No.

Screw that. The fucker pounded at my zipper—and I showed her so by rising, rubbing at the prominent bulge in my crotch.

"Do you have any god damn idea what you do to me, Natalia?"

She darted her gaze up. Let out a sharp gasp before plunging it back to her lap. "Y-Yes?"

"Is that a question?" I leaned in close. She was still sitting on Fletcher, who swallowed hard. I pressed in yet again, until I could feel her breathy exhalations.

"N-Not really. But...I was thinking..."

I wrapped a hand in her thick hair, just at the base of her skull, before tugging her head back. "Don't play shy with me, Tolly. I've learned you're far from it. Tell me what you want, woman. You know it's yours. You know we're yours."

She looked directly at me. The afternoon sun shone into her eyes, making them sparkle like chocolate diamonds. "I-I thought...maybe if you showed me...I would know for sure."

Fletcher chuckled crazily. He pushed to a sitting position, getting more intimately involved in the conversation. With that one movement, shifting himself into Tolly's personal space, he sent a gorgeous shudder through her body. Damn. Damn. She was wearing poured-on jeans and some kind of a fluffy cotton top, ending up like a sexy Daisy Mae. I suddenly, really wanted to change my name to Li'l Abner.

"Fuck." Fletch addressed me but didn't veer his gaze from her. "This innocent shit...it's really hot. I'm not gonna lie, man."

"I have an idea." Abruptly, I let go of her hair. I rose, walking over to the saddle bags I'd pulled off Marty before the picnic. Anticipating—hoping?—we'd have this opportunity during the ride, I'd stowed a few extra supplies in the pack.

I pulled the Ziploc bag out of the pack, shielding it from

her view. "Take off your pants, Natalia," I instructed. "Then sit back on Fletcher, just the way you are now."

Her answering stare was priceless. I was tempted to yank out my phone and snap a picture, but doing that, right now? Hammer on a seashell, anyone? I was already pushing her. Besides, I had a damn good memory—especially now, because it danced with so many memories of her different facial expressions. This one, a mixture of "are you serious?" and "I can't wait to see where this is leading," was one of my favorites. Her curiosity would forever be one of her most endearing, fascinating qualities to me—probably because there was so little in life I could be that way about now. It was second only to the bravery and ferocity with which she tackled the items of that curiosity.

"Drake?" Her voice was a whisper.

"Yes?" Mine was a snap.

"What if...well, what if...someone comes by? I'd be mortified."

Her eyes were thick with a plea. She was truly concerned about being discovered. I flashed a glance to Fletch. Her disconcertment was no more a surprise to him than it was to me. I dipped a fast nod, nonverbally asking for his unique touch with the situation.

"Tolly," he said in a soothing voice. "Look at me." As soon as she did, he posed, "Would either of us ever put you in harm's way?"

"No." Her lips twisted. "No, of course not. But—"

"Would either of us ever want anyone else to see what is ours and ours alone?" My own voice was anything but soothing.

She bit her lower lip before responding to it equally. "No, Drake."

I chose silence as my rejoinder for that. If she was still hesitant in another minute, then I'd—

Shit.

She'd worked through the hesitance.

Fletcher and I watched, enraptured, as she opened the button on her jeans and slowly pulled the zipper down. Tucking her thumbs into the sides of the waistband, she wiggled the denim over her trim hips and thighs before stepping out gracefully. Neither of us missed her sassy little bend from the waist to pick up the discarded pants, giving us a full view of her perfectly peachy ass, white lacy thong sinking into the center.

And that officially did it. My dick and the term "stranglehold" became new best friends.

"Panties too, sugar. Very nice. Now, back to Fletch, baby." I offered my hand to steady her but also as a gentle reminder that I'd keep her safe, despite demanding her compliance with this scary, uncomfortable scene.

Because, deep down inside, part of her liked the scary. And the uncomfortable.

And the knowledge that Fletch and I would always keep her safe.

Fletcher, now naked himself, raised his ocean-blue eyes to watch her straddle him again. He sucked in a breath as she slid her glistening pussy over his stiff cock. I bunched up one of the picnic blankets next to his shoulder and then kneeled, resting on my heels to get comfortable. If things went as planned, I'd be at this vantage point for a while.

As soon as I settled in, Talia gazed at me. Her eyes, still as magical as the pond but emulating its depths instead of its shallows, regarded me with open trust and love. Would I ever be able to meet that gaze and not feel the bottom of my fucking gut drop out? Did I ever want to find out?

She visibly swallowed—tempted to say something but pushing the words down. Waiting on me. Waiting to pleasure us.

"Does his cock feel good between your pussy lips, baby?"

"Yes," she answered at once. "Always." Talia closed her eyes and rocked her hips, dragging her pussy along the length of Fletch's erection.

"Is she wet, man?" My voice was gritty with arousal. Watching them grind on each other was torture and ecstasy at the same time.

"God, yes," Fletcher groaned. "Wet and creamy and—" He braced his hands on her waist, easing her pace. "Slow down, babe. I'll come before this jackass makes his point."

"Screw you."

"Can she?"

"Please?" Talia added, nearly hissing it.

I folded my arms. Leveled a steady, commanding stare. "You may keep moving back and forth on him, Natalia—but don't let him inside that heaven just yet."

They shot me evil glares. I softly chuckled.

"Oh, don't worry. You'll both thank me in a few minutes. Perhaps even scream about it."

"Shut. Up," Fletch gritted.

"Drake, please!"

"Patience. I have a great idea. Trust me."

"That's what you always say." Talia's voice was full of breath and impatience, like smoky fingers gripping my cock.

I took a few seconds to rub my hard-on through the denim of my jeans. My beauty's gaze traveled to the juncture of my thighs. For a moment, she stilled—captivated with watching me grip myself.

Reaching forward, I wrapped my rough fingers around her neck and waited for her stare to return to mine. Her eyes grew impossibly wide. A tense swallow worked down her throat.

"Have I disappointed you yet?"

"No. Never." Quiet words, close to a whisper, escaped.

"Then?"

I kissed her swiftly, still holding her in place, a careful distraction so I could slip the travel-sized lube bottle out from my back pocket. I lingered long enough to let Fletcher see the action, hoping he climbed on board with my plan. I was confident he would. He and I had privately talked about our fantasies of fucking her ass, and this was the perfect time for setting the plan into action.

When I released her from the kiss, I moved so I was sitting outside Fletcher's knees. From here, I could reach her ass and pussy perfectly.

"Let me taste you." Fletcher took over, rising to thread through her hair with one hand while bracketing her jaw with the other. Their mouths collided in a full, hot, consuming kiss. Fletch snarled. Talia moaned. Her body quivered as if electrified, and she began grinding harder in his lap. As they continued nipping at each other with lips and tongues, her needy clit worked up and down his board-straight cock.

Perfect.

I didn't waste another second in taking advantage of her preoccupation with Fletcher. Quietly, I slathered my index and middle finger with a generous amount of lube—and then slid my hand down the crack of her ass. Fortunately, Fletcher's cock was pushed up in front, so I had a stunning view of the woman's amazing ass. It was shaped like an inverted heart, the light-pink globes parted to reveal the wicked rosette at their middle. Just beneath, I was treated to a peek of her glistening pussy.

Fucking paradise.

Fletch leaned back, inch by inch, taking Talia with him. Not once did he break the heated contact of their drugging kiss—making her legs widen in order to stay with him. I damn near groaned. Her ass was even more perfect, angled higher toward me.

Hell, we made an amazing team. This, right here, was why Fletcher Ford and I would never be complete without one another. We worked as one silent, syncopated unit with one singular goal in mind—driving our girl to the edge of ecstasy. Once we'd done that, we'd hold her there and then catch her when we finally let her tumble over.

The breeze kicked up, sifting through the grass, carrying Talia's tangy arousal heavier through my nose. I put a little more lube on my fingers, returning to the opening at her behind—dipping in more this time.

Slipping my touch beyond her tight entrance.

She started.

I pushed.

She stiffened.

I pushed again.

"Relax, honey." Fletcher began soothing her with his whispered praise and encouraging touch. "He won't do anything you can't handle. Concentrate on me for now. Listen to me. Listen to my mind, baby."

Yeah, he'd really said that with a straight face—because it was true. The two of them spoke without words, a connection most would find unnerving. Like ESP but different. They'd tried explaining it to me once. They said they could just feel each other on a level separate from anyone else, even me. I loved them both too much to let it bother me, knowing I got them both on other unique levels. The love. That was the most important thing. It forged our relationship into an unbreakable bond.

Talia's sagging shoulders let me know she was more relaxed as Fletcher kept crooning into her ear and drawing lazy circles around her nipples, now tight and protruding through her bra and top. Her eyes were closed. A dreamy smile spread across her lips. She was a picture of total contentment.

I went in again.

Slowly, I pressed my index finger into her anus. Deeper now. Deeper. Fuck. She was so beautiful and tight. Her eyebrows drew together slightly but eased off when Fletcher leaned forward, quickly unbuttoning her top so he could replace his finger with his tongue on her nipple.

"Not all bad, is it?" I spoke as gently as I could.

She shook her head marginally.

"Words, Natalia."

"No. It's not that bad."

Now, I could practically read her mind. Her thoughts always changed the gorgeous angles of her face, betraying the war inside—what she truly felt versus what she thought she should feel. I almost grunted. We'd been down this road a thousand times.

"Good girl," I murmured instead. "Thank you for being honest with yourself and with me."

When she smiled from the praise, my heart swelled—along with my cock. This woman would be my undoing. Maybe she already was.

"How about some more?" I leaned closer, inhaling the wind in her hair, and then burrowing in to kiss her shoulder as soon as Fletch pushed her blouse all the way off. She tasted so good. She felt even better, all soft sleek curves and breathtaking obedience. I tightened my jaw, resisted the urge to just pump my fingers into her. It wouldn't do us any good to give her a bad first experience. But the animal inside fought me harder by the second. Fletcher and I had been with so many women—had done so many unmentionable things to those women—but Natalia Perizkova was different. So fucking different. Our precious gift, to care for and treasure. How had we earned this? How did we deserve her? It still felt so...fragile.

Stupid. Paranoid.

I knew I was letting the nagging of my gut chip away at the knowledge in my heart, but the marine in me wouldn't let that reminder go.

It could all be ripped away in a second. Treasure every god damn moment.

I began right now. With a determined dip of my head, I licked a path upward from her shoulder, over her slender neck, to the hollow below her ear and back again. As I reached the most sensitive part of her neck, I slid my finger in by another significant length. Talia shuddered. I persisted, feeling how she began to embrace the pleasure along with her discomfort. Going slow would keep the experience positive in her mind.

Fletcher continued to toy with her firm breasts, both nipples glistening from his attention now. They were incredible, dark and erect from her arousal.

Finally, my knuckle hit her ass cheek. I cheered inside. She was one step closer to the bliss.

I slid my finger all the way out and then back in. There

was a little friction with the movement. Her inhalation broke the air. I quickly assessed her face, her pulse, the tension in her body. All conveyed pleasure, though to be sure, I insisted she put it into words.

"Talk to me, baby. How does that feel?"

She gulped deeply. "It's...it's nice."

"Nice? How?"

"Better than I thought," she admitted.

"Is that good?" Fletch chuckled as he leaned back, fully taking in her face.

She nodded but quickly added more when I made a sound low in my throat. "I-I mean, yes." A flush took over her face. "It's embarrassing to say it—but, yes, it feels good."

"Why would you be embarrassed to feel good? Our sole purpose in life is to bring you pleasure. What about that don't you understand?"

The challenge erupted harsher than I intended, prompting her to reply with quick defensiveness. "It just—it seems like it shouldn't feel good to have something...there."

"Something where?" Fletcher prodded.

"In my—" She huffed through her nose. "You know...in my...you know."

"You can say it, Natalia. Ass. It's sexy as hell, baby. The word and the ass itself." I caressed a smile into my voice as I slid my finger out from between her globes, long enough to grab the fleshy cheeks in my hands. I squeezed her with deliberate roughness. "You have a beautiful, sexy-as-sin body. It's made to be enjoyed. To please us and for us to please. There isn't a single thing wrong with what we do when we're together."

She broke into a smile while staring at me over her shoulder. Her gaze was thick now, with entrancing eddies of heat, lust, adoration, love. Filled with possessive need, I dug my fingers harder into her flesh, until her lips parted and the pain became too much. And yeah, I liked watching that too. Loved the knowledge that she'd let us take her to the edge of her limits...and reward her well for doing so.

She moaned again. I growled in return, right before adding my index and middle finger to the penetration of her ass. They glided in easily, as she was more than aroused from my rough handling and hadn't had time to tense up.

"Good, baby. So good," I praised. "Just wait until Fletcher gets to work too."

Her moan changed into a groan as she turned around and buried her face in Fletcher's neck. I kept up the thrusts, slowly pumping my fingers in and out of her ass. The sight of it was mesmerizing, knowing I touched her as no man ever had before. A bit more lube made everything good and slick—and transformed my cock into a fucking ramrod.

Finally, I forced myself to meet my best friend's stare over her shoulder. Fletcher's gaze was as wide and intense as fresh-cut lapis, especially when I gave him the nod of approval. If he took it slowly, our girl was ready to let him fuck her ass.

She was a naturally giving woman. Her body was compliant with her will as soon as she gave herself over to it—but that final step was always our biggest challenge. With patience and a little command, I'd moved her past the step this time. Her body got it. Pleasure could be had with anal stimulation. Now, if her mind stayed out of the way, she'd enjoy herself.

Screw that. She'd be in heaven.

If we could stay the course...

"Tolly?"

Fletcher's rasp was answered by a muffled squeak from

the crook of his neck. It was adorable and sexy wrapped up in the same sound.

"Will you help me?"

Clever bastard. This was the advantage of having that direct connection to her mind. If I paid attention closely enough, I learned from his actions. He knew she couldn't say no to helping either one of us.

"Help...you?" She scooted back a couple of inches. Though she still straddled him, his erection bounced free between them. Fletch's face was stiff with stress, but he managed to pick up the lube from the blanket and hand it to her.

"This will work a lot easier if we use some of this."

"Oh, babe." She tsked at him, a look of cute confusion on her face. "I'm really ready. We won't need this."

"Tolly." He stroked his cock, the pain on his face joined by a hint of amusement. "This isn't going in your pussy today, baby."

He lifted a tawny brow. Then waited. And waited.

As soon as the puzzle pieces snapped into place, her small mouth fell open. Fletch and I chomped back chuckles as she jerked and gasped, snapping the whole top half of her body toward me. "What the hell?"

"Natalia."

"Uh-uh. I can't—do I—?" She let out a husky huff. "Really? Do I have to?"

I brushed another kiss across her shoulder. "Of course not. You never have to do anything you don't want to do. You know that." I looked up, emitting sultry heat with my eyes. "But we'd really like you to try."

She shot back a glower before quickly turning back to Fletcher. She'd heard my disappointment—but felt his.

A few moments passed.

Still. Weirdly windless.

The stream gurgled in the distance. Marty whinnied as he nuzzled the ground, looking for a fallen crab apple blossom.

Talia sighed loudly and reached for the bottle on the blanket, but Fletcher's long fingers wrapped around hers, stopping her.

"I won't force you to do something you're not ready for."

She snorted. "Shut up. I'm ready."

"Are you sure, baby?" I had to say something—although my cock was ready to go rogue if I did so again.

Resignation washed over her elegant, exquisite face. "I love the two of you so much," she confessed. "And you always make me feel so good...better than I always imagine, even when I try picturing things you suggest. I-I trust you. That's what we have."

She took my free hand with one of hers. Scooped one of Fletcher's with the others. We were joined, a triad of solid strength. "I trust you two to care for me. To take care of me. To always have my best interests in the forefront of your thoughts. That's what I give to you—and in return, I care that way for you. We made those promises to one another, remember?" She emphasized it by pulling in a long, deep breath. "So, if this is something the two of you want, I have to trust that I will want it too." She met my gaze fully now. "And I will admit, that with your fingers...back there—"

"In your ass, Natalia. You can say it."

"Yes. Fine. In my ass. There? Happy?" Her eyes danced with mischief as she plunged on. "It did feel good. Really good."

I angled over, smoothing a hand over both her gorgeous globes and then across the slicked aperture at their center.

"And it makes me feel very good to hear that."

She nodded and then turned back, eyeing Fletcher's erection. "So...how this is going to work?" She sucked in another breath. "I trust you. I do. Hopefully, I haven't killed the mood...?"

"I'm not seeing a problem." Fletch gripped his cock, still swollen like a bachelorette party favor.

"Well." She let out a husky giggle. "It's always like that, I think."

"Only when you're around, sugar. Only. You."

"Fletcher."

He cut her off by grabbing her by the nape and then swallowing her yelp with a searing, devouring kiss. The embrace was more aggressive than Fletch's usual style, but our girl didn't seem to mind. Before he even let her go, she reached between their bodies to stroke his cock. The sight elicited a moan from my throat. Fuck, that was hot. The sight of her hand wrapped around his dick, slender feminine fingers clutching tightly, painted fingernails meeting each other on the far side...

Incredible.

Perfect.

My cock throbbed in my jeans, begging me for escape—and to be clutched in that exact way.

After Fletcher set her mouth free, her lips twisted into a pout. "Ummmm...can't we just put this in me first? Get it wet that way?"

Fletcher and I shared another silent laugh. The query was downright bold for our woman, who'd been so guileless from the first moment we'd all met. To the rest of the world, she was still very much an elegant lady—but at times like this, we celebrated how far her dirty talk had come.

"Not a bad idea," Fletcher ensured. "Of course, getting inside you in any way always sounds like a great idea."

He'd barely finished speaking before she'd aligned his cock at her entrance, preparing to take him into her pussy.

"Oh, God, yes!" She feverishly rode up and down on his shaft—seemingly in a race for the finish line now. For several seconds, all I could do was watch. Her bold moves were so fucking beautiful...

Thankfully, I shook myself out of it. In a flash, I realized exactly what she was doing.

And exactly what was required to stop her.

I reached out, putting full reverse thrusters on her by grabbing a handful of her hair. At once, she stilled.

Fletcher glared daggers over her shoulder at me. I scowled back. Yeah, fuck you too. He'd fallen just as deep into the minx's little trap. In a minute, the bastard would be thanking me.

"I'm on to you, Natalia." I pressed my chest against her back, rumbling directly into her ear.

Her eyes popped wide. "Wh-What?"

"Do you think if he spends himself inside your cunt, no one will take your ass today?"

"N-No. I-I didn't—"

"Nice try, Tolly." Fletcher's aqua-blue eyes twinkled in the afternoon sun. He grinned, catching on but never getting angry with our girl. Not that I was truly angry, but sometimes the woman would only listen to full Dominant mode.

"I-I wouldn't do that," she protested again.

"No. Not you," I rebutted dryly, pushing the lube into her hand. "Now rub this on his dick, like he asked you to the first time."

She huffed softly, curling her fingers around the lube. With another pout, she slid her body off his cock. The dude's dick jutted straight up, now glistening and twitching in anticipation of her touch.

Talia didn't let us down. She slathered on a good amount of lube all the way to Fletch's base before snapping the lid shut.

"Damn," he grated. "That's...good, beautiful. So fucking good. I'm so hard for you. Can't wait to do this."

His sensual celebration didn't ease her nervousness one inch. She looked back to me for more instruction, grinding her lower lip with her teeth. I wished to hell I didn't find that so captivating—but only because I knew exactly what joy she was bound for.

"Straddle him like you were before." I let my voice soften. "And relax. You're going to feel so good, baby. I promise."

She settled once more across my brother, leaning her hands on his chest. He moved forward again, kissing her with passion and force, easing a lot of her worry away—though not all. Couldn't fault the guy for trying, though. As he kept kissing her, he caressed and tugged on her breasts. Her nipples rose like tight little berries in the breeze.

"We're going to go really slow, okay?" he whispered.

Talia nodded.

I stroked a hand down her back, scraping my nails softly over her skin, watching goosebumps form in my wake. Because I couldn't help it, I used my other hand to grasp myself through my jeans. My balls were tight and painful. My cock moistened the denim with more precome by the second. I'd played voyeur to Fletch plenty in the past, but this had to be the most erotic sight I'd ever witnessed—and he wasn't even penetrating her yet.

Fletcher continued kissing Talia, sucking and nibbling her

lips, while lining up the head of his cock at her back entrance. Carefully, he circled over her opening a few times, coating her sweet hole with lubricant so the initial entrance would be easy.

"How's that look, D?" he asked me. "She all slicked up?"

"Affirmative," I managed to reply—not easy, since it required a thorough stare at the juncture of his cock and her rosette, waiting for him to breach her in such a forbidden way. "You're clear for advance, man."

For the love of fuck, my dick nearly screamed. Advance already.

Fletcher kissed Tolly again, with infinite more gentleness. "You're in control of this baby," he coaxed. "The motion's just like when my cock's in your pussy. Just lower yourself onto it. The head will be the worst part. Take it fast or slow. That's up to you too. It helps to open your muscles and push back at me, like you want to push me out instead."

Talia snorted. "Is that an option?"

"No," Fletch and I ordered it in unison.

"Just go easy," Fletcher assured. "Keep the ring relaxed…"

"Oh, because you've done this before?" she snapped. "Had something that size up your bum?"

"Well, no," he stammered. "But it's my understanding—"

"Fletcher?" she interjected.

"Yes?"

"Just be quiet."

"Yes, dear."

Her determined look was adorable, until Fletcher distracted her with another string of fervent kisses. From my vantage point, I watched the head of his cock sink into her ass. Slowly, it disappeared between her cheeks.

A rosy flush spread up Tolly's back and shoulders. The

normal tan of her skin soon returned. She had worked through the first-time anxiety and discomfort, and I was so fucking proud. I showed her so with a lingering kiss to the slick flesh between her shoulder blades.

"You're amazing, baby," I rasped. "How does that feel now?"

A long pause went by before she answered between harsh gasps. "So...much. Oh, my God. So much." She panted, utterly frozen above Fletcher's torso. She looked confused about whether to move or be still.

"It's okay, love. Take it nice and slow. It's all pleasure from here. Slide down a bit more. You can do it. Lighten up those nerves."

Fletcher shifted a hand down her belly to her clit. He began lazy circles on the hard nub, widening Talia's stare.

"Ohhhh shit," she moaned. "Ohhhh, Fletcher."

"You're doing great, baby."

"I-I don't know if I can take this too much longer." She tremored, looking around with a panicked stare. "Are you going to come in there?"

"Don't worry about me, baby." He didn't stop caressing her clit. "This is all about you right now."

A tiny snarl left her. "Seriously?"

Fletcher grinned. "I have an idea."

"I was afraid of that."

She ended that in a sharp yelp as Fletcher executed a few deft moves to place her under him. The guy even had the guts to ask if she was comfortable without surrendering a millimeter of his cock from her body. After giving her a second to grasp her bearings, he slowly started to move. With a forearm braced on each side of her face, he loomed over her as if taking her like a stuffy missionary—only there was nothing stuffy about this scene. My cock was right there to remind me of that exact fact.

"How's this?" he murmured. Genuine concern filled his voice, even when he chided her for the simple nod she gave as answer. "Say words, baby. We need to hear it. You know that."

"It's...good," Talia conceded. "It feels really good, actually." She ran fingers from the back of his neck to the back of his skull, tangling in his hair. "Thank you for taking over."

Though I could no longer see his face, I knew my buddy was smiling. The energy of it permeated his voice as he instructed, "Okay, baby, let's move a little. Tell me if it gets to be too much, yeah?"

"Yes."

Her answer was so sexy and breathy, I had to squeeze myself again, staving my orgasm. Her face only intensified the torment. She looked up at Fletch like he'd protect her from one of the world's ugliest monsters, even though he fucked her in such an intrusive way. Many even found the practice foul, but to the rest of us, it was connective and pure, the most sincere form of surrender and possession.

Fletcher pulled his hips back slowly, sliding his cock almost completely from her ass. He stilled for a beat, then another, before gliding all the way back in. His hips bumped her ass cheeks, and his balls pressed into the valley between them. Again and again he lunged, several more times, filling the air with his groans and her gasps. Finally, he angled her legs up and then out, wider than before.

"Oh, my God. Fletcher."

"Feels so good, baby," he responded. "So fucking good. So warm. So tight in your sweet ass. Okay?"

I couldn't find words—so I watched like a mesmerized

voyeur. No more directions, no more encouragement. I was purely, greedily, fascinated with the way they loved one another.

Talia's breathing had gone ragged. Her face was flushed. Her eyes were glassy. All the signs pointed to her body's race for a monumental orgasm. She was on the edge...

Almost there...

Because of his height, Fletcher's body easily stretched over hers. He had full access to everything else about her as he kept stroking his cock in and out of her ass. He sucked a nipple into his mouth, biting down softly at first, increasing the pressure as her breathing spiked. When she moaned, unable to take that anymore, he moved and repeated the treatment to the other breast. By the time he was done, both peaks jutted into the air, stiff and bruised, a red tinge to the normally brown areolas. They'd probably be sore tomorrow, reminders of how thoroughly she'd been fucked in the meadow before our return to the real world.

Fletcher reared up, staring intently at her passion-filled face. "You like it now, baby? Feeling my cock take your ass like this?"

"Yes," Talia gasped. "Oh...my...yes."

"Good." He growled in satisfaction. "Because now I'm going to make you fall apart—and I want to watch. I want to see you crumble as I come in your ass."

Her mouth opened to protest, but he slammed down, kissing her senseless. Talia moaned again from under him.

"Are you ready?" He pumped faster.

"Yes. God, please, yes. Fletcher. Please!"

He wrapped an arm around her waist, lifting her body to him. With a long, lusty snarl, he thrust harder into her ass. His head curved in, and he buried his face in her neck. "So good," he whispered against her skin. "Invading your tight hole like this. Your sweet, wicked little body. I feel it shuddering for me, baby. I feel your ass trembling, your clit vibrating, your blood rushing...wanting to come for me. Wanting to come hard as my cock plows into you..."

Her head arched back. Her face, painted in ribbons of the sun, was exquisite. Her hair tangled with leaves and apple blossoms, like a modern-day Eve succumbing to carnal sin—and loving it. "Fletcher. Oh, my God..."

"Now, baby," he finally snarled. "Come with me, Tolly—now!"

She bowed her back toward him, her mouth dropping in a silent scream. Fletcher went completely still, his teeth openly gritted. They clung to one another for what seemed like an eternity—in what had to be the most beautiful, earth-shattering climax I'd ever witnessed without being a part of. I found myself wishing I'd thought to record it with my phone, but the footage would be a shitty substitution for what the real thing had been. The energy of it. The power exchanged because of it. The heart-stopping beauty of it.

Our girl now knew the magic of anal. Her joy filled me with such bliss, I didn't even care about being just the observer. Honestly, I felt...blessed. Fulfilled. Humbled. Blown away.

I waited until the two of them started emerging from the postcoital bliss and then stretched out on the blanket with them. When Fletcher carefully pulled out, I helped him clean her up before tucking her against me, spoon style, and stroking her from shoulder to elbow and back.

Unbelievable. I was actually spooning with a woman and liking it.

Fletcher dozed off for a while, content to have her leg thrown over his hip. A sated smile spread across the bastard's face.

I began threading my fingers through Talia's hair, toying with the ends of the silky strands. "You okay?" I posed in a whisper. "Not too sore?"

"I'm good. Fine, actually." She slowly turned, trying not to wake him. Fletch was softly snoring, content after the explosive orgasm. "He was really gentle. You guys are so amazing."

"What is it?" It was a low demand, given as her forehead discernibly crunched.

"I just—" She shrugged and blushed. "Did I...do something wrong?"

I grunted hard. "Good God, girl. What would make you ask that?"

Talia smoothed a fingertip over my neck. "Well...you didn't join in. Like, at all."

"And my dick's still not speaking to me because of it." I added a chuckle, but she didn't respond in kind. "Honestly, I was so blown away watching you two," I tried to explain. "It was more than enough. It was...incredible. Sometimes with you two, it's just like that for me."

Finally, her concern seemed to lift. A little. "Hmmm." She patted my pecs. "You know what I think, Mr. Newland?"

"Oh, God," I groaned. Mr. Newland. That could be a good thing or a bad thing.

"I think that behind all this tough-guy exterior, there's nothing but a big ol' teddy bear waiting to get out."

I snort-laughed. "Only when it involves the two of you." My gaze narrowed. "By the way, tell anyone else your theory, and I will tie you to my bed and have my nasty way with you."

She pressed a few fingers over her mouth. "Not your nasty way."

"Very nasty."

"Oh...well. Maybe I'll have to test that theory?" Mischief twinkled in her eyes, pressing gold flakes into the luxurious chocolate of her gaze.

I raised a brow, trying for menacing—which clearly didn't work, since she dissolved into a fit of quiet giggles.

Christ.

I was definitely losing my touch. Going soft. As a god damned teddy bear.

Being head over heels in love might have had something to do with it.

And that sounded just fine to me.

★ ★ ★ ★

I hated flying commercial. Even in first-class, for which we'd paid eight times more, it had been tedious. Because of it, the "teddy bear" was a little—fine, a lot—grumpy as we waited for our bags to come off the carousel. Still, the pause gave me an excuse to touch our girl once more. I toyed with Talia's ponytail while she leaned against me, her hoodie-covered back to my front. Fletcher stood facing her, turning her into our cute sandwich filling. His hands splayed her waist, and he kissed her smiling lips.

As soon as he let her go, she sighed with obvious contentment. "That was a fun vacation. I had the best time, you guys." Her peace radiated, a separate sunshine of its own, fueling the we're-the-shit-and-we-know-it look I traded with Fletch. For just a few more minutes, life was our perfect bubble of existence. I yearned for the authority to give Father Time the day off.

"I dread what's waiting in my inbox."

Now, I wished for the freedom to knock my buddy's block off. "Now?" I snapped at Fletch. "You really can't wait?" Normally, I was the one anxious to dive back into work.

"Brother, there are at least seven fires needing my attention five minutes ago." He grimaced as a buzz came from his pocket again. "Make that eight." He looked back down to Talia, an open mope on his face. "I wish we were back in the meadow."

Talia sighed again, though not with as much ease. "Me too."

Fletch pressed in, ready to kiss her again, but a burst of giggles made the three of us turn. A group of coeds nearby, dressed in matching T-shirts, leggings, and high ponytails, gawked and whispered at our blatant affection.

Immediately, Talia stiffened. She jerked, trying to pull out of my arms.

Trying—and failing.

"Where do you think you're going?" My voice was low but serious.

"Ssshhh," she retorted. "I don't want to cause a scene, okay?"

"We aren't causing a scene, sugar," Fletch chided. "Just standing here like everyone else, talking about our trip and work for tomorrow."

Her lips, so perfect and berry red, pursed. "People are staring."

"No," I interceded. "Teenagers are staring."

"And wishing they were you," Fletch added.

"I don't—"

I silenced her by whipping her around—and impaling her with my stare. "Are you embarrassed to be seen with us? Or me, at least?" I charged. "I mean, Fletch I can understand, especially with that hair. But me, Tolly? Really?"

At least that made her laugh a little, just as the conveyor belt lurched into motion. She was saved from the discussion—for now. I had to push things to the back of my mind, but they would be revisited, likely the next time I had her strung up and on the edge of a screaming orgasm. Yes. Best to wait until then. I smiled at the thought. I'd make damn sure she had a thorough lesson in letting go of insecurities about people watching the three of us in public. Let them all watch, as far as I was concerned. They'd only walk away steeped in envy, jealous they didn't know a love as profound as ours.

After retrieving the luggage, we loaded up the Range Rover and headed toward the condo. As the familiar, bold silhouette of Chicago's skyline appeared on the horizon, I smiled at the sight greeting me in the rearview. Fletcher was sprawled across the back seat, his head in Talia's lap. She toyed with his messy golden-brown hair, a sublime slant across her elegant lips.

"You really do need a haircut again," she murmured absently.

Fletcher emitted a sleepy hum. "Yeah, yeah. I'll handle it. Just not right now."

She mock-frowned. "How does this grow so fast?"

"Genetics?" He mumbled his answer into her thigh, drifting off from her soothing attention.

We pulled under the front awning of our building, a skyscraper with a mix of old and new to the architecture.

We'd picked the place for practical reasons—it was close to FF Engineering, Fletch's company, as well as the major construction projects I was involved with—but it had never felt like home until Tolly had become a part of the picture. Ironically, we hadn't met her through either of our professional pursuits, either. It was the task force for which we'd volunteered on for our buddy, Killian Stone, that had led to the woman who changed our lives.

As we unloaded our bags, the night doorman rushed out to help. "Welcome home, gentlemen—and Ms. Perizkova." He was a new guy but scored major points by including Talia in the greeting.

"Thanks, Maurice," I said, shaking hands with the smiling guy. "Where's Ralph? I thought he was on nights?"

He chuckled. "You have a very good memory."

"That's what they pay me for. Or so I'm told."

"I took on a few extra shifts this month," he explained. "My wife is due next month, so we're trying to save up a little."

"Ah." I nodded, approving. "Makes perfect sense. And congratulations." I said it and meant it. Funny how it was so much easier to encourage the happiness in others when the stuff overflowed one's own heart too. And mine was a busted dam of joy, especially as I scooped up Talia's hand. It seemed impossible to not be touching her all the time.

"Thanks, Mr. Newland." Maurice grinned. He was a lanky, attentive guy. He'd make a great dad too. "I'll have these up to your place in no time."

"Outstanding." I tossed the keys, and he easily caught them. "We won't need the car again tonight, so you can go ahead and park it too."

"Sure thing, Mr. Newland."

I tugged Talia toward the elevators. She pulled back in the opposite direction, dipping her head in the direction the bank of shiny gold mailboxes. "Hey. Let me get the mail. It's probably overflowing since we've been gone."

I pulled her back against my chest like a rubber band. "I had them bring it up to the condo," I explained against her lips. "No need to worry, baby. What?" The prompt tumbled out when she openly pouted.

"It's nothing." She actually looked a little flustered. "You just think of everything. For once, I thought I could be useful."

I lifted a hand, wrapping it to the back of her neck, yanking her yet tighter against me. "For once?" I arched a brow while staring down into her luxurious eyes. Damn, they were beautiful. They turned a little gold when aroused but darkened into a rich sable when confused. Like right now.

Just like that, she'd dropped her gaze entirely. Quietly, she added, "You know what I mean."

The elevator door slid open. I pulled her inside the lift. As Fletcher stepped in beside us and entered the code for the condo, I made eye contact—but he was already with the plan. Without hesitation, he moved in right behind Tolly. She was trapped between us in the corner of the car.

I watched as my brother leaned in, quickly unraveling Talia with kisses, suckles, and small but harsh bites down her neck. From ear to collarbone, he kept up the torment until she sighed and sagged backward, into my embrace.

"Tolly, Tolly, Tolly," he rasped into her ear. "Do you piss Drake off on purpose? I'm starting to think you like being punished."

She let out a high gasp but finished with a sly smile. "Never." Another sharp breath as he bit into the top of her shoulder. "Ooohhh, jeez...please, Fletch."

"Please?" he taunted lowly. "Please what?"

"Please...don't...don't stop." Her body dissolved like a sandcastle under a wave. "Feels—dear God, feels so good."

Fletcher chuckled. "We've created a monster, man."

"A gorgeous, sexy monster." I added it in a heavy breath atop her hair.

The elevator slowed, and the doors slid apart. The condo stretched before us, and I almost said something along the lines of "home sweet home." It truly felt more like home every time we came back with Talia—though all three of us sensed the time was coming to make a decision about where our roots would be planted. We had danced around the topic before, of course, but we still couldn't decide on here or San Diego—so for now, we kept hopping back and forth between the two.

Fletcher punched the release code into the alarm keypad while Talia made a lap around the living room, quickly turning on lights, for the "inviting" ambiance she liked so much. As soon as she was done, she announced, "I'm going to go freshen up a little bit and get out of these clothes. I'll be right back."

I watched her disappear down the hall into the large suite we'd created for her, once we'd all decided to give our relationship a try. Most nights, we all slept in there together. When she wasn't with us in Chicago, Fletcher and I slept in the two guest bedrooms. The master was a special space, exclusive for the three of us.

There was a mountain of mail stacked on the breakfast bar. I absentmindedly started sifting through the envelopes. Fletcher's pile was double the size of mine, with all the fashion catalogs sent in his name. Everyone in the fashion industry prayed he'd be caught by the paparazzi in something from their latest line. Many times, the designers also sent sample pieces, but those usually went to his assistant at the office, rather than directly to our home.

I jolted my stare up as he tossed back his last piece of mail, a thick ivory parchment envelope, with a furious thwack. On the front, his name was etched in classic calligraphy. The words "and guest" followed below.

Uh-oh.

I'd seen envelopes like that before. Instinct told me to react to this one by burying it ASAP among the catalogs, but Fletch and his manicured fingers were too fast. He swooped in, grabbing the thing up again. Even so, I was tempted to wrestle him for it—if the damn thing was what I thought it was.

While we teased Tolly for being our little monster, the two of us battled real ones of our own. Ghosts that reared up in our minds, souls, and lives with epically shitty timing.

Mine was called Iraq.

His was called family.

"Gee. Isn't this lovely. And here I thought they'd forgotten about me," he snarled.

I shifted forward. Carefully. "Fletch. Let it go for now. Just—"

"But look, man. How special, right? They sent it to me in the mail. Guess they thought that was a better thing than calling their own damn son."

"Fletcher—"

"The mail. How fun. Just like every other person on the guest list. Why should their own fucking son be different, right?"

"Dude." I force-fed a growl into my voice. "Just leave it until the morning. You'll be clearer then. Why are you getting all riled up now? We had such a good trip—"

His violent sneer cut me off. "You do not get it, do you, man?" He raked a glower up and down my form. "No. Of course you don't, Mr. Perfect Family Life."

I backed up. By a giant step. Best friend or not, some lines didn't get toyed with. "You're hurting. That's real, and I get it. But that's the only reason you're standing right now, brother."

"Says Mr. Perfect." He swept a hand down, as if unveiling me in a magic show. "Who can say that, on his perfect ranch. In a perfect little town. In a perfect little world. With such perfect—"

"Enough." I braced my stance. Squared my shoulders. Fired up my unwavering glare. "This will be your only warning, Mr. Ford." My voice was equally low, ensuring my anger seeped into every syllable.

At once, Fletch's mouth clamped shut.

A few beats passed. A handful more.

Finally, he dropped his head. "Fuck." When he lifted his stare again, red heat darkened his face. True remorse flooded his features. "You didn't deserve that. I'm sorry."

"It's okay," I grumbled.

"It's not."

"It is, God damn it." I punched his shoulder. The move wasn't playful. "I get it. You forget how long we've known each other, man? And remember"—I motioned to the envelope with my chin—"I know how easily they can get under your skin."

He huffed. "Which, in and of itself, pisses me off." His head fell again. As he slowly shook it, his arms and shoulders went taut as lead cage bars. "Why do I still let them get to me after all this time?"

"Because we all want our parents' approval, no matter

how fucked-up it is."

The answer wasn't mine. It belonged to our beauty, newly arrived, clearly relaxing Fletch's tension like a human balm.

"It's in our very nature, so there's nothing wrong with it."

We both looked at her in mild surprise. Neither of us had heard Talia come back down the hall, but she must have overheard enough of our exchange to issue her comment. On silken steps, she approached Fletcher again. She wrapped her arms around his waist and rested her cheek on his back. I watched, relieved, as he visibly relaxed into her embrace. An exhalation left him, matching the inherent surrender of the move. "I love you," he murmured. "Both of you."

"As we love you." Her whispered words were finished by a wide, long yawn. "Can we go to bed?" she said after that. "I'm exhausted from our trip, and I bet you guys are too."

She started down the hall, extending a hand backward for someone to take. Adorable girl. Amazing woman. I longed to be the guy grabbing on to her, but Fletch seemed equally exhausted. I nudged him toward her and directed, "Go. I'll turn off the lights and lock up."

He gave me a grateful nod before taking her hand and letting her tug him toward the master suite. In that moment, I thanked myself for letting him go with her. They were gorgeous together, so connected they almost seemed twins instead of lovers, and they filled my heart to every limit it possessed.

I loved them.

More than anything else in the world.

They were my world.

If only we could shut out the rest of the bullshit and exist alone, just the three of us...

Yes.

Perfection.

At least for tonight, we still held on to it. Still had all the moments to call our own. And perhaps that was how we'd have to exist from now on, stealing the moments for ourselves where we could get them. If I had to live the rest of my life being a time thief, then so be it—as long as my two partners in crime were with me too. As long as the three of us were together, I only had three matching words for the grand masters of fate, destiny, and life.

Bring. It. On.

CHAPTER TWO

Fletcher

My head was going to burst into a million tiny pieces.

I swore it was the truth as Aunt Petra's nasal giggles peeled through the Italianate living room, down the marble hallway, and across the two-point-five miles of kitchen, to jab me where I stood pouring my third gin and tonic.

"Whoa. Easy, cowboy." Drake appeared from somewhere in the Aunt Petra hell and immediately tried to upright the gin as I went for a double.

"Fuck off."

"Nice try, dick." He yanked the booze out of my grip, not realizing I was desperate enough to switch gears and go with vodka and tonics instead. "Slow the fuck down," he ordered, voice low. "You'll regret getting shitfaced around all these people, Fletch."

"Well, I already regret coming at all, so let's go for the big money."

His brows drew together. "What happened?"

I jerked a glare his way. "What makes you think something 'happened'?"

He rolled his eyes. "Beside the fact that the tension between you and your folks is thick as a medium-rare Porterhouse? Come on, it's me. I could feel it from the second we got here."

Well...shit.

"Where's Tolly?" I didn't want to have this conversation in front of her. If Drake had noticed all that crap in the air, she was definitely aware of it too—probably explaining why I'd transformed into the king of the assholes, avoiding the two of them for the last hour and a half.

Ninety minutes of agony. And fury.

Ever since Mom's lovely little comment, murmured just beneath her breath, as soon as she and I had been within earshot of each other.

Thanks, Mom. Not.

Francine Ford could have reduced the queen to tears given the motive and opportunity. No one was off-limits to her venomous tongue if she thought they deserved a dressing-down.

"I think she's still cooing over your cousin's newborn. Shit." He interrupted himself with a quirk of a laugh. "Maybe it's time to go break up that party before her ovaries explode and we have a whole new problem on our hands."

He finished it with another chuckle, but I didn't bite on the humor. Didn't stop me from noticing how his eyes sparkled as he made his way back to the living room.

Yeah, I'd really just thought that.

His sparkling eyes.

But he'd given me an awesome thought to chase for a minute. Our woman with a round belly, swollen breasts, glowing skin, and shining hair, nourishing our child inside her own body...

One day.

One day...

Who the fuck was I kidding? Mom's and Dad's small minds had nearly exploded before Talia, Drake, and I had crossed the threshold tonight, as if our presence alone would taint the sanctity of their marriage, let alone this anniversary celebration. How the hell would they take us starting a family together?

I was confused. And hurt. And now, thoroughly pissed. My lifestyle had never been a secret to them. And they loved the crap out of Drake. Well, as much as they were capable of loving someone beyond themselves. My father had always delighted in hearing details of our "escapades," as he called them—but maybe that explained it all too neatly. Maybe Dad had actually just given the cause lip service. Maybe he thought we were young and sowing our wild oats—getting certain "predilections" out of our systems—and that we would eventually settle down into more traditional relationships.

Not anymore.

In the three and a half words he'd spoken to me tonight, Dad's "new" viewpoint was clear. He was in Mom's camp about this and staying there.

What a difference a real relationship made.

When Drake, Tolly, and I had laid out our ultimatum to Natalia's parents last summer, I'd never suspected we'd be set for a repeat performance of judgment from my own. At least not to this degree. Ironic, how the most accepting of our three clans was Drake's middle-of-the-Bible-belt kin.

So much for stereotypes.

Or my ability to read the minds and hearts of my own family.

Dad had to be the biggest stunner. While I'd picked up a strong Dominant vibe from Drake's father, I'd always thought my own was just a horny player. Perhaps he'd tried a nontraditional relationship before meeting my mother, but if he had, it was only to pay homage to "the bucket list factor," as Talia had once tagged it. But overall? Dad just didn't have the personality to thrive off sharing a woman with another man. Hell, he could barely stand being in a room with other people most of the time. God forbid the spotlight wasn't on him and only him. Mom wasn't much different.

And there was that truth, smacking me soundly in the kisser.

My parents were narcissists. Serious ones. They probably had been since their youth—so why the hell was I just seeing it now?

Paging Dr. Freud.

"Shit," I muttered, finishing on a chuckle. Could it be the therapy was...working? I'd spent a lot of time on his couch lately. More than the one in my own damn living room. Nice to know my spending money on the good doc hadn't been a total waste.

"Well, there you are. Why are you in here by yourself?"

I turned in time to watch Sasha float into the room. My little sister was a beautiful, elegant clone of my mother. Jutting out her visibly bony hip, she leaned against the marble-topped island in the center of the kitchen.

"Fixing myself a drink." I let my tone fill in the logical conclusion to that. Because I need it. Badly.

She folded her arms, spreading long, French-manicured fingers against opposite elbows. Her lips, perfectly painted in the on-trend pink of the week, pursed. "Mother has a bartender in the study. Why not just have him make you a drink?"

There it was, right on cue. The subtle accusation, tippy-tapping just beneath the surface of her tone, ensuring it would sneak its way under my skin.

As it did.

"Because the good gin is in here." I poured the double shot, tossing Drake a secret gloat about it. Fuck. I needed to gloat about something tonight. Or maybe not about anything. Maybe that was the point.

"Liar." Her challenge was quick and sharp, perfect Francine Ford-style.

"Why do you say that?" Casual and noncommittal always drove Mom crazy. I wondered if it worked on the mini. But the fact that I'd even entertained the thought made me consider chugging the drink and then pouring another. Once upon a time, Sasha and I had been close. Maybe even friends. She was a stranger now.

"Because I know you." Was that a hint of affection in her tone? Or a gloat of her own? Either way, how much more wrong could she be? She didn't know me at all. "And I know when you're hiding out."

But I couldn't refute that one. Yeah, so she still knew me in the little ways. Even that rankled.

"Not exactly my crowd of people out there, Sash."

"You mean our relatives, brother? Our own flesh and blood? How much more of 'your crowd' can it get?"

She exaggerated brother as if both syllables were raw acid. My gut twisted on strange emotions.

"You're serious, aren't you?" I growled, though didn't wait for her just-ate-a-lemon look to go away. "Can you name even one memory, happy or sad, that you've had with anyone out there? 'Our people' are people we don't even know, Sasha. I'm surprised they even showed up for this thing." I almost corrected myself with the proper verbiage from the invitation. An anniversary gala. Celebrating what? Nearly two hours into the shindig now, and I hadn't seen Mom and Dad speak to each other, let alone touch or kiss.

Sasha made a little pish sound. "Please." Rolled her wide blue eyes. "You know Mother throws the best parties in town. It's a crush out there. Everyone will be talking about it for weeks." The ice in her eyes warmed to a light cobalt, pride taking over as she spoke of Mom. Not because the woman had been loving, attentive, and active in our lives. Because she threw "the best parties." Soirees where people air-kissed on their way to the lobster buffet and the free booze, saying shit like "Hey, you!" and "Sweetie, you look great!" because they couldn't remember one another's name.

I peered harder at Sasha. Had we even been raised in the same house? Some days, I couldn't be sure.

"For weeks, huh?" I finally muttered. "Uh...okay. If you say so." I swallowed the rest of my drink in one gulp. Soon the edge would soften.

"Well." Sasha adjusted her weight, cocking her head with a knowing tick. "If they weren't before you walked in, they will be now."

Yep. Here it was. The moment of truth I'd been waiting for. And dreading.

Despite the hammer of my heartbeat, I forced out an easy smile. "And that means?"

One second of silence. One more.

"Fletcher."

"Sasha."

"Are you kidding?"

"No. Not really in the mood for jokes. If you have

something to say, sister, say it." I swept out a hand, clearing the stage for her. If she wanted to make a show out of this, I was damn well going to let her. The gin finally spun some magic into my blood. My nerves dulled, clearing plenty of room for the anger.

She added a little grunt to the annoying pish. "Come on, Fletch. Did you see Mother's and Father's faces when you got here with Drake and that woman? When the three of you walked in, like nobody could tell what you're all about?" Her head rocked, tilting the other direction. "You're seriously trying to be disinherited, aren't you?"

"And why do you care?" I volleyed. "I have a feeling you wouldn't lose a wink of sleep over it, sister."

I sucked in a deep breath, hoping it accomplished double duty. I needed to stay calm while shoring the walls of my heart. Proclaiming true feelings in this house was often an exercise in pain and disappointment. I didn't expect this occasion to be any different.

"I love them."

At first, Sasha didn't move. It was almost as if I hadn't spoken. But in subtle degrees, her face changed. Disapproval flared her gaze. Disappointment flattened her lips. Her nose wrinkled as if a skunk had paraded across the room.

Every reaction my head had predicted.

Every reaction my heart wouldn't let pass by.

Making me slam down my glass, frustrated words tumbling out.

"I don't care what you all think. It's good, it's real, and I'm not going to hide it."

She shrugged. Shook her head. "You're hopeless, Fletcher."

"And you're a snob, Sasha."

"Well, oh, my God. Alert the press. Gasp. There are snobs among us!"

I didn't want her stab to hurt so much. I didn't want to care so much. But in a weird way, she was right. Family was family. Though I hardly recognized them anymore, they were my blood—and it did hurt.

And as the pain grew, so did my anger.

"You've become just like her," I spat. "Just like them."

"And that's bad?" She gave a haughty laugh while attempting to look down her surgically sculpted nose.

"It could be—if you keep it up. You really want to end up like her?"

She flashed an impish grin. "Oh, that's pretty funny—coming from you."

"Because she's the picture of happiness, Sash? Stability? Is she really what you aspire to be? The 'marriage' they're celebrating out there...is that really what you want for your life? Your heart?"

Redness crept up her face. Oh, I'd struck a nerve—probably more. I'd attacked her role model. Questioned the marriage—well, the farce of one—she held in such high esteem. I hated myself for doing it. This wasn't just teasing my baby sister about smooching with her teen idol posters. I'd hurt her. Sure, I'd spoken nothing but the truth, but it had caused her pain, nonetheless.

"So, let me get this right," she finally ventured, rocking back on her four-inch heels. "You're concerned about me idolizing Mom and Dad and their not-quite-normal marriage... but you'll go back to the city tonight and sleep with a woman... and another man?" A quip of a laugh fell from her. "Sorry, brother, but ewww."

I pinched the bridge of my nose. "We don't sleep together, Sash. Well, we sleep, but we don't—oh, fuck it. That's just not how it works. Jesus."

"Enlighten me, then. No. Wait. Don't." Her hand went up, giving me the full stop signal. "I want to keep my mind free of that image."

"Never asked you to go there in the first place." I leaned back against a counter, once more dropping into diplomat mode. If she wanted to keep up with the self-righteous society girl on me, she'd have to work for it. I wished that meant her haughty little huff wasn't so gratifying, but then I'd be the liar of her accusation.

"Oh, Fletch." Her voice dipped and she pursed her lips, as if chiding a dog for messing the carpet. "What did you really think was going to happen, bringing both of them here?"

I tilted my head to the side, as if in thought. It was strictly for dramatic impact, and she probably knew it, but it was fun watching her squirm a little anyway. "You want to know what I really thought?" I edged my stare back down at her, proving noses didn't have to be artificially sculpted for damning impact. "I thought my family would be happy for me. One thing strikes me as interesting, however..." Inserting an acerbic snort felt as good as the dagger stare. "Have you noticed the only people who really care about it are Dick and Franny?" Using the snarky nicknames for my own parents didn't feel as good as I'd expected. Neither did Sasha's incensed reaction. I plunged on. "Oh, and now you." I finished by arching a brow toward the hallway. "No one else here has so much as batted an eyelash. So fascinating."

Well. There it was. The ball, firmly back in her court. I

watched as a return play turned her eyes to uncut sapphires. She wasn't going to let the play roll out of bounds.

I braced myself.

Sure enough, she spun me a one-hundred-eighty-degree play. In an instant, the patronizing, saccharine-sweet little sister was gone. In her place? A bitch on wheels to put even the glory days of Margaux Asher to shame. A she-creature with a snarl on her lips, a stance like a MMA fighter, and a vicious glower I barely recognized.

"Don't be a damn fool, Fletcher. And don't turn your back. You think those people out there aren't watching every move the three of you make? That they aren't whispering about you like the sharks they all are? You just became the chum in the water, brother." She cocked a hip out, raising both perfectly tweezed brows. "Such a shame too. I really like Talia, you know. She's a lovely woman."

Well, that did it.

She'd purposely brought Tolly into the mix.

In return, I eagerly took my own turn in the Come-to-Jesus game. Like second nature—because it was—I shucked any hope of salvaging what little "family" ties I shared with this woman and eagerly climbed into executive office mode. At once, I became the man everyone saw at Ford Engineering—the no-nonsense, no-bullshit businessman who'd swum with real sharks and built my professional reputation around the world. I'd just never unleashed it on my younger sister before. That all changed now. She'd poked the hornet's nest and was about to be stung.

"Hmmm. Speaking of scum—" I see-sawed my head. "Ohhhh, wait. You said chum." Hitched a nonchalant shrug. "Where is Marshall tonight? Not like your boyfriend to miss an opportunity for crawling farther up Dad's ass."

I stopped there, hoping the subject of Marshall Golde would be closed by her announcing they'd broken up. No such chance. Sasha preened as if referring to one of those teen idols from her pink bedroom walls. Her love-struck teen thing went on as she professed, "He was going to be here but couldn't be."

"That so?"

"Yes." She sighed dramatically.

I wanted to roll my eyes. No. I wanted to shoot myself in each foot. My bombshell would probably have to be dropped.

"Well, he couldn't help it," she explained. "The partners assigned him a project at the last minute. He couldn't say no. You know how things like that go. What's that look for?"

"Oh, come on, Sash. Are you that naïve?"

"Naïve? Ha!" She tossed her head back. "Says the guy who can't make up his mind for a partner?"

"Yeah? Well, you may want to put a tracker on that walking teabag you call a 'partner.'"

Her head dropped. Her glee went manic, darkening again. "Be very careful where you're treading, Fletcher."

"Advice you may want to give Marshall as well," I parried. "Either that, or put a cowbell on the douchebag. I've seen him at the club a few times, you know—when you think he's doing a project for the partners." I jabbed air quotes around the word project, to emphasize the awful affect. It seemed to work. Her gorgeously manipulated face began reddening, betraying how her own gut recognized the fact of my words and didn't want to. "Believe me, darling. The only project Marshall's working on right now is how many ways he can get into Lorena Clemson's snatch."

She turned red as a beet now. "Take it back."

"Or what, Sash? You'll out Drake, Talia, and me? Sounds like that boat's sailed and you're still standing on the dock. Be careful where you're looking, though. I think I see Marshall making sure Lorena Clemson notices his mast."

"Fletcher!"

She twisted her lips before stamping her foot. I fought the urge to pull out my phone and Snapchat the moment. It was that fucking priceless.

"Suit yourself, sister." I sneered the word, imitating her use of brother earlier. "Keep sticking your head in the sand. I'm pretty sure that's a patented Francine Ford move too. You'll have all of them mastered in no time." I pumped a fist into the air. "Gooooo, Sasha."

She stamped the other foot. I was damn near impressed. That shit couldn't be easy in those heels. "You're disgusting."

I shook my head slowly. Almost ruefully. "And you're clueless."

"If Mommy and Daddy don't throw you out by the end of the night, they will when I tell them how awful you've been. Awful. Spreading those vicious lies about the man who's going to be your family. Your brother-in-law!"

"Baby, until that douche nozzle gives you a ring, I wouldn't be making too many 'Reserve the Date' cards."

No more stamping feet. Instead, she drove down both fists atop the chopping block. A couple of the booze bottles even jumped from the impact. "Take. It. Back." Her reiteration was snarled from bared teeth.

"Won't make it any less the truth." My reply was, strangely, the exact opposite. Maybe, like the harpies of old, she'd hogged all the rage in the room for herself. Or maybe I just realized that the woman in front of me was no longer the sister I'd loved and wasn't worth one more drop of my emotion. Of any emotion. "Marshall is having way too much fun sleeping with half the city to get tied down to anyone, sweetheart—let alone to a shrew like you."

She dragged her hands back in. They were claws now, screeching against the custom tiles atop the block. "That's it. I'm telling them. Then you'll be thrown out in front of everyone."

"Don't bother. I'm leaving." I pushed forward, moving into her personal space while whipping up a hand to shield my stage whisper from an invisible audience. "And don't worry, darling. I'll take all my embarrassing little secrets with me."

As she fumed, I simply couldn't resist a final pièce de résistance. With speed only a big brother would dare, I grabbed her, yanked her close, and planted a sloppy, wet kiss on her cheek. She gasped, but I persisted, hauling her into a breath-squeezing hug. High-pitched blustering ensued as she battled to push me away, but I answered her demand before she could vocalize it, releasing her to barrel toward the doorway back into the living room.

Drake. Tolly. They were my only targets now. I needed to find them and get out of this hellmouth of a house before any more of this sick energy could seep into us by osmosis.

I searched the crowd for Talia first. There, in the cluster of women gathered near the fireplace, her beauty enhanced tenfold by the light from the grate and the cream-colored sweater dress she wore. Her eyes sought mine at once. I inhaled deeply and then started a path toward her, concentrating on pushing out all the frustration and anxiety on the exhalation. A new breath in, and I envisioned the poison in my soul being edged out by calm cohesiveness. Another breath, and I was back to sporting the collected front everyone was used to seeing.

I could move again. Thank fuck.

But Tolly was already on her feet. She discreetly excused herself from the clutch of women chatting away about God knew what and then slipped around the neighboring bunch of men who were embroiled in local politics talk. Her stare, fixed on me like a laser, never wavered. She already knew something was off, and no way would she let me get away with hiding. I needed her insistence on honesty the way a beached fish longed to be thrown back into the ocean.

God damn, I loved this woman. Craved her. Needed her.

But I needed the other fish in my ocean too. Drake. Where the hell was he?

He appeared from the direction of Dad's den, concern stamping his face as soon as he saw me. My chest compressed as all my senses recognized my own truth. It was so simple. So perfectly right.

If the world suddenly fell away from the edges of this house, my life would still be complete. The only two people who mattered to me were here, rushing at me from opposite directions, converging next to me—

Completing me once more.

"Ghost?" Drake muttered for our ears only. It was a term he and I had always used for getting the hell out of somewhere. Time to disappear like a ghost. Most of the time, it had been our exit strategy from clingy women, but the metaphor fit this situation just as ideally. In more ways than one.

As in, I felt like a ghost in this house. Just a visitor now, though I wondered if I'd ever really fit in here. For that matter, anywhere. I'd always had just places to live—I'd never really called somewhere my real home. I wanted to find that place now—and make it come alive with the two of them.

As in, perhaps I'd seen a ghost. In Sasha. My mother had been reincarnated before death, haunting me in the form of her exact replica, a hissing harpy confronting me in the kitchen while the original model held court in the living room.

As in, I was about to become a ghost to them.

The deepest, and hardest, blade to accept.

It'd be a long time before I was welcomed back in this place again. Yeah, I'd been the black sheep most of my life, but when Mom and Dad learned about the way I'd spoken to Sasha...on top of that, breaking every guy code ever invented by selling out my sister's boyfriend? It'd be months until another invitation came. Maybe years.

"Let me just grab my coat and bag from the guest room," Talia murmured. "I think that's where they put them."

Before she could turn away, I pulled back on her hand. Her warmth and strength...they were keeping my very sanity together. Thankfully, Drake picked up on that too.

"I'll get your stuff." Drake stuffed the keys to his Range Rover into her slim fingers. "Just take him out to the car. I'll be right behind you." He turned for the hallway to the guest suite. He knew his way around my parents' house as well as I did.

"Well." Talia said it on an airy sigh. "Guess that's settled." She tugged lightly on my sleeve. "Come on, you. Let's go." But I didn't budge. "Fletcher. Come on. Fletcher, look at me. Look." She tugged harder, followed by pinching my forearm. The snip of pain was enough to clear my mental fog and focus solely on her face for a moment.

On her face...

That beautiful face.

The brown eyes, cutting to my soul. The half smile, speaking to my heart. The determined chin, fortifying my resolve to get the fuck out of here.

My sweet Talia. My one and forever.

"I love you." I mouthed it more than spoke it, not trusting my voice to stay solid. I suddenly felt removed from my body, as if I could control nothing. As if the world were happening to me instead of because of me. My heart rate sprinted. My blood pumped hard, as if wanting to explode from my veins. But outwardly, I was a zombie. I caught enough of that disgusting reflection in her eyes.

Eyes getting closer as she rose to her tiptoes to give me a quick kiss. I wanted more—she tasted so damn good—but she was leaning in tighter now, almost as if hugging me.

Instead, she spoke to me. Tucked her lips close enough to my ear so I could hear every whispered word. "Okay, listen to me, big guy. We need to get out of here before there's a bigger scene. People are looking, but they only think we're sharing a little love moment over here. I need you to help me. You have to put your feet in front of each other and start moving toward the front door, okay?"

I felt my head dip in what was hopefully a nod. I'd follow this woman through a pit of snakes. Across a burning bed of coals without shoes. I would follow her to the ends of the fucking earth—because with her, I finally had peace. My forever.

So, yeah, I did what she asked. Didn't say a word, though. Everything inside still careened with conflict, dicing and slicing my brain as it struggled to process the ugly reality known as my fucking family. Not that the effort worked. I was numb, so I just let her tug on my sleeve a little more, guiding me out to the front sidewalk.

The nighttime temperature had dropped significantly, the cold acting like a wicked slap in the face. It caused me to stop in my tracks and stare at Talia. "What's wrong?" I asked.

She shook her head, but there was an adoring smile at the edges of her lips. "Not a damn thing. Not anymore."

I unfurled a grunt, conveying how I believed her as much as a kitten hiding a dead mouse. "I'll just get it out of you in the car." The challenge, issued while I fished the keys out of her hand, was finished by the chirp of the fob. "Come on," I added, craving more than anything to kiss her in the surprisingly romantic ambiance of the Range Rover's dome lights. "Drake will be out in a minute. The second he is, I want away from this House of Lannisters."

"Who?"

I rolled my eyes. "One day, I'll awaken you and that buddy of mine to the awesomeness of Game of Thrones."

"Because it has families like yours in it?"

She had a point, and I wasn't in the mood to pose a debate. "Just get in," I urged while opening the car door. "I want to go home. We can all take a bath, or sit by the fire, or crawl into bed and eat chips."

"Which Drake will never approve of."

"Meh. He'll come around."

She giggled at that and bumped me with her shoulder. I returned her grin, but the assurance behind it was a fast fade.

This was bad.

Really bad.

I had just laid the groundwork for a major upheaval in my life, and only a small portion of me cared. When I gazed at the woman trying to persuade me to get into the car with her, her big brown eyes so careful and concerned, even that small part fell away.

Until my head butted in on my heart again.

What was wrong with me? It had to be abnormal, realizing your entire family wanted to wash their hands of you—and you didn't care. What did that say about me? Maybe I really was broken—beyond just the normal "broken." Missing some essential component everyone else had. That weird, wacked-out part causing people to love blood family even if they were disgusting excuses for humanity.

Even if, on many occasions, they felt like someone's worst enemy.

"Fletcher."

I was conscious of my head snapping up. "Huh? What?"

"Get inside." There she was again. My sanity, pulling me toward the joy of my future instead of the defeat of today—and from this point, the garbage of my past. I fixed my gaze on her incredible face as she held the door open to the back of the Range Rover. "Come on. Get in the car, Fletch. Sit in back with me. Drake will drive us home. You can put your head in my lap and I'll scratch your head, just the way you like."

My lips kicked upward of their own accord. This smile for her...it was honest and good and real. Everything I felt for Talia Perizkova was real. All my hope, my energy, my vitality, my determination to become a better man...a better person. She was all the best parts of me. The best parts of both Drake and me. The discovery that had completed our friendship and made us whole. Along the way, we'd sure as hell lived a lot of life—and made a lot of women's dreams come true.

But that had always been the catch. The fantasy fulfilled was always theirs, not ours. All incredible women, even mind-blowing lovers—but not our one. Not the woman we kept looking for, bound by some strange, tacit agreement that we would find her. Perhaps she'd even come to us...

Drake's deep voice interrupted my poetic thoughts. "Dude."

"Huh?"

"Want to tell us what the fuck happened in there?"

He turned over the engine. It was the only sound in the car. I didn't add to it—unless my stare had a soundtrack.

Drake threw the Range Rover into gear, grunting hard. "Ohhhh, goodie. I love this version of you. Moonchild Ford."

His frustration seeped through in every syllable. I snorted in return. I wasn't too out of it to issue that.

"Don't be mean, Drake." Talia funneled the plea into her stare, turning into a sienna glow beneath the passing streetlights. "Not now."

"I'm not being mean," he defended. "Trust me, he needs to be smacked around a little right now. If not, this stargazer shit goes on for hours." After stopping at a four-way, he shifted to Park and swung around to face us, all but ordering me, "Lie down. Let Tolly calm you—and then you can explain why your sister ran to your mother in the middle of their anniversary celebration and broke down in hysterics."

"What?" Talia, still shivering from the chilly night, gladly accepted the coat Drake had retrieved for her. She turned to look at me with newly concerned eyes. "Come here," she beckoned, pulling me close. We embraced, and I simply listened to her heart thudding, silently comforting me through the shitty moment.

Several long minutes passed as we eased into traffic on the main stretch back to downtown and the condo. I really didn't want to re-tell what had happened with Sasha, but the air in the car was thick enough to cut with a butter knife. Both of them waited, exercising incredible patience, as I dug deep to find my balls—and own up to the mess I'd just created.

"I went into the kitchen to fix a drink for myself. The bartender was watering stuff down, so I went for the good gin in Dad's freezer."

"Got that much," Drake conceded. "But when I left, trying to find Tolly, you were in there by yourself."

"Not for long," I filled in. "She came in seconds after you left. I'm surprised you two didn't pass in the doorway."

"I had more important things on my mind." Drake's voice was a velvety spread of affection for our girl. Like he could be blamed.

I took advantage of the moment to force down another long breath. "As soon as Sasha discovered me, she started in at once with some judgy crap, transparently clear as a message from my mom and dad."

Talia stiffened, though I felt her dismay before it even hit her muscles. "Judgy crap?" she echoed. "About...what? Us?"

"Not worth going into." And I meant it. No way would I subject the two of them to the blow by blow. "She just started in and wouldn't let up," I summarized. "And I lost my cool. Said some things I shouldn't have said."

I wrapped it up with a fast shrug, like there wasn't more to tell. They'd have to accept it. I wasn't digging out the gory details.

"Dude?"

"Yeah, D?"

"That story is more watered down than the shit that bartender was pouring tonight."

"Fuck you."

"Stop." Talia huffed. Pushed away from me, throwing a pleading gaze at us both. "Please don't keep things from us, Fletcher. Most of all, from me. I can handle it, damn it, and you know it. Lord knows, I know my way around a family argument."

Her desperation instantly tore down my walls. Fuck, fuck, fuck. I had no barriers with her around.

"Fine. Okay. You're right, baby, and I'm sorry. I still just want to protect you from so much. But you're strong. One of the strongest people I know. It's easy to forget what you had to go through to be with us."

"And the shit before we came along," Drake added. His ominous undertone was tough to miss. Talia had told us bits and pieces of the crap she'd endured with her asshole ex, but we never pushed her for more details. She'd tell us when she was ready.

I couldn't afford to be as coy about what had happened tonight. Exes were way different than blood family. One could write the former out of the picture. Not so easy when DNA bonded you to someone.

Talia coaxed me away from that brood with her sublime curve of a smile. She gave it the perfect accompaniment, patting her lap in invitation. "Do you want to lie back here with me for a little bit? It's the best we can do until we get home."

Did I want to? Better question was, how could I resist? Her nearness was my balm. Her hands, threading through my hair, de-jangled my nerves.

As soon as I'd become putty in Talia's hands, Drake started in again. "So, what about any of that would have Sasha carrying on the way she was?" Clearly, he wasn't satisfied with my details so far. I couldn't blame him. In his boots, I'd be pressing harder too.

"I dropped the bomb about Marshall and Lorena Clemson on her." I damn near muttered it, not proud of what I had done.

"No. You. Did. Not."

At once, Talia snorted out a laugh. While meeting Drake's glower from the rearview, she quickly covered her mouth. "Sorry, sorry." She half-giggled it all out. "I know it's not funny, but you sounded more like one of my girlfriends, Mr. Newland."

I laughed too. "She's right, dude. You just did a good one of the blonde with the Southern drawl. Taylor."

"Yeah," she concurred. "Just too funny, coming from you."

"You're wearing off on me. Making me go soft." He winked at her via the mirror. Her eyes twinkled in response. "But back to the subject. Fletch...you really told her?"

"I did," I reposted. "And would do it again in a heartbeat."

Drake slid out a low whistle. "God damn." He gave his astonishment another break. "What'd she do to bring that on?"

"Saying shit I didn't appreciate." Talia's caresses or not, I defiantly jutted my jaw. "So, I went for the slam dunk."

"Slam dunk?" Drake drummed nervous thumbs on the steering wheel. "Dude, in her tea-and-finger-sandwich world, you just dealt a finishing move. A figure-four leglock of sisterly destruction."

"Did you just stick a WWE reference in the same sentence as finger sandwiches?"

"Damn right."

"There's a new one for amazing me, Newland." Hopefully, he'd bite on the praise and we could shift off the subject. The guy wasn't immune to flattery all the time. Just most of it. Right now, I was trying everything to avoid the rest of this. The pain I'd have to give them by exposing them to the truth about my family.

"Ohhh, no, no, no, no. Don't go there with that buttery flattery wannabe humor shit, man." Drake sure as hell made that part clear. "This is serious. You just pummeled that girl into no man's land. You either got really toasted really fast, or Sasha must have said something pretty shitty..."

Ding, ding, ding.

I could literally feel the air shift as the truth clicked into place for my best friend.

"That. Little. Bitch."

Talia started. "All right. Confusion, party of one." She tried to sit forward but couldn't get very far due to my head in her lap. "What the hell are you two talking about?"

Drake's dark eyes found mine in the rearview mirror as I sat up once more. This explanation wasn't the kind of thing you gave a woman from the middle of her lap. I nodded some reassurance at him. I got this. And yes, I'll really talk this time.

"My sister was saying things, Tolly. Not-so-nice things." I took both her hands, stroking thumbs over her knuckles. "Things about...the three of us. That I shouldn't have come to my parents' party with you two. That we would be the talk of the family, and probably the whole town, with the way gossip spreads in their circle."

She let out a watery laugh, though her fingers trembled against my grip. "So? Let them talk. Haven't we traveled down this road before? Last summer, anyone?" She shook a bit harder. Reliving that mess wasn't easy for any of us. "Look, I won't be separated from you two ever again. I don't care what people are saying when we walk by. They don't understand what we have. I'm through living my life worried about what others are going to think."

No more finger shivers. She actually squeezed my hand tighter, as if urging me to give the same brave declaration.

"Tolly." I freed up one of my hands. Scrubbed it down my face. "It's just not that easily said and done with my family."

Pussy. Why did it feel like I was defending them, even after the three of them had rolled over, spread wide, and shown me every speck of dirt in their judgmental souls?

And why did this woman suck the very breath from my lungs with her sweet, trusting little shrug?

"They'll come around," she said simply. "If my family did, yours can too."

"It's not that simple, Toll. Not close to it. Believe me, I wish it were."

"Explain it to me, then. Why is it so complicated?"

"My father is very..." I let out a heavy sigh. "Shit." More face scrubbing. "How do I explain this?"

I directed the question to the front seat. Shock of shocks, I was actually at a loss for words. Sometimes, Drake had the perfect set of syllables for my needs. Could step into the side of my brain that wasn't working.

Thank God now was one of those times.

"Richard Ford is a powerful businessman in this town," he started. "If he sets his mind to it, he could make a lot of business dealings much more unpleasant for Fletch."

Talia worried her bottom lip. "And you too?"

"Probably. Likely," he amended. "Luckily, he's pretty self-centered and lazy, so a lot of it would take more effort than he's willing to expend—but he certainly jumps to the bidding of his wife, and if this shit blows up with Marshall and Sasha, that'll be a brand-new mess. Marshall works for the legal counsel serving as advisor to the city manager. If we start having permit issues on job sites, just as a starter, we will know exactly who to thank. That slime ball is getting what he deserves, but he'll take down as many innocent bystanders in the process."

Talia ceased biting her lip. She pushed that soft pillow out again, tapping a finger to her chin in deep thought. "Hmmm."

"Hmmm?" I pressed.

"Just thinking," she mused. "And coming up confused. I mean, wouldn't your sister be grateful to you?" Her voice carried a matter-of-fact clip now, despite how my expression must have been clear with its own bafflement. Was she nuts? "Okay, maybe not right at this moment," she clarified. "But when Sasha calms down and realizes you just saved her from wasting more of her time with this guy, not to mention the rescue from becoming a fool, I think she'll want to thank you. And further, why do you all sit back and condone that? That kind of sickens me, actually, the more I think of it."

"Hey." Drake's comeback scythed through the shadows in the car. "We don't condone it, okay?"

"Sometimes you just have to mind your own business," I cut in, attempting to explain one of the trickier aspects of guy code. "Let karma do her thing and catch up to the fucker. Things have a way of working themselves out. Eventually, Marshall would've slipped up and Sasha would've caught him. It wasn't my place to make a mess of her life, especially because I did it out of anger and not love. That's the wrong motivation for anything."

Regrettably, Tolly hadn't stopped shaking her head. "I think you're wrong. Both of you. She's your sister, Fletcher. You should do what you can to protect her. That's what family does."

"I know you believe that. Hell, I love you for believing that—but I was raised in a different world than you. In your world, there was always right and wrong, good and evil, black and white. The right things were the right things, period. But in the world of the Fords? Of Chicago society? It's just not always so cut and dried."

She hunched back against the cushion, huddling deeper into her jacket, and then angled her gaze toward the blackness beyond the car's windows—the ones not on my side. "Then I don't think I like that world very much—and I'm glad you won't be a part of it any longer. It's a wonder you came out so normal, if those are really the values your parents taught."

I settled against the cushion as well, my body humming with tension. I was so tired. I knew that. I was drained. I knew that too. But I'd had enough judgment for one night, so I chose the riskier discussion path—but the one that brought more vindication. "Huh. That's sort of funny coming from you, baby. Your own parents all but forced you to stay in a relationship with an abusive asshole—and you've stated, every way but straight-up, your sister is probably being abused by her husband too. Want to tell me, with that kind of a family, how 'kin' are supposed to treat one another? I don't think you have room to judge that."

Yeah. It had felt good—for all of two seconds. Then immediately, I wanted to take it all back. The crestfallen shock on her face tore through my chest and then clamped my heart in a torturous vise.

"I'm...sorry." She wouldn't look up while she whispered the words, fretfully tugging at her hands.

"Fuck. No. I'm sorry. I'm so sorry. Please look at me. Please." I waited, through what felt like a thousand years, for those bottomless brown eyes to reach mine. "That was unnecessary. I apologize. I'm an ass. I've had all I can take for one night, but I should've never lashed out at you like that."

"It's okay." Her voice held ration portions of warmth, not shared with any part of her face. "Fletcher...it's okay."

Yeah, she'd said the words—but every roiling inch of my gut told me they were empty and patronizing. It wasn't okay. I'd royally screwed the pooch, opening up on her like that. I would just have to spend the rest of the night making it up to her.

Drake made the final turn into our driveway, rounding the bend to the porte cochere. A new night doorman hustled to greet us, swinging the front passenger door open. He looked a bit confused when the seat was empty. Drake hitched a thumb over his shoulder, indicating he had passengers in the back, and the new guy quickly compensated, opening the rear door with a smile.

"Sorry about that, folks. Not used to everyone's habits just yet." His smile was warm and genuine.

"No worries," Drake responded. "Hey, does this mean Maurice's Mrs. is in labor?"

"I believe so, sir. I'm not completely sure, but I received a last-minute call from the agency about the shift tonight. They mentioned something about 'someone making an early appearance.' With the other residents asking similar questions as yours tonight, that's what I'm piecing together."

"How exciting!" Talia sure got animated about that. "We'll have to check in the morning with the desk and see if the little one arrived." Her face was bright as a Christmas display, playing up every aspect of her beauty. The new guy assisted her out of the car, chatting her up while they walked toward the building's door. He swung it wide for her. I followed closely behind, not wanting to let her get too far, deep in my damage-control mode. Drake, gone nearly to radio silence, brought up the rear.

"We're in for the night. Sorry, I didn't catch your name." Drake handed him the keys, following up with a quick self-introduction.

"I'm Harold," the jolly man replied. "It's an old-fashioned name, I know, but I was named after my grandpa and—"

"Sounds good, man. Have a great night." After a hearty pat to the man's back, Drake stepped up on the other side of Talia. Using just the subtle press of his big body, he pushed her a little closer to me. I shot a fast nod of gratitude. Yeah, he was on board with moving our party along as fast as possible too.

"That guy would've talked all night if you let him," I commented as we waited for the elevator to arrive. "I think he liked our girl too."

Hopefully, I could start winning her back with some teasing. The compliment earned me at least a small giggle. It was brief but suffused her cheeks with a light blush. "Stop. He's a harmless old man. Probably gets lonely sitting down here by himself all night."

The elevator chimed, and we moved as a unit into the car. I entered the code for the condo, and the door slid shut...then silence.

"Who wants a cup of tea when we get inside?" Talia finally murmured. "I think that sounds nice. Hmmm?"

Drake and I exchanged a new glance of trepidation. Tea? I was relieved to see it wasn't the mood enhancer he'd been thinking of, either.

"Well." Drake spread a wolfish smirk, crowding into her

again. "I had something else in mind." His voice dropped to a sensual growl.

Talia giggled again, but there was a husk in her tone too.

"Me too, brother," I added softly. "Though I'm thinking... whiskey."

Talia's brows knitted. "You're always a gin guy."

"Not anymore."

And just like that, my mind zipped back to the scene in my parents' kitchen. I might not ever look at a bottle of gin and not think about those minutes that had turned into one of the biggest letdowns of my life.

"Doesn't matter, really," Talia replied. "You've had enough for tonight."

"Excellent point." Drake all but pleaded at me with his stare while hugging Talia to his chest. "Let's just go to bed and have hot monkey sex until we pass out."

"Mmmm." Her voice was muffled, thanks to Drake's tight embrace. It was still an adorable, arousing-as-fuck sound. "I think I could get on board with that plan."

"Agreed." I growled it while pressing close and kissing the back of her head. "But first, I need a shower. Gotta wash off the stink of the night."

"Stink" said it perfectly—and maybe scrubbing my body would wash off the stench of the self-pity in which I now slogged through at knee level. Maybe spending some intimate time with them would be just the healing medicine for us all.

Talia went down the hall to the master suite, and I took a detour into the smaller one delineated as mine. When I came back into the master, Drake was already in bed with Talia. They both had iPads in their hands and were busy tapping through screens.

"We look like an old married couple," I mumbled. "Except for the obvious."

"Speak for yourself. We aren't old." Drake looked up, closing the cover on his pad and putting it on the nightstand.

"Not that part," I groused. "I meant—we aren't a couple."

As soon as the complaint spilled, I wanted to cane myself for it. So the shower hadn't helped at all. Fuck, I was getting on my own nerves.

"No." Leave it to Talia to go full with the raised hackles while still looking every inch the lady. Even in her cute sleep tank, makeup stripped and hair in a messy bun, she was as regal as the Queen of England. "We're a family now," she clarified, even making that sound like the royal we. "So, stop being so grumpy and come join us." She pulled back the covers in invitation.

But I was bolted to the spot. My sister's wretched words came back, taunting me. Her insistence there was something wrong with what we were doing. Saying that people would talk about us behind our backs. Yet so many people at that party had known about Drake and me for years—almost ten, to be exact.

So why the fuck was I letting it all bother me now?

One look back to the bed answered that unequivocally. When I beheld the two people I loved more than anything in the world, all the reasoning notched into place.

And I simply knew.

This bullshit wasn't just about me taking the fall anymore. It was about Talia. And Drake too. They were in this relationship willingly, but no sane person would sign up to have a target painted on their back by the Ford family. It wasn't fair to put them in my parents' crosshairs, but I was too damn selfish to set either of them free.

I would take the whole ship down with me because I was too much of a coward to face the churning oceans of life without these two people.

CHAPTER THREE

Talia

"Come to bed."

So, this wasn't setting a good precedent, solving problems with sex, but screw the shrinks right now. I wanted—needed—to get reconnected to Fletcher. To them both. For the last half hour, Drake had been my rock, reassuring me in verbal and nonverbal ways that this garbage with Fletcher's family could be overcome with the force of our patience. I'd listened because, deep inside, I knew it was true. For all the brightness and laughter Fletcher could bring to the world, his lows sometimes resembled an icy tundra of sadness. It simply meant he felt everything with intensity and passion—and I wouldn't change him for all the rice in China.

But now it seemed he didn't even want to move from the tundra. Drake and I, already snuggled close under the covers, stared at his immobile form next to the bed. The same lost, angry look dominated his normally beautiful face, unchanged from when we'd left his parents' home.

Finally, he pulled the covers farther back with a heavy sigh and then climbed in. Drake and I traded a frustrated glance. Not a lot of ego boost when one's bedmate sounded like he faced a firing squad rather than two people wanting to share some awesome love with him.

I resolved not to take it personally. Fletch had endured a terrible night at the anniversary party. Maybe we could make him forget all about it.

So here went nothing.

Or maybe...a whole lot of something.

I wouldn't know if I didn't try.

I took a deep breath. Folded my hands against the coverlet, almost laughing at myself. Look at me, I'm Sandra Dee...

"Guys...I think we need to try something a little different tonight."

"Different?" Drake's bold features flared.

"How different?" Fletcher's tightened.

I almost laughed. Together, they looked like a pair of nervous colts. Our bedroom dynamic was incredible on a bad day, off-the-charts amazing on a good one. Why mess with the norm? Or so that was what their faces conveyed.

I didn't care.

It was time to push some limits.

I started the process by reaching for Fletch. "I want to show you how much I love you, Fletcher. How much I really care about you."

His lips twisted. "I don't need pity, Talia." His tone was a bitterly perfect accompaniment.

I pressed on.

"Well, that's good, because pity isn't what I had in mind." It was time to put on my bravest face...my big-girl panties, figuratively speaking. I'd been bold and not worn any panties to bed, and the soft brush of the sheets against my mound definitely gave a measure of sensual courage. I turned a little, looking up to him through half-closed lids, hoping I appeared seductive. "Lie back, Fletcher. Let me love you."

With a thoroughly masculine hum, Drake propped up on an elbow and stretched his big body out. He was at a perfect distance to stroke my arm or back or whatever came within reach but gave me enough space to crawl atop Fletcher.

"I think we need to get rid of this." I tugged Fletcher's T-shirt over his head, thankful he cooperated in getting the garment off. Without breaking the connection of our stare, he tossed it to the floor.

"Mmmmm. Better."

I leaned down, kissing him, drawn in by the deep-blue oceans in his eyes. So much torment there still, like angry waves crashing on the shadowy shores in his irises. The blue grew darker toward the center, until it nearly blended with the ink of his pupils. The creases at the corners were deep flares of stress tonight, more pronounced than I ever remembered. I hated the circumstances that made them that way but loved him for not shying away from their intensity.

I traced those precious grooves with my thumbs. Finally whispered, "You are so beautiful, Fletcher."

And so uncharacteristically quiet.

Another wrenching observation. He usually had a sassy comeback, or at least a gentle thank you. Now, he just stared with unblinking force, as if seeing me for the first time.

Insecurity swirled. Was that good or bad? What was he thinking? Was I making him feel worse? Should I be doing something else? Maybe taking charge was a bad idea. Maybe I should've left well enough alone...

But then Drake was there.

He stroked along the back of my thigh, his hand big and warm and reassuring, as if he sensed I needed the contact for my very grounding. I beamed him a quick smile, silently thanking him for the solace. He gave me courage to keep trying with Fletch.

With growing boldness, I worked my way down Fletcher's chest. I spread my fingers, touching every inch of his light-gold skin, marveling at the corded strength beneath it. His muscles, already strung tight, pulled and bunched as I stroked him—though in my mind, in that special place where he alone dwelled, I didn't feel arousal or excitement. His presence was defined by tension, hesitation, darkness.

What am I doing wrong?

I rose up again to kiss his mouth. A sigh loosened in my throat as he let his mouth open, accepting the slip of my tongue. The kiss was quiet and easy, working up to a low sizzle. I accepted that, knowing he needed it. We didn't have to be in a hurry. I had one goal alone. To make him to feel how loved he was.

"Fletcher?"

"Yeah, baby?"

"Can I...do more? I mean, will you let me—?"

Oh, my God. Could I get any more awkward about discussing sex? I was in a hot, passionate, incredibly sexy relationship with two gods turned into human form, yet naughty bedroom talk was like learning ancient Greek for me.

Maybe I'd just show him.

I tugged on his pajama pants, hoping he'd get the hint and let me off the dirty chatter hook. Relief flooded in when he raised his hips off the bed, allowing me to slide the pants all the way down. Quickly, I dumped them atop his T-shirt on the floor. At the same time, Drake shifted up higher on the pillows, his heavy-lidded gaze betraying his motivation. He wanted a better view of what was about to happen—but no way was he going to interfere.

Well, shit.

I was a little lost without his usual direction, but I could almost hear his voice in my head, guiding me what to do next, so I went with it. Trusted it. I had to before uncertainty chomped in and ate me alive. No room for that right now. This wasn't about my needs or feelings. Fletcher needed the consummation of our connection, and I was determined to deliver, despite how completely unfamiliar this felt. Amazing, how sex was a totally different experience when I was being told what to do, rather than taking control myself.

I had to leave all the doubts behind.

Just...go for it.

I lowered my attention again, sliding everything down his etched torso this time. Along the way, I nipped at the sculpted striations of his pecs and abs. He was so incredibly made. Leaner than Drake, but not by much. If they'd both become sports stars instead of businessmen, Drake would've been perfect for boxing and Fletch for swimming.

I didn't stop until my face was level with Fletcher's groin. His erection pulsed in front of my face, full and ready, the slit at the top glistening with a pearl of milky fluid. Wow. So hot... and needing my attention.

I tore my sights away long enough to look back up, met by a pair of gazes like hungry wolves, waiting for their next meal. Drake's jaw was tense and his bare nipples hard points against the coarse hair on his chest. Fletcher was even tauter. He gripped the sheets bunched at his hips, his knuckles straining against the skin stretched across them.

I smiled.

They both growled.

Drake's instructions flowed through my head again. Remembering how he'd told me to do this in the past, I wrapped all my fingers around Fletcher's cock, squeezing with firm pressure.

Fletcher groaned.

Oh. Wow.

I got more adventurous. Licked his tip with the end of my tongue, teasing enough to make him hiss with pleasure. I glanced up again, just to make sure I was reading him right, and was met by Drake's approving wink and quick nod. I moved in for another swipe, taking more time, using the flat surface of my tongue on the sensitive underside of Fletcher's crown. His answering groan was my new superpower. I moved down, determined to fill my mouth with as much of him as I could. Slowly, I slid over his pulsing shaft, tightening the suction on the pull back up.

He didn't hiss anymore. Or even groan.

He was stock still and breathing as though all the air in the room wasn't enough to satisfy his lungs.

I was pretty sure that meant he was enjoying things.

I continued the motions several more times.

"You're doing so good, baby." Drake's voice was rough and strained. His praise sank right into my bloodstream, which proceeded to rush between my thighs. When his voice dropped like that, amazing things were about to unfold. My pussy knew it too. Every intimate fold in my body was a fresh throb of arousal—of anticipation I'd never known. I couldn't wait to be fucked by one—or both—of them.

The wait was already killing me. I ground my crotch onto Fletcher's leg, hoping for some friction to ease the building ache.

"Shit." Drake's harsh hiss made me proud inside. I was getting to them. "Look at that. Fuck."

"Looking," Fletch confirmed, though his tone was a dark timbre I barely recognized. It was permeated with arousal but also with anger...and frustration.

It was also kind of hot.

"My dirty little bitch," he rasped then. "You're so fucking sexy. Do it again."

No doubt about it. He was commanding me this time. While the voice emerged from his lips, it was barely his own. And while the filthy words took me by surprise, they also ramped the pressure in my core to nearly unbearable need. I pulsed. I gushed. I ached.

Once more, I rubbed my pussy against his leg. This time, he raised the limb too, creating even more resistance. I moaned around his cock. If we kept grinding like that, I'd have an orgasm from just that.

"Greedy thing, aren't you?" He swept a hand from the sheets to my hair. "Keep sucking me. Then grind on my leg again."

My mind spun. My senses reeled. I obeyed him without question, giving over to a wild animal inside. A hot, horny, needy creature, driven only by instinct and a near-Pavlovian response to his dirty tone.

"Yeah," Fletcher praised. "Yeah, that's it. Your cunt is so wet. It's soaking my leg. My needy whore."

"Dude."

Drake's reprimand was quiet, but I heard it. I tried to censure him with a glance. Stop. I want this. Oh, God, how I wanted it—and how I dreaded him interrupting it. Fletcher's words should have been degrading, but they felt like adoration.

NO BROKEN BOND

I was so turned on, so hot with anticipation of what came next. How did I let them know without breaking the moment?

I waited until Drake met my gaze. Sent out a silent shout, ensuring all was okay. The man, a master at reading my expressions, would hopefully understand the look on my face. The need in my eyes.

"Fletcher." I breathed it more than spoke it. "I need you. I need you so badly."

I took his cock again, impaling my throat on his hard length, not stopping until I nearly gagged. I was in a frenzy. Needed to please him. Was nearly losing my mind because of it.

He threaded his fingers deeper into my hair, taking control of my movements. Inwardly, I rejoiced. I wanted him to use me. Wanted to feel like I gave him all I had. I breathed deep, relaxing into his guidance, letting him take over completely. My eyes watered from the sting of how tightly he held my hair, but that also added to the magic of this moment...the sorcery of all these amazing sensations in my system.

More.

"Please. Fletch."

But he quickly choked my sigh off, ramming his cock farther into my throat. It was deeper than either of them had ever gone. I panicked and began gagging, instinctively pulling back, only to get nowhere against his firm hold.

"No. Take it. Take all of me." I'd never heard his voice so stern. My pussy juices were a tiny river of lust, running down my leg now.

I looked up at him, eyes clouded with tears, mind crazed with desire. It was agony, but I wanted it. Needed him to push me, consume me, take everything he could from me—and to take everything from him in return.

He thrust his hips up, again and again and again. His face was fierce and his cock was brutal as he fucked my mouth the same way he'd pound my pussy. My gagging and moaning did nothing to deter him.

Drake's deep voice broke through our sexual fog. "Enough! It's too much for her."

I tried shaking my head, letting him know I was fine. And I was. I was on the verge of coming, exactly like this, lost to the wicked paradise of Fletch's rude, filthy handling. I didn't let my rhythm break on his cock, not that I had a say by that point. Fletcher was sweating, drops falling from his brow, running down his aquiline nose and spattering on his taut, straining abs. He was utterly carnal...completely beautiful.

"It's not, God damn it. She's loving it."

"Fletch—"

"Feel her," he ordered. "Do it. Do it. Reach down and feel her pussy. I'll bet her naughty cunt is soaked. I'm right, aren't I, sweet Talia? You like the way I fuck your pretty mouth, don't you?"

His voice came to my mind with rasping detachment, but I agreed with every word. I prayed Drake would just do it—how I yearned for his long fingers on my clit, stroking so I could finally know the best climax of my life—but Drake didn't move. He was motionless against the pillows. True, he enjoyed what he saw, since there was no mistaking his own tall erection, but his lust and his brain were clearly at war. He grimaced, craving to protect me. He hissed, yearning to fuck me.

Time to take the initiative again.

Desperately, I grabbed his hand. Luckily, he was close enough to touch. At once, he wrapped his fingers around mine.

I responded with a quick, reassuring squeeze. After that, he kept his words to himself but kept his attention completely on my face—double-checking every damn movement Fletcher made.

Fletcher...so incredible in his control.

Fletcher...healed by my surrender.

Fletcher...giving to me, even as he used me.

"I'm going to come, Talia. It's all for you. For your beautiful throat. Don't waste a drop. Do you understand?"

Every phrase was timed to a slide in or out of my mouth. I could only moan now, and I did. My jaw hurt. My throat was raw from his thrusts. But I was beyond aroused...and far past confused. Why did I love this? How could I crave this?

Questions for later. Much later.

If I started examining it, I wouldn't revel in it. Right now, I wanted nothing more than to please Fletcher in the most explosive way possible. To take the very essence of his body, deep inside my own. Then, dear God please, to find my own release.

With one final thrust, Fletcher roared in ecstasy. A rush of fluid coated my abused throat. So much. He had so much for me. I forced it down as he kept pumping, cupping my chin in a brutal clamp—holding my mouth tight around his shaft.

"Every drop," he ordered, his voice a husky mandate.

At last, our gazes met again. His eyes were ablaze. His nostrils flared with each inhalation. He was unspeakably sexy. Ruthlessly virile.

I yearned to climb onto his still-raging erection and ride him until I was spent too. I had never been so turned on and so ashamed at the same time. What the hell was going on?

Once more, a question for another time. I only wanted

to keep focusing on him. To rejoice in how thoroughly I'd pleasured him—and hopefully brought back the man I'd known before this horrible night with his family.

At last, he slid his grip from my face. He fell back onto the bed, chest heaving, skin gleaming, cock softening.

As Fletcher's breath returned, Drake was still speechless. I studied him harder, wondering where he was at. Though I couldn't reach into him as I did Fletcher, I'd become an expert at the dark angles of his face—and right now, they said danger.

On the other hand...I'd never felt closer to Fletcher.

So, where did that leave the three of us?

Worry and tension still flashed across Drake's face like a bar room's neon sign.

Maybe if I could just give him a smile...

But my mouth had never been so sore.

I licked my lips while reaching up, tenderly exploring my abraded skin. I felt bruised and used—a recognition that ran another thrill up my spine.

I gave in to instinct, crawling back on top of Fletcher. Drake pulled the cover up over my sweaty back.

When I buried my face into Fletcher's neck, he wrapped his arms tightly around me. Not tight enough, apparently. He cinched me in even harder, simply letting me breathe in and out, matching our heartbeats against each other.

After a few long minutes, he finally spoke in my ear. "Are you okay?"

"Yeah." I turned my head, kissing his neck below his ear.

"Tolly." He swallowed hard. "I'm so sorry."

"Don't be."

"But—"

"I loved it, Fletcher. Every single minute of it. Truly."

"No," he growled. "No, God damn it, you didn't. Don't say that to make me feel better. I was an ass."

"Like I tried to tell you?"

I lifted my head, shooting a glower at Drake and his snide snip before pressing my forehead to Fletcher's. "Do I really need to show you how hot that made me?"

He grunted. Shook his head. "You deserve to be treated like a queen, not a whore."

"Apparently, I like to be treated however you want to treat me." I attempted a laugh to finish it off, but the stubborn ass refused to heed me. "Please, Fletcher." I framed the side of his face with one of my hands. "Please, listen to me. That was hot, okay?" I took a turn to shake my head, though added an awed smile. "So hot, I can't find words. I don't regret a single thing. I would do it again in a heartbeat."

"Natalia."

I flung a new glare at Drake and his Dominant growl. "Don't with the 'Natalia,' Mr. Newland. I'm telling you the truth." As he snorted, I nearly gave myself a wedgie with the big-girl panties. Necessary move. I would not let them ruin this moment or make it into something it wasn't, and that meant standing up for myself too. "But...there's just one small, remaining problem."

Fletcher's face fell. "I fucking knew it. I knew you were holding something back."

His self-disgust was a bigger neon display than Drake's protectiveness, now vanished in favor of a visage of gentle concern. Their Freaky Friday switch-up should have weirded me out more, but I was on a mission now, not to be stopped.

"What's wrong, babe?" Drake queried in a voice like silk.

"Well..." It was as far as I got before the nerves took over again. No. Time for the game face. I could do this. My throbbing pussy demanded it. "I'm...ummm...seriously horny now."

The guys paused, glancing at each other in wolfish commiseration. Drake broke the contact first, gazing up at me with a full-on smirk. "And how can we be of service, ma'am?"

I practically growled back. They were really going to make me say it. "Fine," I huffed. "Can someone please fuck me?"

They shared a soft chuckle. Gorgeous bastards.

At last, Drake drawled, "I think that can be arranged." But as he pulled me from Fletcher's arms, he took a moment to cradle me close. "Are you sure you're okay?"

"Yes," I answered at once. "But I ache..." Even more with all his mighty muscles and dark sexuality pressed close. "A lot."

"I can take care of that."

His kiss ripped away the rest of my worries. He was commanding, controlling, consuming. He mastered me with his mouth, thrusting his tongue against mine, before exploring my neck, ears, and chest with incredible nibbles and kisses. The whole time, he ground his erection into my belly. Yes. Yes. This was exhilarating but familiar, passionate but patient—the kind of loving I was used to from him. And tonight, it was perfectly timed. I knew what to expect now...and moisture coated the juncture of my thighs because of it. As soon as Drake settled his cock there, the head was soaked with my cream.

"My God," he grated, rolling his hips so he could get every inch covered. "You weren't kidding, were you?"

I shook my head, all innocence and demureness now. The contrast from ten minutes ago was too comical to ignore, though I craved his cock too much to waste time on a laugh. I needed him. Everywhere. Right now.

"Spread your legs for me, baby. Let me inside."

I couldn't comply fast enough. As soon as I widened my thighs and lifted my hips, he plunged his erection in, sinking fully into my heat.

"Oh, my God. Drake!"

"Feels so good baby...yeah?"

"Yeah." I panted and writhed, letting out an approving cry as he shuttled in and out, in and out. "This is going to be the quickest orgasm in history."

"Only if I say it is."

I looked at him in complete panic. I couldn't hold back now if he told me to.

His deep chuckle sent relief through my system. I wrapped my legs around his hips, bracing for his thrusts. Needing every single one of them.

"Fuck. Talia." His gaze widened with wonder. "You really did like what Fletch just did. Your pussy is so hot and creamy."

I didn't say anything in response. Just buried my face into his neck, now weirdly embarrassed about my enjoyment of the degradation. I would have to figure out what that was all about when I wasn't concentrating on so much pleasure. On so much frustration. I needed to come like a star going supernova. I just wanted to focus on Drake's body. On what his incredible cock could do to my throbbing pussy.

"Natalia?"

"I'm—I'm okay."

"Don't be shy now." His chide was velvety but wicked, a dark and sensual tease. "I watched the whole thing, Tolly. Remember?"

"Yes, I remember."

"You were amazing." He angled his hips just right to slide against the inside of my channel, lighting up my nerves with every stroke. "So sexy. So giving. Just like you are right now, only in a different form. You're a beautiful, sexual creature, Talia. Don't ever be ashamed of it. Not with us. Not ever with us."

His thrusts lengthened. His cock swelled. He was doing it right. So damn right. "Oh, Drake! Please. God!"

"I love when you beg me. So sweet."

"I love you." The words came freely now, flowing from my lips just as my pussy flowed for his dick.

"I love you too." His voice was guttural, sensual. "You ready to come for me?"

"Yes!" I nearly screamed it. "Please...yes."

He pushed my knees to my chest. "Hold these here."

I willingly obliged. Whatever he had in mind, I trusted. The pleasure he delivered was always ridiculous. He thrust deeper and deeper while I gripped my knees, moaning in pleasure. Beautiful sensation gathered in my bloodstream, shimmering at the edge of my consciousness. The release I'd been chasing...it was almost here. It was going to be so good.

"God! Drake!"

Every single one of my muscles contracted at the same time, sending shivers through my system, bits of light through my bloodstream, sparkling out through my toes and fingertips in fantastic tremors of utter pleasure. It was just the start. The paradise of paroxysms went on and on as Drake orgasmed deep inside me, filling my pussy with his seed, fusing our mouths in a searing kiss, binding our souls once again.

As my climax receded, my thoughts clarified.

I was so completely in love with these two men. They were the molecules of my atmosphere. The tide and waves of my ocean. I could never take a breath without them both in my world.

They completed me.

Which was why, nearly at once, I noticed the stillness that still seemed to define Fletcher.

He'd been right beside Drake and me during our lovemaking, though had fallen again into noticeable silence. Though he'd never relented any contact with us, his somberness was palpable.

Soon, we all snuggled into our usual heap of postorgasmic bliss. I was exhausted and sated, so I didn't notice which one of the guys performed the blanket-wrapping duties—for my sake, of course. Both of them were furnaces, but I was always the cold one. Even between their two overheated bodies, I always preferred the covers too.

Such a minor detail, but it reminded me once more of all the concessions they'd made for me. So many, I'd lost track now—but because of all he'd done for me, it wasn't hard for me to be what Fletcher needed tonight—then for Drake to be what I needed too.

Concessions were easy, even natural, when people loved each other.

I'd even gotten lucky with mine tonight. Fletcher's rougher handling had shown me a new aspect of my sexual self—a part I liked. Both the guys had loved it too—so why go down the path of embarrassment or regret about it? The logic even sounded ridiculous, now that I started to weave my way through it.

Giving a part of yourself to the people you loved was one of the best parts of being in a relationship. It meant you trusted them and that they'd reward the trust by keeping that part of you safe. Nobody had ever kept me safer than these two men.

If Fletcher wanted me to do that again for him tomorrow, I would—and happily.

There was just one massive roadblock to that plan.

Fletcher himself.

How did I convince the man he'd done nothing wrong? The tension around him seemed to thicken by the minute.

My answer to that consisted of two parts.

One—convincing the man of this one was going to take a monumental effort.

Two—I wouldn't be alone.

Tomorrow morning, first thing, it would be time to enlist Drake in the battle too.

CHAPTER FOUR

Drake

Warm.

Too warm.

No. Too damn hot.

I tried to roll over and escape the sauna, but my legs were instantly entwined with someone else's. Or were those furnace coils? They were the source of all the heat, for sure.

"Mmmmph." It was my half-asleep way of saying "let me the fuck out of here." I followed it up by opening my eyes—then bolting all the way awake. I realized where I was. Still in bed, tangled with Talia and Fletcher, where we'd all passed out after I'd fucked her senseless.

The memory got me even hotter.

Damn, how the woman could unravel me. Incite me. Enflame me.

Now, even more than ever. Shit. For someone who was always cold when conscious, she was a damn radiator once she fell asleep.

Another minute of this heat, and I was going to go Doctor Manhattan on her and Fletch. I needed some space. Now.

I slowly slid out from the bed, trying my best not to wake Tolly. When I glanced at the farthest side of the bed, it was to realize our third piece was nowhere to be found. No telltale sounds from Fletch using the facilities, either.

Why didn't that surprise me?

After quickly pulling on some joggers, I sneaked out of the bedroom, subtly shutting the door behind me. Down the hall, in the kitchen, I found a dim glow from the light over the sink, as well as the digital readout on the oven. Two eighteen a.m.

The breakfast nook was dark. So were the dining room and living room.

Still no Fletcher.

I turned around, wondering...

Until spotting the open whiskey bottle on the counter, its contents partially gone.

I let out a long, rough rumble. "Fucking. Great."

Score one for Ford. Another wasted self-beating.

I had half a mind to just go back to bed and let him mentally flog himself into tomorrow, in whatever the fuck corner he'd crawled into. Maybe a royal-level hangover would do the man some good. If it were just the two of us here, and my own bed waited for me, the option would've won by a landslide.

But we weren't the only ones here.

The woman of my soul was here. Slumbering just down the hall...through dreams in which she was happy with Fletch and me.

And sometimes, happy took some work. From everyone involved.

Even after two o'clock in the god damn morning.

As I ruminated on that theory, I spotted the open slider to the patio. It was one of Fletch's favorite spaces in the condo. He liked how he could see a lot of Michigan Avenue. Said the bustle of the street calmed him, helped him reflect on things. I'd always responded that he had probably been one of those kids who had fallen asleep to the vacuum cleaner too—though asking Francine Ford to verify that was impossible. The woman literally had no memories of Fletcher when he was still in diapers. I'd often wondered if the woman had popped him out and then pretended he didn't exist until he no longer smelled like Pampers and poop.

So, maybe it wasn't so shocking that he did this crap from time to time.

I grabbed a jacket from the back of a chair before pushing the door a little wider and stepping onto the landing.

Sure enough, his dark form was sitting in the corner, curled up on a chaise lounge, bundled in a throw from the living room sofa. A dark hoodie was pulled over his head, white wires from his ear buds glowing in contrast to the shadows in which he was shrouded.

He raised his head as I slid the glass door shut behind me. I quickly zipped up my own jacket. The night air was brisk. Unbelievably, I longed to be back in the furnace-bed with our woman.

I pushed his feet off the lounger and replaced them with my ass, coming down with a decisive thud. He grunted, lifting one of his feet back up. Damn thing jabbed into my hip. I resisted the urge to whack at him. Wouldn't do any good. This was a pity party for one, and I was an unwelcome guest to the soiree.

Too bad, motherfucker.

After sending out that uplifting mental message, I waited. Eventually, he'd say something. There was one upshot of having a best friend who'd logged more time on professional therapists' couches than most docs spent in med school. Fletch simply couldn't not talk when given the opportunity. It just required waiting him out...letting him find the right way to get rolling.

He played that ball quicker than usual.

"She'll never forgive me."

His voice was husky and jittery against the relative silence of the night. Hell. Had he been crying?

"Fletch," I volleyed back instantly. "She fucking loved it. What about that don't you get?"

"Doesn't matter." He took a huge gulp of the amber liquid in his glass. Yeah, the glass. Bastard had poured himself a glass of whiskey like most people served orange juice. "She shouldn't forgive me."

"It doesn't matter if she loved it?" I growled. "Do you even hear yourself?"

"She's our queen. She deserves to be treated like one." He gulped and looked away. Another swig of the whiskey—like that was helping—before he confessed, nearly whispering, "I called her a whore."

"Did you mean it?"

"Of course I didn't mean it! I-I just got swept up in the moment."

The violent defensive bite in his answer was exactly what I'd hoped for. He wasn't completely lost on this. Not yet. "Then why are you beating yourself up?"

"It's what I do," he groused. "It's my superpower."

He chuckled sloppily. I didn't join in.

"I think being an ass may be your superpower."

"Fuck you," he snarled. "Just...go back inside. She's going to wake up if we're both gone."

"Good. That means you can explain all this shit to her— because believe me, man, I'll bet she's already dreaming about ways to make you explain it to her."

He kicked me, disguising it as a restless readjustment. In the name of our friendship and of the woman inside, who'd probably clock me for breaking Fletch's ankle, I let it pass.

"Why are you being such a dick?" he finally snarled.

"Oh. Now, that's funny." I paused for a moment. "You giving me the dick statement."

With a moody huff, he slammed back against the headrest of the chair. With an equally weighted breath, I rose. This whole night had been one fuck-up after another. It was time to get to the real problem.

"Listen," I began again. "I'm not going to deny the thing with Sasha is probably going to haunt you for a while..."

"Us," Fletcher countered. "It's going to haunt us, man." He brought his other leg back up, using the motion to mask how excruciatingly he measured his next words. "And there's the rub, Newland. You and Tolly don't deserve that bullshit. None of it. Me? I've grown a Teflon hide against it—but you two..."

"What?" I fired solidly into his telling pause. "You think we can't?" I stomped to the rail. Gripped it with a fist matching the iron it was made of. "Were you listening to a word she said tonight? Do you really need to be reminded about what she went through last year with her family? That woman of ours... She's a warrior, man. We may enjoy treating her like a delicate little bird, but Talia Perizkova is a fucking condor, talons and all. I wouldn't put anything past her." With my free hand, I stabbed a finger his way. "Don't insult her by selling her short."

Fletch's head reared back as if my finger had shot lightning bolts. "Condor or not, that still doesn't make what went down at my parents' right."

"Maybe not. Probably not. But it is what it is. Now, we

deal with it. Together. End of story."

He leaned forward, straddling the bench now. His newly lifted gaze was a study in blue flames. "Why do you do that?"

"Do what?" I whipped back.

"Oversimplify everything."

I twisted my grip harder to the rail. Ground my teeth together. No composure-saving trick was working—because now he was really pissing me off. "What would you rather I do, Fletch? Sit around and have a drunken pity party for myself, like you're doing? Is that a better plan?"

"Fuck you." His voice drifted off as he gazed out into the city lights. "That's not what I'm doing."

"Really?" I fired. "Because that's exactly what it looks like from here. And what are you showing Talia? That this is what she can expect from the guys who want to be her husbands? That every time something goes wrong, you hit the booze and emo eyeliner music in a dark corner?"

His head snapped up, unshed tears making his eyes gleam in the mix of moonlight and city lights. "Why the hell not, Drake? Why the fucking hell not? At least I can listen to this 'eyeliner music' and know what it's talking about. At least I can connect myself emotionally from A to Z."

"What the hell does that mean?" I snarled.

"Do you care?" he flung. "Wait. Hold on. I remember now. The answer doesn't matter, as long as you get to sweep in and save the day. Get the white hat out—here comes Drake and his mile-long cavalry."

I let the rail go. Jammed both arms across my chest, telling myself he didn't really mean any of that. He was hurt. Defensive. And drunk.

"Don't lash out at me." I was stunned by the diplomacy

beneath it. I really longed to back it up with five, perhaps ten, knuckles. "This is unnecessary, Fletch."

"Right." He shook his head. "Of course it is, Mr. Newland. Whatever you say, lord god on high."

"Can you stop being such a dick for one second?" I spread my arms. A few inches higher from their forty-five-degree angles, and I really would look like his lord and savior—which wasn't off the table yet. "I'm trying to help you look at this shit storm a different way. You see that, right? You're too smart for all this crap"—I emphatically pointed at the glass he still clutched—"and she doesn't need to see you like this."

"But she does need to see the crap I pulled in the bedroom tonight?" he retorted. "You see that, right?" He surged to his feet. Swayed for a second and then fell back onto the chaise in a clumsy heap. "Jesus. I'm a damn basket case, Drake. And now, with my disgusting excuse of a family messing shit up..." He dragged in more whiskey. How the guy could chug good Macallan like ball park beer, I couldn't—and didn't—want to understand. "Maybe I should go away. Neither of you need me around, fucking things up."

"Christ and the fucking angels." I couldn't remember speaking to him with such venom in my tone. Ever. "I can't get through to you, can I?" Only when cold pain shot through my fist did I realize I'd driven it down onto the railing. "Tell you what, asshole," I muttered. "I'll just go get the bottle for you. Sit out here and get shitfaced all night if you want. Have fun with the hypothermia you'll have by morning too. Just see how that will 'fuck her up,' Fletcher." I took two steps, fully intending to cut him off there, but fury stopped me short right before the doorway. "You're not a basket case, Fletch. You're a selfish prick. If you can't see that yourself, I'm sure as hell not going to get through that pretty-boy skull of yours, either."

With that, I pivoted and went back inside. Though I was tempted to ram the slider closed, I forced myself to push the glass door with gentleness. The asshole's bender was sure as fuck not going to ruin our lady's rest.

I made my way back to the bedroom.

I slid back under the covers and pulled Talia into my arms. Her sleep-soft body instinctively curled into my side. Sleep would be a long time coming for me, if at all, but I was content to feel her curves against me and listen to her soft breathing.

Finally, thank fuck, Fletcher came back in too. He crawled in and then scooted over, wrapping arms around Talia from behind. With a long but shaky breath, he buried his face into her dark hair. Within minutes, he was asleep too, more than a little aided by his whiskey chug-fest.

Sleep was definitely not coming now.

Or so I'd thought.

When the alarm went off at six, I was roused from dreamless darkness though felt like I hadn't slept at all. When something was off between the three of us, the balance of the universe was affected. Ridiculous? Maybe. But true? Hell, yeah. Our rhythms were so synched to each other, our lives so intertwined, that we literally fed off one another's energy. But the day was new, and the slate was blank. I chose to face it with confidence that we'd get shit back on track. Then, tonight, we could screw our sweet girl back into another great night's sleep—and this time, join her for it.

Talia met my eyes in the bathroom mirror while we stood side by side, brushing our teeth. She didn't say a single word, nor did she have to. The questions and pleas in her stare spoke volumes.

"All right," I finally told her after a quick rinse and spit. "I'll talk with him tonight, if I can't connect with him today." The first option felt more doable than the second, as I explained, "I think he's already gone."

Sure enough, the bastard had sneaked out without saying goodbye to either of us. Beholding the empty space on the foyer credenza where his wallet and sunglasses usually were, I made a promise not to let this bullshit go on until tonight. I'd be the man's worst texting nightmare until he agreed to meet me for lunch. His wrecking ball had to be stopped before gaining any more destructive momentum.

I dropped Talia off at Stone Global Corporation, making sure our goodbye kiss was one to remember, and then headed farther into the city to my own office. The streets were a nightmare, worse than usual even for a Monday morning. Traffic alerts on my Rover's nav unit screamed about a two-car accident ahead, near Wacker.

Just excellent.

I dialed the office on my cell since State Street had become a parking lot, letting them know I was stuck in traffic. I had a meeting in fifteen minutes that would need to be rescheduled. I thought about texting Fletch, since I literally had the car in Park by now, but decided he likely needed a little more space. Or maybe I did. His disappearing act from this morning was like a kick in the god damned balls. That shit was going on the household no-fly list as soon as possible.

Traffic funneled into one slow-moving lane, ensuring everyone got a nice gawk at the accident's leftover debris of the accident. The cars, or what was left of them, were being loaded onto a flatbed truck on the opposite side of the lanes.

My stomach lurched.

One of the vehicles was a BMW Alpina B6.

The same size and custom paint as Fletcher's—with the same dual sport exhausts.

I shook my head rapidly. That didn't mean a damn thing, despite the chill invading my spine. Plenty of rich idiots in Chicago were just like him, insisting on fast black cars with tons of custom shit despite the city's insane winters.

This means nothing. This means nothing.

Nevertheless, everything that had happened in the past twenty-four hours came screaming back to mind—giving me a crazy case of paranoia as I rolled slowly past the wreckage.

This means nothing. This means nothing.

Besides, FF Engineering was at least three miles away, on the other side of town. Why the hell would Fletch have any reason to even be in this neighborhood, especially at the early hour he must have departed the condo?

Not particularly a believer, I sent up a quick prayer anyway. Judging by the damage done to those cars, the humans involved would be lucky to be alive, if not badly injured. Glancing at the B6 once more, I vowed to call Fletch the minute I was parked at the office. Now that traffic had picked up past the accident scene, I would be there in less than thirty minutes.

When I finally settled in behind my desk, I hit Fletcher's number on my desk phone's Speed Dial.

One ring. Two.

A third. A fourth.

Voicemail.

Again.

"Shit," I muttered. Where the hell was he? I had also sent a text and an invitation to FaceTime. He never blew me off for that, even if he was sulking.

A meeting. Yeah, he was probably already into the thick of things. That would explain the ice-out, which really wasn't an ice-out—as I kept reminding myself.

I launched the chat client on my computer and then clicked on his profile.

His message was still set to its weekend auto-greeting.

"Shit." It spewed from me more forcefully this time. Had he even made it to the office?

Fuck.

My mind flashed back. That car, on the flatbed...had there been a license plate on it? I couldn't remember. All I thought about was the mangled steel—and the thought that nobody in that machine could have really survived what it had been through.

"Shut up," I snarled at myself, next dialing his assistant.

"Fletcher Ford's office."

"Meagan." I force fed composure to my tone. Told myself that in under a minute, I'd be listening to the asshat's tired grumble and then verbally reaming him a new one for leaving without goodbyes this morning. "Good morning. This is Drake Newland."

"Good morning, Mr. Newland," the woman greeted smoothly in return. "You must have ESP."

"Why?"

"I was just going to call you."

I straightened in my chair. "Why?"

"Well, I'm having a hard time tracking Mr. Ford down this morning. Do you know what his personal schedule is today? He didn't show up to his first appointment, and he's not answering his phone. Errr...Mr. Newland?"

Her voice faded beneath the stunned buzz in my brain.

The static of it shot to the base of my skull, making every hair on the back of my neck shoot to attention. As my senses spun harder, the painful prickles darted down my spine, becoming a web of dread throughout my body.

Something was off.

I knew it now.

Way the fuck off.

"He...uhhh..." I rubbed my forehead, ordering myself to form words. "He left the house this morning before we had a chance to talk." There. That was a full sentence. I could do this shit. "So...I'm not really sure where he was headed."

"Okay." Meagan's reply sounded hollow and far away. "I'm sure he'll turn up, then," she continued from the same strange tube. "Probably stopped to get a coffee or something and got delayed. Would you please tell him to check in with me if you hear from him before I do?"

"I-I will. And please—do the same. I have something important to discuss with him."

"Will do. Bye now."

As soon as she disconnected the call, my phone slipped from my numb fingers. It clattered to the desk, the screen taunting and dark—but only for a few seconds. When it rang again, I whipped it to my ear and growled, "Are you trying to give us all a heart attack, you bastard?"

"Uhhhh. No. Drake?"

"Shit," I muttered. "Tolly. Baby, I'm sorry. I didn't look at the caller ID." And, because of it, would now make her worry too. "I thought you were that shithead partner of ours."

"It's—it's okay."

As soon as I registered the wobble in her voice, all the ice in my body turned to raging fire. Nothing, and no one, put that shiver into my woman's voice without regretting it. "It's not okay." Not a request. Not a question. I slammed it out as the fact it clearly was. "What is it? Talk to me, baby." Tell me whose face I need to bash in for you. Because punching anything sounded like a good idea right now.

"S-Something's wrong," she finally whispered. "I know it sounds crazy, but Drake, I know it. I just do. I can't put my finger on it, but...you know how he and I are. Something's wrong." She stopped, pulling in a quivering breath. "I-I can't feel him anymore. That little hum I always have in my head, because of him. It's...stopped."

Her choked-back sob stabbed the center of my chest. I hated hearing her upset. Hated. It.

Before I could wrap my mind around the right words to reply to her, she already had more for me. "Why did you answer your phone that way just now?" she questioned. "Drake? What's going on? Do you know something you aren't telling me?"

Too smart, this one. The blessing and curse Fletch and I had signed on for with her.

"No." I pushed it out with suspicious speed but added just as fast, "You remember what I promised you, right? That I wouldn't hold anything back from you ever again?" Last summer, when I'd let her father sway my mind so badly that I'd left her and Fletch in the name of their domestic bliss, the three of us had endured a nightmare of separation. From that point forward, we'd made a three-way promise. We'd never play "I have a secret" again.

"Yes. You did." She exhaled just as shakily. "But I can hear something in your voice. You're worried about him too, aren't you?"

"I won't deny that." I rose, feeling restless...explosive. Wasn't there anything in my chrome and glass office that wouldn't break if I threw it? "His behavior this morning..." Maybe verbalizing my shit would help. "Well, it was unusual, even for a drama king like him." After she gave a watery laugh at my jab, I went on, "I've tried calling him a few times this morning, and he's not picking up. I finally got through to Meagan, who asked if I knew his schedule for the morning. He didn't show for his first appointment."

I hated being the one to break that all to her, but no secrets meant no secrets. I listened, chest aching, as the line scuffled at her end. She was probably pacing too. "That's not like him."

"At all," I concurred.

"What can we do?"

"Nothing. He'll turn up. He'll turn up, baby. I know it." By now, I stood facing the wide window of my office. The morning sun was crisp and brilliant over the skyline, bouncing off all the iconic structures—Chicago Place, Olympia Center, Park Tower, John Hancock—a view that normally inspired the hell out of me. Today, the kniving angles and sharp light were intrusive, abusive, infuriating. "Listen...he was in a bad funk last night after you went to sleep."

From her end, utter stillness.

"Talia?"

"A funk?" she rasped at last. "A...bad one?"

No. Secrets.

"Yeah. Pretty bad."

"How? Why?"

"He started blaming himself for everything from what happened at the party, to how he behaved with you afterward, to the color of the sky not being the perfect shade of blue."

"That's just silly."

"I know and told him as much." I pinched the bridge of my nose. "We fought. A little. I'm sorry." I rushed out the apology. "We were both tired and edgy."

Again, a weird quiet from her end. "Then this morning, his hum is gone in my head."

"It probably doesn't mean anything." I held back on adding that the reason she didn't "feel" him was likely due to the fucker's monstrosity of a hangover. "Let's not get all worked up. We just have to wait until he calls one of us back. Why don't you leave him a message? Or text him? He may still be giving me the electronic middle finger, but you he'll answer."

Her shivering breath vibrated over the line. It sounded small but ghostly, making me shiver though I stood in a patch of sunlight. "I did, Drake," she said. "That's what made me start freaking out."

"Don't freak out." Damn, I craved a teleportation machine. I'd beam myself to her this very fucking second. I couldn't turn my voice into a comforting embrace, a reassuring kiss. "Baby—"

"He never leaves me hanging when I reach out to him. And if I can't feel the bond..." Her voice broke. "Our bond, Drake. Our head thing. It's gone. Why is it gone?"

"Baby, calm down." Again, with yearning for the teleporter. I'd grab her now, forcing her to look at me by bracing hands to both her shoulders. "It's probably just because you're nervous now. Let's not jump to any conclusions, okay?"

"Okay." Her hesitant nod bled through in her voice. "I'll try. I will. But I think I'm going to be a complete basket case until we hear from him."

"Do you want me to come get you?" I'd hopscotch over the

buildings to get to her faster, if that was what she needed.

"No, no." She hurried the words, as if flustered with her burst of weakness. "I have a meeting in ten min—whoa, it's actually in two minutes." Her breath puffed through the line, indicating her rush to grab materials for her appointment. "I need to hang up. Please call me if you hear anything. I love you."

"I will. And I love you too."

After ensuring she was really gone, I slumped back into my chair. I was still nervous as hell, so I pushed back, letting the chair's castors carry me until I bumped the bookcase behind me.

Not a great occurrence when attempting to forget a car accident.

The scene consumed my mind again. That car, resembling a soda can doomed for a recycling bin. The smell of burned rubber. The chaos of police lights. Twisted steel and glass littering the highway, so many destroyed pieces. Somebody's life, now in a million little shards.

No. No.

Fletcher's office wasn't even near that intersection.

But he hadn't been bound for the office. Meagan's voice careened through my head, confirming it.

He didn't show up to his first appointment...

What if...?

"My God." Again, a true plea now. I almost dropped to my knees as I repeated it. I sure as hell clenched all fingers together, turning it into my lame version of a heartfelt petition. "My God...please...no."

It had looked so much like his car. How many Alpina B6s were there really in this city?

"Please," I rasped again. My stomach churned. In the same rumble, it reminded me and thanked me for not eating yet this morning. My nerves all clenched in prayer too. My heartbeat was frozen.

Waiting.

Waiting...

My cell phone chimed again.

I bolted the chair forward and reached for it.

When I observed the number, an unfamiliar caller with a Chicago area code, my stomach stopped roiling—and jumped straight into a bile bath.

"This is Drake Newland." My voice shook.

Right before the nightmare took over.

I'd never forget the moment I practically lip-synched the words as the other voice began. I had no idea why. It was like I'd seen this conversation take place in a dream or maybe another life all together. Either way, the ghost of it had caught up with me. In horrifying spades.

"Mr. Newland. I'm so glad I reached you. My name is Andy, and I'm the admissions nurse at Memorial Hospital in Chicago. A man has been brought in through the emergency room. He's...not in great shape. His personal identification had your name written in as emergency contact."

For one second, I closed my eyes. Talia made us do that. One day she'd insisted we all write "Emergency Contact" on the back of our own business cards and stow them in our wallets with our drivers' licenses. Fletcher's wallet had my card. Talia's had Fletcher's, and I had Talia's in mine. Then we promised one another other we'd never have a reason to use them.

You broke the promise, Fletcher.

But if this guy is calling, then you're still alive.

Thank. Fucking. God.

"Mr. Newland?"

"Yes. Sorry. I'm...I..." Well, for starters, I was suddenly a bumbling idiot. Pull. It. Together. "Wh-What?" I finally stammered.

"I'm sorry. I know this is a lot to take in at one time, but are you able to get down to the hospital?"

"Of...of course." I jerked to my feet. Stopped short. "Why? He's all right, isn't he?"

Weird images flashed to my mind. That wreckage again. All that glass again. But weren't there YouTube videos of people in accidents just as bad, who'd walked away with nothing more than scrapes and bruises?

"Mr. Ford is being prepped by the trauma team. There will be paperwork and decisions to make. Since your name was in his wallet, I thought you would want to be here."

"Right. I'm on my way. Memorial, you said? Where do I go?"

"You can just come in the front door. A docent will help you. We have senior volunteers on hand to help in times like these."

"Times like these?" I all but bellowed it. "What the hell? Is he dead? Or going to die?"

"No." Andy's voice wavered, acting like a mirror back to me. I didn't like what I saw. Don't alienate an ally, shit for brains. Get your shit together. "As I said, he's not in great shape, but he's under the best of care. We're doing everything we can for him. Our facility is one of the finest—"

"I don't need a god damned commercial. I just need the fucking truth, Andy. If this isn't it, I'll hunt you down when I get there."

So much for that shit being together.

"Mr. Newland, threats aren't necessary. I'm being straightforward. Mr. Ford's injuries are numerous, and we're handling them in order of priority..."

Andy went on and on, but I couldn't admit I was too freaked the fuck out for comprehending a single word. Finally, I just had to cut him off again. "I'm leaving now." I was lethally calm about it. "I'm downtown, so I should be there within a half hour."

But before I got into the car, I needed to call Talia.

It would be the worst phone call I'd ever made.

I stormed out of my office, down the hall to my project manager's office. Ducked my head in and growled, "I'm leaving. Fletcher's been in an accident. The hospital just called."

Before I could leave, Jim stood to his full height, grasping my shoulders. "You want me to drive you over? You look like hell."

"Yeah. No. Fuck it, I just have to go. I have to call Tolly. Then I have to go."

Mr. Bumbling Idiot, reporting for duty.

I had to get it together. Why couldn't I just pretend the Range Rover was a Humvee, I was in the middle of some desert shithole, and I was sprinting to be at the side of a battalion brother?

Because this was my brother.

Because if anything fucking happened to him, I couldn't lie down in my rack and dream of leaving the war behind. This was the war.

In the parking garage, I stared at the controls like a dumbass.

"Start the fucking car," I ordered myself in a mumble. "Now, seat belt. Reverse. No. Fuck. Wait. Call Tolly first."

I pulled back into the parking space. Had barely gotten the car stopped and idled before banging my palm on the steering wheel so hard the horn sounded. I did it again, exactly the same way, taking violent delight in the blares bouncing against the cement, pounding against the air, unleashing my own enraged shout.

"Fuck this!" Bang. Honk. "Fuck him!" Bang. Honk. "God damn you, Fletcher Ford. I'm going to fucking kill you if you live through this!"

I shouted it at the windshield, continuing to beat and honk, emotions trampling my nerves like a fucking wild mustang stampede. I let the ponies come, stomping every square inch of my senses, until my fury was spent enough for my thoughts to clear.

Finally, with shaking fingers, I punched the Speed Dial for Talia's number.

She picked up on the first ring. "Drake? Did you find him? Did he call you? I'm telling you, I'm going to throttle him for worrying us like—"

"Natalia."

Her babbling halted at once. My tone left very little confusion about the purpose of my call. Something bad had happened.

No. Secrets.

"Drake. Wh-What is it? You...you're...scaring me."

No. Secrets.

"I'm coming to pick you up, baby." I pushed my forefinger and thumb into my eye sockets, telling the tears to take a fucking hike. "Be out front in ten minutes, okay?"

"But—"

"Fletcher's been in a car accident." I barreled over her gasp, needing her to hear the determination in my voice. The very little strength I could impart right now. "Memorial Hospital just called me. I'll pick you up."

"No." Her reply was immediate and stringent. Too much so. Already, I could hear the manic threads of her composure, and they were unraveling fast. "No, Drake. Go straight there. I can drive myself."

"I don't want you driving, damn it. You're already too upset. I'm coming to get you."

"Damn it!" She all but screamed it. "You're wasting time, Drake. Get to him—you must get to him."

"And you think you can drive?" I bellowed back. "In that condition?"

"You don't understand." She was broken now. Sobbing. "Drake...we're losing him. I-I can feel it. I can feel him... slipping. I can feel it all in my bones. Please...just go to the hospital."

I almost begged the mustangs to come back. My jaw ached from gritting so hard. "Fine," I finally growled. "But I'm going to call Killian. He can have the SGC driver bring you. Swear to me you will not get behind a wheel. Swear it, Natalia."

"Okay. All right. Okay. I'll wait for Mr. Stone to find me. Please be safe."

"I will be." I should have hung up but took a huge pause, letting her listen to my weighted huff. "Thank you, Talia—for relenting. I couldn't bear it if—"

"Hush," she admonished. "I'll be safe. I'll see you at Memorial. I love you."

"I love you too."

After disconnecting with her, I immediately dialed Killian. His assistant, Britta, answered in her pleasant and professional manner.

"Britta. Drake Newland."

"Well, good morning to you."

I normally spent time in good-natured ribbing with her. We were both Walking Dead fans, so Monday mornings were exceptionally ripe times for casual conversation. Not so much today. "Is he around?" I demanded at once. "It's an emergency."

"One moment. He's in a meeting, but for you he'll want to be interrupted."

I engaged the Bluetooth on my phone to take the call over the car's speakers. Stone Global's Hold button music was a strange injection of Zen in the midst of these harrowing minutes, filtering through the Range Rover as I put it into reverse for real.

"My brother!" Killian's exuberant voice was a burst of excitement after the green-tea-and-eucalyptus tune that'd been massaging my ears. I winced, turned the volume down on the system, and began the strange ordeal of finding the right place to start this horrible tale.

"Kil." Fuck. "Killian."

"Damn." His subtext was a scratching record, yanking him from swaggering to serious in two-point-five. "What the hell is up, man?"

"I need your help. Right now. Fletch—he's...he's been in a car accident."

"What? Fuck. How? Where?"

"I don't know. Memorial called me about ten minutes ago."

"How can I help?" He was suddenly the Killian Stone

familiar to the entire corporate business world. Granite composure. Steeled resolve. Self-control matching his last name to the iota. "Tell me, and it's yours."

"Talia's at work today—but I'm scared to death to let her behind the wheel."

"I'll bring her myself."

"Not necessary. I was thinking one of the company drivers—"

"Fuck you," he growled. "I'm bringing her myself."

I clenched my jaw harder—mostly to stave off more ridiculous tears. Fucking Killian. He knew, as only a friend and a brother would, that I needed more than just wheels for my girl. I needed him. Stone Global's fiscal year end was approaching, which meant he likely had back-to-back meetings clear into the night, but at this very second, as I listened to his fingers clacking computer keys in the background, he was clearing them all in the name of our friendship.

Fucking Killian.

"Thanks, Kil. I—" I love you, man. "I just—owe you one."

"You owe me about twenty-one, but who's counting."

"Dick."

"Uh-huh." He inserted a fast, wry laugh. "See you in twenty."

As I disconnected, I realized I was already halfway to the hospital. My speedometer read eighty-two. As tempted as I was to just keep it there, I needed to slow my shit down. No sense in two of us being fucked.

"I swear to God," I muttered, hating the new crawl at sixty-two. "I'm going to kill him for this." Again, the windshield was my new best mate.

The miles seemed to creep by. Finally, I pulled into the

hospital's parking lot. I swung into a spot marked Physicians Only, threw the Range Rover into Park, and was on my feet, sprinting for the main entrance. The loafers I'd slipped on a few hours ago did nothing to improve my pace.

The elderly folks milling around the counter inside the front door saw me coming but were unfazed. It occurred to me that they'd probably seen my panicked look and frenzied charge before—on a dozen other people each day.

Stay calm. Stay calm.

The mantra marked my steps toward a little woman who looked like the love child of Betty White and Yoda. "Can you please help me?" I entreated. "My brother—my friend—was brought here not long ago. He was in a car accident. They called me and told me to come here. Said you'd tell me where to go."

Yeah, I sounded like an idiot. A full-on, beyond-control, babbling straightjacket case. But the woman smiled as her kind eyes found mine. "Okay, young man. Let's just see what we have here."

She eased her frame into a chair in front of a computer screen. I clenched my fists, resisting the urge to lean over myself and scroll through their database. She was trying to help. Worse, if I bit her head off as I had Andy's, I'd likely be escorted to the trauma unit with a bar of soap jammed in my mouth.

"Now. What is your brother's name?"

"Ford. Fletcher Ford." Now wasn't the time to explain how the word "brother" was used very figuratively in our household.

"All right," she stated. "Here we go. According to the computer, he is being prepped for surgery in the trauma suites."

"Where's that?" I barked it, wincing when her wrinkled gaze shot up. "Apologies, ma'am. I'm freaking out here. I shouldn't have— Can you point me toward that unit, please?"

She gave a brief nod, accepting my contrition. "Just take this elevator to the fifth floor. Follow the signs to the trauma unit. Someone will be able to help you from there."

I took off at a run toward the elevator and then remembered Talia. I skidded across the floor, fighting to change directions, moving faster than physics wanted to accommodate in slick-bottomed loafers.

"Fuck!"

"Excuse me?" Yoda White admonished.

"Sorry, sorry. Two more people will be coming through those doors asking for Mr. Ford. Tall, good-looking guy with jet-black hair, escorting a beautiful young lady with eyes like chocolate. Can you send them there too?" I turned and then spun back. "Please?"

"Of course. Of course."

"Thank you."

Once inside the elevator, I mashed on the number five. When the lift doors closed, I caught my reflection in the stainless-steel panels. Thank fuck no one else was in here with me. I seemed certifiable. I felt worse. Like I was falling apart. I stared down at my feet, certain they'd be splattered with my spleen in a second.

On the fifth floor, I broke into a new jog. As the docent had told me downstairs, the overhead signs guided me correctly. Once I arrived at the trauma unit, a young red-headed man looked up from the nurses' station computer.

"Mr. Newland?" He stood and strode toward me, hand extended.

"Yes. Are you the guy I spoke to on the phone?" I dragged an embarrassed hand through my hair. Shit. I'd treated him so badly on the phone. "Andy, right?" I injected it with respect this time.

"I am." He smiled a little, acknowledging my overture. I wasn't the first asshole he'd likely encountered in this job and wouldn't be the last. Still, he said gently, "Let's go down the hall a bit. There's a private room there. We can talk."

I nodded with as much composure as I could summon before following him to a door. After we walked in, he flipped on the lights. Four blue upholstered chairs circled a basic wooden table. A box of tissues was the centerpiece, a lone flag of flimsy white flying from the box in surrender.

Fucking. Great.

I slid into one of the chairs. Andy lowered quietly next to me. "So, we need to be up-front about what we're facing here."

I swallowed. Then again. My sights seemed to tunnel, making the walls go fuzzy but a single striation of the wood sharpen. Less than a dozen words in, and I already sensed the agony ahead.

"Mr. Newland."

"Stop." Again, my voice was a damn drill officer. I honed my sights on my clenched fist, using it as an anchor to bring my tone down too. "I'm sorry, Andy. Can we just...wait a minute or two? Our fiancée is right behind me. She'll want to hear this too—from a medical professional." I rubbed my forehead with my fingertips, finally confessing, "I'm so jacked up right now. I'll forget what you say or miss something."

"That's fine. Can I get you something? Water? Coffee?"

"No, but thank you. My stomach isn't the greatest at the moment."

Because I'm living a god damned nightmare.

"That's understandable," Andy murmured.

I glanced up. "Just tell me, while it's still you and me...how fucked-up is it?"

Andy laid his file and papers on the table. Squared his lean shoulders while resting hands to either side of the pile. "Your brother is very lucky to still be alive," he said. "The EMTs got to the scene quickly and made all the right decisions. Now, it's up to the surgical team."

Again, it probably wasn't the right moment to explain our unique ties to one another, so I let him go on thinking we were brothers—although I'd just referred to Talia as our fiancée and Andy hadn't skipped a beat. As soon as possible, I'd need to let Talia in on the little "engagement" detail too.

I knew she was coming before I heard Killian's deep voice addressing one of the other nurses at the desk. Andy and I stepped back out into the hall, where Tolly all but leaped into my embrace.

"Have you seen him? Can I see him? Please, Drake. Tell me. What's happened? Are they helping him?"

She was as frantic as a squirrel trying to cross the road. Darting, furtive, indecisive, unpredictable. Not good. Squirrels in the road got flattened.

I pulled back but kept my hands on her shoulders. Dug my grip in, forcing her to look me directly in the eyes. "Natalia. Listen to me. Look at me."

She complied—for all of two seconds. Then her gaze went rogue squirrel again, racing between Andy, Kil, and me. "I'm so scared. Drake, I'm so scared."

"I know." Fuck, did I know. It hurt to breathe. It was agony to think. It was infuriating to accept any of this as our new reality, when only twelve hours ago, Fletcher had been guiding Talia through one of the most incredible moments of her sexual awakening. He'd been that bold. That brave. Taking a risk even the big bad Drake Dom had shied away from.

I wanted that man back. Every audacious, courageous, messed-up, morose, crazy, intense inch of him.

Tolly threw herself against my chest again. I circled both arms around her, wishing I could unzip my skin and haul her all the way inside me. I needed her near. Having her close was having him close in some ways. In so many ways...

"I know. I'm scared too." I whispered it into her hair, not sure if she even heard me. Maybe if I didn't say it too loudly to the universe, the fucker wouldn't acknowledge it—and I could hold up a bit longer.

For her...

...and for myself.

CHAPTER FIVE

Talia

Wake up.

Wake up!

Wake! Up!

I pressed the heels of my hands into my eyes, willing it to happen. I had to just do it. I had to just wake up. Then this nightmare would be over. I'd be back in our big bed in our beautiful bedroom at the condo, tangled in silken sheets with the dual lovers I owed everything to. They'd warm me. Secure me. Dare me to face my day with all the fearlessness their love had given me.

But I opened my eyes to the same dull hospital walls. The same antiseptic smell, attempting and failing to cover the stench of tragedy.

The same harrowing nightmare, now unfolding as the reality of my life.

How had this happened? How had we gotten here?

It's all my fault.

It was my natural fallback position, often driven by ludicrous logic—only this time, it made complete sense. This horror...I'd brought it here. To Fletcher, who was alone in a blackness I couldn't comprehend. To Drake, who'd held me as if his life depended on it and let me cling to him with the same terrified desperation.

It was all my fault.

All of it.

The things my parents had drilled into my head, every day of my childhood... They were all true.

You reap what you sow.

Karma takes no prisoners.

Fate will find a way.

Rain falls into every life.

And a million other ditties carrying similar tunes. They collided through my brain, a philharmonic concert of grief.

And they were all true.

Fletcher had left the house this morning angry—too angry to even say goodbye. At himself, yes, but also at us. I'd sensed it when we'd gotten home from his parents' party. Things would be easier with his family—not perfect, but easier—if Drake and I weren't the ones his heart wanted. That likely explained why I had thrown myself at him in bed like that, leading to a result that had only brought him more conflict and spiraled him into that dark funk.

I'd ruined everything.

My heart shrieked it, though my head fought back with the obvious logic. There'd been three people in that bed last night. Three consenting adults. But every time I looked up at Drake's face, I yanked the entire burden back on myself. As worried as I was, he was clearly twenty times worse. I'd never seen him racked with so many emotions at the same time. His face was gaunt. His eyes were bloodshot. His normal healthy color had vanished, leaving a pallor betraying his stark fear of losing his best friend.

His brother.

I lifted an urgent hand to his jaw. It was like a boulder beneath my touch. "Hey." I curled my fingers in, compelling him to focus on me—to see I was here and would take care of him. "Hey. We're going to get through this, okay?"

With hesitant jabs, he nodded. "Okay."

"Let's find out what we can right now and go from there."

"Yeah." More lost nods. "Okay."

A few feet away, Killian Stone paced like a monarch, cutting a zigzag swath across the hall, cell phone at his ear. Thirty minutes ago, he'd barged into my meeting with a solemn look on his face, motioning without words for me to follow him. I'd barely issued apologies before running after him—literally jogging to keep up with his long strides—out of the building and into a waiting town car.

As soon as the vehicle had pulled away, I'd been full of nonstop questions. Killian hadn't answered any of them. Instead, after a reassuring squeeze of my hand, he'd started punching numbers into the cell he held in the other. I'd pieced together my own conclusions based on the facts I could gather. The grim lines of Killian's jaw. The white ends of his fingers as he pinched the bridge of his nose. And most significantly, the words he'd finally bit out to the person he'd called. Somebody named Mac—though from his tone, I surmised he had a few other choice nicknames stored for the man.

"He's like my brother, damn it."

"He needs the best. You're the best."

"The car was totaled."

"They're prepping him now."

"Then don't do it in the name of family. Do it in the name of money. How much do you want?"

Killian had ended the call when we'd arrived and

immediately made another. Now, tension defined every molecule of the air, resonant with beeping monitors, squeaky-wheeled carts, ringing phones, and Killian's continued pacing.

As soon as he ended the call, Killian motioned to Andy. The nurse rushed over, attention defining his demeanor. Clearly, he'd added two and two by now and realized his newest intake was best friends with the CEO of Stone Global Corporation standing before him.

"My cousin, Dr. Maclain Stone. The surgeon. You know him?"

Andy nodded at once. "Who doesn't?"

"Good." Killian dipped a short executive nod. "He'll be here in fifteen minutes, and he'll be taking over Mr. Ford's case."

Andy shifted from foot to foot. "Uhhhmm..."

"Yes?" Killian prompted.

"I just...didn't receive word of the attending switching." The poor guy looked ten kinds of torn and twice that in uncomfortable. He likely sensed Killian wasn't used to being questioned, but he took his duties as a nurse seriously.

"Well, it's happening." Killian all but yanked out a scepter to seal the decree. "He's the best there is, and my best friend needs him. So, change the paperwork, the orders, whatever. Maclain Stone is in charge of this—even if he isn't happy about it."

I wasn't sure whether to be happy or anxious about the new development. Killian had just ensured Fletcher would have the best care there was, but between the man's comments in the car and his sinister grin now, he'd obviously strong-armed—or paid a king's ransom to—Dr. Stone for doing this. Pissing the guy off gave Killian the supreme jollies. Was that going to help or hurt Fletcher in the end? I admired Killian for his uncanny business sense, as well as his unfaltering love for my friend Claire, but if he'd bullied Mac Stone into doing this and Fletcher paid the ultimate price, I'd break Killian's neck with my bare hands.

So, gathering the girl balls for my next words was really a no-brainer. "Killian...thank you...but is it really a good idea to have someone caring for Fletcher who doesn't really want to be doing it?"

Yep. I'd really gone there. Andy's eyes widened, conveying a mixture of fear and admiration, but it was only Killian's countenance concerning me now.

The man turned fully to me, dark eyes softening. "It's not Fletcher he doesn't want to help, Talia. It's me. But he's literally the best neurosurgeon this side of the Rockies, and he owes me. Big-time." He extended a reassuring squeeze to my shoulder. "My little cousin will do the right thing. Don't worry."

Drake stepped back in, wrapping me close once more. I sank into his warm, solid chest, wanting to forget all of this already. But we were barely off the starting blocks. This mess was just beginning.

"Just before you both got here, Andy was going to run through what they know so far about Fletcher's condition." Drake's statement was a comforting baritone in my skull, since my cheek still rested on his chest. "There's a private room right over here. We can all sit down for a few minutes and hear what he has to say."

Drake circled around to let me walk with him, still tucked into the crook of his arm. As soon as we entered the room and sat down, he locked his hand against mine.

The area was as Drake said. We had privacy but at the cost

of space. The room was really tiny, even feeling cramped with Drake and Killian looming. They occupied the seats closest to the door, while Andy and I were squished between the wall and the table.

"Christ," Andy muttered while rearranging his notes and files. "It's really hot in here." He flushed, fanned himself with a manila folder, and then croaked, "Is anyone else warm?"

Before I could stop it, a giggle bubbled up and out of my mouth. At once, I slapped a hand over my lips. It was strange and funny, watching the effect of these two alpha guys on an unsuspecting third party. Apparently, I was so used to how Killian and Drake commanded every room they entered, it was just a part of my existence. Poor Andy. Another soft titter erupted from me. I was almost feeling sorry for the cute ginger.

Drake clutched my hand harder, ordering my eyes over to him. His gaze was like titanium, sharp and hard, not seeing humor in anything that was going on.

I cleared my throat. Pleaded an apology with my eyes. Refocused on Andy.

The nurse started to explain what they knew about the accident. I really wasn't laughing anymore.

Fletcher's car had been hit on the driver's side by a delivery truck going full speed. That meant his body had taken a direct impact.

"Didn't the airbags go off? That car has ridiculous safety features." Drake was intense and direct as usual.

"There isn't much that can help when tons of steel are barreling into you," Andy explained. "The airbags did deploy, but they only help so much."

Yeah. Not laughing.

"Is...is he going to die?" My voice was small and scared.

I was surprised it had any volume at all. But I had to get the words out. I—we—needed to know the bottom line here.

Andy's energy overflowed with empathy. "We have a good team, ma'am. They're doing everything they can to help Mr. Ford. The addition of Dr. Stone is well in his favor."

He gave a quick nod to Killian, as if personally thanking him for calling in his famous cousin for this. Killian responded by gritting the one word Andy had left off. "But...?"

"But there are some serious hours ahead of all of us," Andy went on. "Right now, the primary injuries that occurred at the time of the accident are straightforward. There's nothing the team can do to reverse those injuries, so instead the goal is preventing any further, or secondary, injuries to the brain."

I gulped hard. Jerked my chair closer to Drake's, entwining our arms from wrist to elbow. Brain injuries. How severe? And what exactly did that mean? Would Fletcher come back to us as he was before? I still couldn't feel him. The chasm in my mind, once filled with his loving light, was a horrible abyss.

"Our main concern is keeping his blood pressure stable and managing the brain swelling. Typically, when the brain is traumatized the way his has been, swelling occurs around the brain itself from displaced fluid from damaged vessels and, of course, neurons inside the organ itself."

"Of course. Neurons." Drake's tone was dry.

I talk about brain neurons every day...not.

Andy wasn't fazed. "Since the brain is inside the hard shell of the skull, we may have to open the skull to allow the brain to swell due to its injuries—then recede as it heals." He made a motion with his hands, giving me the comparison of a giant football stadium with a retractable roof, opening and closing.

"How long will that go on for? How can you just have your

skull popped open like that? Isn't that dangerous?" This time, Killian asked the questions.

"There are risks involved, of course," Andy replied, "as there are with any surgical procedure. But we maintain a sterile environment, and the surgeons usually use the operation as a last resort. We can try other methods of reducing the fluid before surgery."

There was a loud pager-type sound from the direction of Andy's pocket. "Please excuse me," he said, pacing out of the door.

In his wake...silence.

Killian expelled a long breath. His face was stormy. Drake's was just as dark. He propped his free elbow on the chair's arm and then jammed his chin on a raised hand.

I worked my fingers in and out of Drake's grip. I was so restless.

I was so frightened.

This is all my fault.

Without a doubt, Drake would spank me if he knew what I was thinking. Or hell, maybe he'd agree. They'd had nice lives, once upon a time. They'd been young and rich and free to have all the wild, opulent adventures they desired. But since I'd come along, it seemed we battled one awful trial after another and little else.

The only common factor in the last twelve months...was me.

Me.

"Stop."

My eyes darted to Drake. Quickly to Killian, since I suddenly remembered he was still in the room, but then back to Drake.

"What?" I tried for nonchalant. Ha. His gaze, even harsher and darker, told me how ridiculous the idea was.

"Stop beating yourself up, Natalia."

"I-I wasn't—"

"You really going to try that?" He twisted, staring me down with bunched eyebrows and a determined jaw. "Because I know you as well as Fletch does, baby. In different ways, but just as thoroughly. I know what you're doing to yourself inside that beautiful head of yours."

"Drake. I—"

"Deny it." He challenged it more by pressing closer, invading as much of my personal space as he could. "Go ahead. See what happens. Deny it."

Killian rose to his feet. "I...uhhh...need to call Claire." He looked impossibly tall and awkward in this remodeled broom closet. "I'll give you two some privacy."

Drake jabbed his chin in Killian's direction but didn't relent his attention on me by an inch. His looming size, along with the tight walls of the room and my churning stomach, crashed a wave of dizziness over me, even seated in this chair.

This chair. In this damn closet. In this hospital, filled with so many queasy smells and heartless sounds.

"Let's talk," Drake charged.

"Not yet," I rasped.

"Natalia..."

"I-I need to get out of this room." I shoved at him. "Can we please just get out of here? It's like a dollhouse. Maybe even a dog house." I wanted to laugh again but couldn't. I stood up so fast, my chair teetered on its back legs. The thing would have clattered to the floor but thudded into the wall instead. The room was suddenly a cage.

Panic cinched my chest. Cut off my breaths. I needed air. Lots of it.

"M-Maybe there's a stairwell we can go out," I stammered once we were back in the hall. I looked around, but nothing was marked as an alarm-free exit. The thought of going all the way back down to the hospital's lobby... All my anxiety just got worse. New tears burned my eyes. I gasped in desperation. I couldn't be the only person who felt trapped in a place like this—but that was a Styrofoam life ring in the middle of a damn tsunami. Worthless.

"Talia?" Drake. But so far away now. And fading more by the second. "Baby. Breathe, or you're going to faint. Fuck, you're white as a ghost."

Why was he so far away? And why couldn't I breathe? No. I was breathing, as fast as I could, and it wasn't helping.

Someone help...please.

"Sit her down before you have two head injuries to worry about."

Who was talking? A man? A woman? I couldn't tell. And who were they talking about? I twisted, trying to see, but my mind sank deeper into quicksand, denying my body movement.

I flailed up from the mire, springing open my eyes to find three expectant pairs overhead. What the hell?

My head throbbed as I bolted upright.

"Whoa, baby." Drake's luxurious baritone voice wrapped around me, a blanket of safety. I finally comprehended he was cradling me and now tried to lay me back on the floor. The hospital floor.

Ew.

"Wha'?" It was all that emerged for several moments, before all the proper switches in my head connected back to communication mode. "Drake...what the hell? Let me up. I need to see Fletcher. We were going to see him."

"No," he countered, his tone as calm but steely as his hold. "We were going to get some fresh air, and then you freaked yourself out and fainted. Now, sit up slowly before you freak me the hell out again."

"Yes, Sir."

It popped out, also on autopilot—though the cement brick of his order left little room for any other options. As I took deep breaths, still supported by the cradle of his arms, I glanced up to see that the brick had been formed from the pulp of his own stress, fear, and tension. Damn.

He'd aged at least five years in the last hour. I reached up to the rugged ridges of his face, resolved to ease some of them away.

As soon as I stroked my fingers down his jaw, a rough exhalation escaped him. Yeah, we were cuddled in the middle of the damn floor, in the center of a busy hospital ward, but for that singular moment, it all melted away. It was just us, still just as strong.

"Hey," I finally uttered.

"Hey, there." One side of his mouth kicked up. Damn. Why wasn't the man's face blown up twenty feet high on a billboard over Times Square? A mystery for the ages.

"Are you okay?"

"Am I okay?"

"Yeah."

A sound chugged out him, carrying at least the ghost of a laugh with it. "You're something else, woman." He hugged me so tightly, I squeaked. "Sorry." He eased off on the embrace but remained close enough to press his forehead to mine. "You scared me. Don't do it again."

"Okay."

The edges of his cement block crumbled, giving room for his full smile. Only a moment's worth, but I greedily accepted it.

"Think you can stand up now?" he asked softly.

I sure as hell wanted to try. Though nausea hit me in another strong wave, remaining on the floor was not going to help. Despite really wanting to gag again, I struggled to a standing position.

"Good girl," he praised, kissing my forehead while continuing to support my weight. The contact of his lips lightning-bolted me with a new awareness. I was still sweaty and gross.

"I-I need to splash some water on my face." Andy reappeared with what Fletch liked to call "movie timing." A cast member in the right place, at the right time—like the movies. "Is there a restroom nearby?" I asked him.

"Down the hall, on the left," he replied.

As I peeled away from Drake, his face tightened with new concern. "You want me to come with you?"

"I'll manage. Thank you."

I needed some time alone. Some space. Some minutes just to breathe.

In the bathroom, I leaned close to the mirror. Hell. I'd aged five years too. My face was pale, my normally olive tone looking closer to green. My hair was a mess. My eyes were dull.

I sucked in a cleansing breath through my nose and then turned on the tap. The cool water ran over my hands, refreshing me instantly. I splashed my face numerous times, letting my mind go numb as the water calmed me in visceral ways. As much as I could be calmed right now, at least.

After patting my cheeks and forehead with some paper towels and then gently clearing off any makeup I hadn't sobbed away yet, I turned and leaned against the counter with my hip. Took more full breaths, hoping they brought my courage back along with the oxygen.

You have to get your crap together, Talia. Fast.

There was literally no time for wallowing. I had to get back out in the hall. The thought of receiving an update about Fletcher, or even getting the opportunity to see him, had me tossing the towels in the trash and then bursting back out of the door.

Drake and Killian had moved back to the waiting room and were now in tense discussion with another very tall man. The stranger's stance was firm, his composure arrogant, and his face formidable. In short, he fit in just fine between Drake and Killian. Transport the three of them back in time a few hundred years, and they could have been a trio of noblemen in some medieval court. The newcomer's haircut, a spiky style, probably would've fit in at court too. His hair, like his thick eyebrows, was dark, though his was an ashy brown, contrasting to Drake's mahogany and Kil's ebony.

Really? Hair color is the most important thing going on in your brain right now?

My approaching footsteps made Drake look first. He walked over, grabbing my hand once again. "Feel better, baby?"

"Yeah." I stood on tiptoe, kissing the underside of his jaw. "Thanks. How about you?"

"Much better, now that Kil's cousin is here." He tugged me back toward the two other men before announcing, "Dr. Maclain Stone, this is our fiancée, Talia Perizkova."

My head snapped. My gape ensued. It was weirdly satisfying to watch the same thing happen to Killian. "Wh-What?" I finally blurted.

Killian wasn't so subtle. "Dude. You just said the F-word." He scooped up my left hand. Flipped it over with flourish. With the same dramatic flair, he looked back up to Drake. "Uuuummm. You missed something."

"Not at all." Drake took back my hand, bringing up to his lips for a lingering kiss. As his lips pressed over my knuckles, his stare reached out to me with midnight promise. "It's just a matter of time, my friend." His words were for Killian, but his velvety tone was for me. "Saying girlfriend isn't right anymore." He paused, letting that zip through my bloodstream like rockets of joy, before challenging Killian. "Did you ever consider Claire just your girlfriend?"

Killian snorted. "Not for a single moment."

"Okay, then." Drake brought his other hand up, meshing mine between his two wide palms, once more giving the sounds on his lips to Killian but the adoration in his stare to me. "We understand each other."

Dr. Stone watched the two of them volley back and forth, boredom and impatience defining his face. Finally, he stretched his hand toward me and smiled. Okay, it wasn't really a smile. The expression reeked of forced formality, likely the result of practicing it for years.

"Dr. Stone," he murmured. "Pleased to meet you."

I made sure my smile was sincere. Wasn't hard, considering why he'd come. And was about to do. "Thank you for coming, Doctor. I mean it. We are so grateful. I heard your conversation with Killian while we drove here earlier. I know this isn't something you elected to do, but I want to—need to—

let you know how grateful I am that you came."

All three of the men pulled in harsh breaths. I'd expected as much—but wasn't about to let the bad water under his bridge with Killian destroy his concentration on the man I loved. They'd have plenty of time for their pissing match later. Much later. Fletcher was the only thing that mattered right now.

Without much of another beat, the doctor cocked his head, planted hands on his lean hips, and raised one brow with much the same talent as his cousin. "Ms. Perizkova, I'm a doctor," he drawled. "I fix people. It's what I do. Whether my douchebag cousin initiated the call or not, if there is someone I can help, then that's what I will do."

I nodded. "Well, still." Entwined my hands in front of me, showing him deference. "Thank you."

Mac Stone folded his arms and shrugged. "Hey. It pays the bills."

His steel-blue eyes danced with mischief. He knew he was being an ass—and seemed to thrive on it. Dear God. This one was more full of himself than Fletcher.

Fletcher.

I needed him back. All of him—even that insanely cocky attitude. I needed his waggling brows and mischievous eyes. His outrageous swagger and his magical kisses. His passion and drama and life...

Furiously, I blinked against the tears. They welled and spilled anyway.

He has to be all right. He has to be!

Dr. Mac Stone was a vital key to getting us there. If it meant kissing his boots and putting up with his cavalier act, that was what I'd do.

But Drake had clearly had enough of the guy's bit. He

whooshed out a heavy sigh before asking, "So, what's next? What will happen now? The game plan?"

Mac raised both hands. "Easy does it, slugger. One thing at a time."

I dared a glance at Drake. Yep. As I expected, a vein pulsed furiously in his jaw. "Slugger?" he snarled.

"Hey. No disrespect, man."

"You sure about that?"

Mac chuffed. Rolled his eyes. "Cool your jets. There's a game plan, okay? We just can't put anything in motion yet. We're in a holding pattern until we see how your brother's body reacted to the trauma. Once that piece falls into place, we react with the proper play."

Though Drake relinquished the tic, he didn't lose the growl. "Right. So, we'll just cool our jets until then."

Mac's hands shot back up. "Again, no disrespect. Metaphors are required for what I do. Unless you prefer the twelve-letter explanations for everything?" After he got a new nod of deference from Drake, he jogged his chin back over to Killian. "I also can't help it if golden boy over there puts me on edge."

Killian's face darkened like a sudden thunder cloud over the lake. "Really, asshole? You're going to go there? Now?"

Mac dropped his hands. At his sides, they became fists. "Screw you, Kil-joy."

"God damn it, Mac."

"Hey." Drake planted himself between them. If words could turn into blows, the cousins would've been at it like the Hatfields and McCoys, right here in the trauma wing waiting room. "Is this going to be an issue with you and this case, Dr. Strange?" he gritted at Mac. "Because I won't have you taking pot shots at my friend, in front of my woman, and—"

"I'm a professional when it comes to my patients." Mac's jaw hardened into a near-perfect square. "I just don't particularly care for his presence." His gaze turned the same texture, once more honing on Killian. "Is there somewhere I can speak to you two in private? There are some decisions that must be made and paperwork needing to be filled out. Consent forms, that kind of thing. You said you're his brother?"

Drake's battle-ready stance slumped into an uneasy shuffle. "Yes." He darted a fast glance my way. "And no."

"And...no?" Mac echoed.

"We're not...blood."

"But she's his fiancée?" He motioned toward me with a new jerk of his chin.

"She's our fiancée." Drake's spine re-straightened. His shoulders squared.

"Interesting." As a beat passed, I realized he meant it— though his curiosity in our "situation" seemed more clinical than insidious. "You have medical power of attorney, then? Either of you?"

Drake and I exchanged a panicked glance. We'd been so prepared with the emergency cards. Why hadn't we seen this coming? "No," we answered in unison.

"Hmm." Again, his reaction was damn near dispassionate. "Well, does he have living relatives?"

"Fuck." Drake muttered it nearly beneath his breath, dropping his nose to the brace of his fingers.

"Yes." I sucked it up and issued the answer. "His parents and sister..." Are on a barge in the middle of the Antarctic, where I wished them last night after their stupid party. "Live here. In Chicago."

Seemingly from nowhere, Andy rematerialized. His face was red, his mien feverish. "There was no information about them in his wallet."

"You don't say," Drake growled.

"Well, someone needs to get them here, pronto." Mac smacked his hands together along with the last word. "Hate to be the bearer of shitty news, but without a legal paper saying otherwise, you all don't have jack to say about his treatment. Hopefully, you're tight with the family and they'll let you hang out." He shrugged like it was the least of his concerns, instantly tripling the stiffness in both Drake's and Killian's postures. "So, guess I'll be in the attendings' office. Someone come find me when the family gets here."

As he strode away, digging in his coat for his cell, I honestly didn't know whether to be furious with him or sorry for him. Callousness was probably as necessary as metaphors in his line of work, but I couldn't imagine another result for it other than loneliness. Who was he calling on that phone? Did they mean anything to him? Had he ever known a moment like what Drake and I endured now, letting love in even when it hurt?

We'd likely never know—nor did Drake and Killian seem to care. Remarkably, Drake was the one who gave the moment its best sound bite. The mix of snarl and grunt from his throat was an ideal expression of helpless rage. Killian tacked on with a sound equally as low but not as vicious.

"Mother. Fucker," he pronounced. "I hate that cocky bastard. I always have."

Drake shot out a glower. "Then why'd you get him involved?"

"Because he's the best," Killian retorted. "And right now,

that's what Fletch needs. I'd have called Satan himself"—he glared at the dwindling figure of his cousin—"though I'm beginning to think Mac might be hiding retractable horns."

Drake pushed out a bitter laugh. "You're right. I'm sorry, man."

Killian groaned. "Stop with the apologies already."

"I'll apologize if I fucking want to."

"Dick."

"Ass."

It was hard not to repeat my giggle as Killian hauled Drake into a gruff man hug. When they backed up, Drake's eyes were glassy with unshed tears. Killian didn't make his effort at containment any easier with his next words.

"He's going to be fine, D. He's strong and healthy, and now he's in the best hands possible. We all have to believe that."

"Yeah." Drake nodded hard, taking advantage of the chance to duck his head. "Yeah, man. Okay."

Killian, sensing Drake needed more than those two seconds, rounded toward me. "Claire is boarding the SGC jet in San Diego as we speak. Taylor's with her. Claire says to tell you that the Girl Power Brigade is on its way." He nodded and then grimaced, as if congratulating himself for remembering it all right but then wondering what the hell he'd just said. "I guess Taylor insisted on coming along. That little firecracker wouldn't take no for an answer, and we figured you could use the support."

For long moments, I could only vigorously nod my head. The world had crashed down so hard and so fast, I hadn't even thought to call anyone. Now, to learn two of my closest friends were flying across the country for me... Another tidal wave of emotion drenched me so completely, I couldn't speak. Didn't even try.

When Drake made his way over to me again, pulling me into his chest, that was it. The dam burst. The sobs escaped. Ugly tears, filled with so many different things. Gratitude for our friends. Uncertainty for our future. And the fear, so real it was like metal shavings in my mouth, that we'd never see Fletcher alive again.

I had no idea how long I cried. By the time I was done, Drake's shoulder was drenched. I looked up to behold the tears streaking his face too—which meant I really wasn't done. My sobs began anew, driven by even different emotions. Lingering guilt about the hand I'd played in Fletcher's funk, which might've distracted him in the car this morning. Racking anger at my emotional baggage, which had to sap my men sometimes. Brutal fury for not being stronger for them when they needed me the most.

That had to end. Right now.

I could do this. I could be a better fortification for them, starting this instant.

I began with a few steadying breaths, forcing them to pull up my spine and strengthen my voice. With that renewed energy, I moved back far enough to directly meet Drake's reddened gaze.

"We need to call his parents." There. I did it all in one piece, without a hitch or a sob. The next part would be tougher, but I was ready. "I think you should do it, Drake. I know it'll be unpleasant, but Richard and Francine have known you for years. I'm not trying to push this off or anything—"

"Ssshhh." Drake palmed my jaw, holding me steady for his reassuring kiss. "I don't think that at all. Your logic makes sense." He stepped back, letting his hands slide down over my wringing ones. "I'm going to use the closet of doom." He nodded toward the awful tiny space Andy had used for our little meeting. "Will you be all right out here for a bit?"

Killian stepped over. "Consider it done, buddy. I'll regale her with my sparkling wit. Maybe a few card tricks..."

There was an insult on the tip of Drake's tongue, ready to fly free, but I watched as he reeled it back in at the last moment. After grabbing my nape and taking my mouth in one more fast kiss, he disappeared back into the room though left the door open.

Carefully, I inched over to a spot where I could watch him. At first he just paced, as if waiting for someone to pick up on the line. When someone did, he turned swiftly. I couldn't see his face anymore but watched his head fall forward. With his free hand, he rubbed the back of his neck. Though I was only an observer, I felt every drop of his conflict, grief, frustration. This was probably one of the hardest calls he would ever have to make.

Suddenly, he twisted to lean over the table, supporting his weight on the back of one of the plastic chairs. A few nods. His shoulders sagged. Finally, he disconnected the call.

When he came back out, I opened my arms at once. He took me up on the embrace, sucking in his breath hard, almost as if inhaling me. It fed a need in me too, knowing I could comfort him like this. I truly would give him all the air in my lungs if that was what he needed.

"Christ, that sucked," he finally murmured into my hair. In return, I stroked a gentle hand through his.

"Who did you talk to?"

"Francine," he supplied. "She's hysterical, in her perfect socialite way. I'm sure the Women's League will get a call about it before Richard."

"Drake," I admonished.

"You think I'm joking?" he rebutted. I almost bit on that one but was too afraid he wasn't bluffing. Instead, I threaded fingers through his hair again, lending wordless support until he continued. "Anyway, she said she and Dick would be here as soon as possible. She's taking care of notifying Sasha as well."

Since that felt like a good excuse to sit down, we did. Andy was busy assisting another family, and now that Drake had returned, Killian swiftly excused himself, making a beeline down the same hall his cousin had taken. There was only one other family in the sitting area, watching a Friends rerun with shell-shocked gazes. If someone was camped out in this waiting room, Ross and Rachel probably beat the midday news for entertainment.

It all still felt like a nightmare to me.

As soon as Drake and I settled, I reached for him again. He readily twined his fingers in return. We couldn't be near each other right now and not touch. Even the three minutes he'd taken to call Francine had been unbearable. Staying physically connected seemed the very key to our survival right now. It was strange, but I didn't want to even try to figure it out. It just was.

Finally, I attempted to speak again. "I...wish..."

Drake pushed closer to me. "You wish what, baby?"

I sighed. "I wish I could just wake up. That I'll somehow open my eyes and learn this was all a horrible nightmare."

He swallowed deeply. "It's a nightmare, all right."

On the TV, the Friends gang played a contrived game of Trivial Pursuit. The laugh track was like buzz saws on my nerve endings. "So now what?" I ventured, trying to block out the boob tube. "We sit here...impotent? Now that they know we aren't married, we can't even find out anything new about his condition. You think...maybe...his parents will tell us when they know?" I winced, hating to level my last question. "Was his mother nasty to you?"

"No." His answer brought a stunning flood of relief. "I wouldn't describe her attitude as nasty," he went on, "but she was definitely cool. This'll sound bizarre, but she's a lot more maternal with me than Fletch. It drives him crazy because he knows it's all for show."

On the TV, Courtney Cox screamed, "That's not even a word!"

In my brain, my instincts shrieked back. That's not even important!

No.

Important was behind walls I couldn't break down.

Important was fighting for his life, on a cold table in a cold room, full of people he didn't know.

Important was the dark space that still stretched in my head. The presence I kept begging to wake up, to come back to us, to live.

I felt so damn helpless. All I could do was join Drake in trying to take a calming inhalation. Wasn't happening for either of us. "Maybe we should find some coffee or something."

"Outstanding idea," he agreed at once. He circled a curious glance around. "Is Kil still here?"

I twisted my lips. "I think he went on a cousin hunt."

"Ah. Got it."

"What do you make of that guy?"

I accepted full responsibility for the question. It was a little like asking a powder keg what he thought of the dynamite sticks, but I steeled myself for a gamut of answers.

In the end, Drake picked the one I hoped for the most. "Well, I don't care for his attitude, that's for sure," he conceded calmly. "But I'm not interviewing for a new best friend. All I want is the best care for the friend I already have." He surged to his feet, dragging me up too, before finishing with a guttural grind, "The one I refuse to live without."

We left for the cafeteria hand in hand...two thirds of a broken heart.

And a fear-filled soul.

If Fletcher's family closed us out now, our nightmare would officially become hell. We agreed to tread carefully when they arrived, good-behavior systems on full alert, and hope for the best.

And pray for the impossible.

Maybe, dear God maybe, if they saw how upset and concerned we were, they'd accept us, welcome us. Maybe they'd even understand our relationship a bit better—though I knew not to count on that. According to Drake, they were one self-absorbed bunch. Very likely, they wouldn't notice anything except how this tragedy directly affected them.

We just had to hope that somehow, our interest benefited theirs in a huge way. We had to pray they'd suddenly treat us, two outsiders, with more respect than they'd given their own son for the better part of his life.

CHAPTER SIX

Drake

I thought I'd been prepared for this.

I wasn't.

When the Fords arrived at the hospital, everything spun out of control—including the intensity of their rejection. Like preparing for a key battle, I'd tried envisioning every way the confrontation would go, but I didn't factor in the scathing sting of their outright renunciation. There was no deeper consideration for Tolly and me. No second chance. No chance, period.

Watching them now, wounding Talia, was the worst part of it all. Her trusting, pure heart was so ripe for their uncaring destruction. Seeing them crush her hope, tearing out her soul to get to it, was like observing a second tragedy take place today. She would never give her love so freely to anyone again. Our girl had always believed in the good in every human before, but now I had to stand and witness that belief crust over with an icy layer of disillusionment.

They sent Francine, of course, to wield the crippling blow.

"Drake. Darling." Though Talia was standing right next to me, the woman's greeting remained in the singular. "Thank you for calling us and making sure our son received the critical pieces of initial care, but we'll handle everything from here, sweetie. Why don't you and your girlfriend run on home and get some rest?"

Sweetie? And "get some rest"—in the bed we'd never share without Fletch?

"Please, Drake," she continued in a sappy coo. "I insist. We'll let Fletcher know how much you did for him."

"You—you can't be serious." My tone was incredulous. No. Screw that. I was enraged.

"Drake?" Talia's touch came, soft and insistent, at my elbow. "Maybe we should just...go wait in the lobby."

To her, the option might as well have been a banishment to a leper colony, and her trembling voice reflected it. My wrath simmered right back up to the surface.

"No, God damn it. We should not. He'll want us here when he wakes up. And he'd never leave either of us if the shoe was on the other foot. Never."

"You're right." She sounded small and guarded and defeated. "I know you're right, but if we're not welcome here..."

"I'm not leaving." My words were seethed. My glower was savage. "If you need rest, I'll ask Killian to take you back to the condo, but I'm not leaving."

Richard, apparently roused enough to make his way to the waiting room, strolled into view. "Newland."

I raked him from head to toe, standing there in his Easter egg-colored golf wear. "Dick."

"Really, son—"

"I'm not your son."

"Bah." He waved a hand as if batting away a fly. "Stop borrowing a page from Fletch's melodrama script. There's nothing more you can do here now. This is time for family."

"I am his family!" I sprang at the condescending douche,

seeing pure red. "You know damn well how close we are." With a raging stab of a finger, I pointed at Tolly. "We are in love with this woman. She makes your son happy. You know that, damn it. Pretending things are different won't make them untrue."

A massive harrumph made the man's shirt resemble roiling Pepto Bismol. "This is neither the time or the place for that discussion. Listen to me right now. If you're as fond of Fletcher as you say, you'll honor our wishes. Look at what you're doing to his mother. She's beside herself. I'm barely holding it together myself."

"Yeah. I can sure as hell tell." My statement dripped with sarcasm.

"Just what is that supposed to mean?" Richard snatched the bait but tossed it. "You know what? None of it matters." He shored up his posture, notching both arms at forty-five-degree angles. Oddly, his fists resembled spoons, about to dip into the antacid of his shirt. "At this point, it doesn't matter what you think at all. The sooner you realize that, the easier it will be for everyone. Fletcher's mother and I will decide what happens next, and what happens after that, and after that. None of this concerns either of you anymore." He glared down his beak of a nose. "It really would be better if both of you left."

Kerosene. Fire. That was the chem lesson the man just instigated inside me. Sure, Dick Ford was a big dude, but I'd taken down guys twice his size before, in settings much less appropriate than this.

"With all due respect, Mr. Ford, I'm. Not. Leaving." I motioned toward the nurses' station. "Go ahead. Have them call security to drag me out of here. What a fun story that will make for the front page of tomorrow's gossip section, hmmm?"

Ford cocked his elbows back farther. "How dare you."

"No, sir. How dare you. Why do you people need to be reminded that your son and I have been best friends for over a decade? We've spent more holidays, weekends, and special occasions together than he ever cared to spend with you phony pieces of society page—"

"Drake! Stop!" There she was, saving me in the nick of time with her cooler temperament. Talia pressed up against me, ignoring the wrath burning off me like black smoke from a torched oil rig. "Listen to me, baby. I know you're angry. I'm furious too. But this won't help Fletcher right now. Saying things you'll later regret... None of them will change this awful situation."

I ordered myself to breathe. Again. Though my chest still pumped on those desperate breaths, I wrapped her tight into my embrace, burying my face in her hair. She was absolutely right—and I was absolutely saved. From myself.

"Thank you for that," I whispered for her ears only. "And thank you for not giving up on me."

"I love you," she whispered back.

"As I love you."

"They're awful." Her voice was still quiet, but I could see the tension around her eyes and lips.

"Yes...they are."

"But fighting with them will only push us out of the loop further."

"You're right." I even forced a small smile. "As usual."

Her stare warmed. "Let's just sit over there, under the TV"—she grimaced, because the Friends hour had been followed by a Dukes of Hazzard marathon—"and wait to see what happens next. If nothing else, Killian can probably get his cousin to speak with us in private so they don't know we are being kept abreast of what's being done."

At once, I nodded. As soon as we sat, I wrapped my arm up and over so she could burrow as close as possible to me. For a moment, I sagged against her too. Dipped my head and smelled her, so rich and vibrant and womanly. Then let the words in my heart simply spill off my lips.

"How are you so amazing?"

She tilted her face up. Her features were still soft and warm, the umber in her eyes reminding me of the perfect part of a sunset. "Well, I wouldn't say that."

Her shy smile touched the darkest place in my heart. "I would," I insisted. "If not for you, I'd probably have my fist down Dick's smug pie hole by now. Wait, no. I'd have already pulled back and they'd be hauling me out of here in cuffs for it." I finished with a chuckle.

Talia didn't join me. "Don't even think about that again. I need you right now." She poked a finger into my shoulder. "Fletcher needs you. We both need you to be here, alert and present. And free of handcuffs."

She still wasn't kidding—and her words cut me to the quick. With a few words, she'd hit the damn nail on the head, making me see what an ass I had been.

Shit.

I'd let my emotions get too damn keyed up—and none of this horror was about me. I needed to step back. Way the fuck back. I had to consider what was in Fletch's and Talia's best interests, instead of what sated the worthless beast in me.

"I love you." It bore repeating, especially right now. It was the perfect, and only, way to sum up the thoughts bombarding my brain.

"I love you too."

We settled into each other a little deeper. As Bo and Luke Duke yee-hawed over our heads, we resigned ourselves to a long damn wait.

★ ★ ★ ★

We watched, feeling increasingly helpless, as Francine, Richard, and Sasha were each allowed a turn to go back and see him. At one point, the nurse turned to Talia and me, rocketing our hopes—but Francine was too quick. She pulled the nurse aside, whispering to her like a gossipy courtesan and compelling her to turn heel back into the ward. It felt like another blow to the gut.

And an even bigger one to our hearts.

If Fletcher came through all of this, he would never forgive his family for the way they treated us.

Not if.

When.

I refused to believe any differently.

Eventually, Mac Stone emerged from the closed-off section of the unit. Not openly acknowledging us, but not disregarding us either, he announced, "Well, we have some hard decisions to make."

Richard paced forward. "Doctor, can we have this conversation somewhere private?" He stabbed a glare toward Talia and me.

"We can," Mac readily replied, gouging our hopes he'd have a soft spot for our cause, "but really, what are you all trying to accomplish with that plan?"

I jolted forward in my chair. Talia was with that program, copying the move.

Francine's face took on a fly-up-my-nose twist. "I...beg your pardon?" she fired at Mac.

"No pardon to give," he rejoined. "But sure, if you insist." He lifted his head with new purpose, ticking it just to the side in that nerve-grinding way. "But back to the larger point here." He ticked it the other way—toward us. "You know, I saw those two people when your son was brought in here earlier. They were more distraught than a lot of family members I deal with."

So maybe the guy didn't get on my very last nerve.

Especially as he unleashed the full glory of his arrogance on them.

"Your point, Doctor?" Richard asked impatiently.

Mac volleyed with a pointed glare. "My point is, why are you making this harder than it already is? Your son needs all the positive energy he can surround himself with right now. Creating an environment filled with animosity and anxiety is the furthest thing from his best interest. What harm is it for them—his friends, his lovers, his housekeeping staff, who the hell cares—to know what's going on? You and your wife still hold all the cards, but where is the harm in having more people on Mr. Ford's team who care about him?"

Richard grunted. "You don't know what you're talking about." And now the true snob emerged.

"Really?" Mac's eagle-sharp eyes flared, making his brows jump too. "You seriously think this is my first rodeo, man? I do this shit every single day of my life. I deal with fucked-up families using a tragedy to make a point as often as I deal with the tragedy itself. And let me tell you something I've observed about all that, Mr. Ford. Those shenanigans never end well.

"Your son will wake up if I have anything to do with it. And when he does? You're going to have to answer to him." He shrugged his broad shoulders and worked his square jaw back and forth. "So do what you will—but I'd just like, one fucking time, for people to do the right thing and treat each other with the same respect they'd hope for if the situation were reversed."

Mac turned from us all, rubbing at the back of his neck. Tension stretched through the muscles there until they could be seen under the bright-blue scrubs he now wore.

So...not the last nerve, for sure.

Maybe not even the one next to that.

As a matter of fact, my outlook on the good doctor might've just peeled out a full one-eighty.

Dick shuffled over to Francine, who glanced around her husband to hurl one more visual dagger at the doctor. Then her catty regard found Talia and me. Was she expecting us to cower? Hadn't she realized by now that we were the wrong damn kids for that game? Emboldened by Mac's mandate, we stuck to our glares—daring the woman to make the right decision.

She dipped a nearly unnoticeable nod at Dick and Sasha.

At once, they opened their conversational circle toward where we sat.

"Mr. Newland? Ms. Perizkova?"

Mac's voice was an invitation for us to join them. We jumped up, nearly tripping each other in eagerness to make it to the pow-wow. If they wanted to change their minds, it was too damn late now.

Talia gripped my hand tightly in hers. I was thankful for the anchor. But before Mac could begin, she reached out with her free hand—

To touch Francine's forearm.

As one, we all gaped at the gesture with open shock.

"Thank you." Talia's gorgeous brown eyes brimmed with impending tears. Fuck. There might have been a few hundred stinging the backs of mine too. Two simple words, saying everything for us. I was so fucking proud of her, the beating organ in my chest literally threatened to rip its way out. In that moment, she proved why she was the woman who'd won my heart—and the human I would strive to be.

Francine was having a much harder time dealing with the overture. For a moment, she almost looked ready to throw up. Then her eyes, usually a shade lighter than Fletcher's, turned the same Caribbean blue from her own tears. But before they became worse, she ducked her head, halting any more chances of the moment becoming a new emotional foundation.

That, we soon learned, was just the start of the fun.

One hour stretched into the next, interminable and nearly unbearable, as Mac Stone went to work on our guy. The surgery, performed to relieve the pressure in Fletcher's head, entailed making burr holes in his skull and then placing a catheter so the collected fluid could drain, reducing the swelling of the brain tissue.

The risks? Try about a thousand. All the normal dangers for surgery applied, with the addition of the sensitive condition in the skull and brain itself. Everyone was excruciatingly aware of all this, so hours passed with few words spoken in the waiting room.

Thankfully, someone turned the TV off. The first family was replaced by a second, though they wore the same haunted looks on their faces. Must've been an unwritten admission ticket to the place.

Once again, I vowed to kill my best friend for putting us all through this. But first, God damn it, he had to survive. No other outcome was allowed in my mind. None. He would survive all this. He had to.

Eventually, Talia drifted off in my arms. I gently laid the top half of her body across my lap and began absentmindedly stroking her spine and hair. The movements felt essential, her closeness my comfort, using her steady breaths as my focal point. A hospital volunteer came in with a light blanket, arranging it across Talia's back. I mouthed my gratitude so my girl wouldn't stir.

Our girl.

She needs you, Fletcher. Damn it, we need you.

As we closed in on the fourth hour of waiting, the door to the room swung open. In swept Killian, with Claire and Taylor right behind.

As soon as the commotion hit the air, Talia bolted upright. In a flurry of squeals and cries and gasps and "ohmygods," the females converged on their friend, all but hauling her off my lap.

"Oh, baby. I'm so sorry." Claire gathered her close and rocked her gently.

"Is he okay?" Taylor was more impatient, firing questions as Talia struggled to fully wake up. "Have you seen him yet? What's going on? When was your last update? Did they even offer to text you every hour? They do that now. They should be doing that."

"He's in surgery right now." I kept my voice modulated while addressing the willowy blonde who'd come up through the SGC sales and marketing ranks along with Talia. I'd heard Taylor had earned the nickname "firecracker" and now knew why. "It's been close to four hours," I added. "And the last we heard, everything was going according to plan. He's holding up well. We opted out of texts because we want everyone in that room one hundred percent focused on helping Fletch. His surgeon will come out when they're finished and tell us how everything went."

"How long...was I asleep?" Talia yawned in the middle of her question.

"Not long enough." I went irked grizzly with the comeback though bussed her forehead with a tender kiss. "Will you please let the girls go back to the condo with you? You could get some actual sleep."

"Absolutely not." Her stare was a mixture of a plea and a dare to say otherwise. She tangled the tips of her fingers with mine, confirming she still needed that constant physical contact as much as me. "I'm staying here with you."

My soft smile spread as I brushed hair from her eyes. "Stubborn girl."

"I don't want to miss when he wakes up."

"Did Mac say how long he expected the procedure to take?" Killian took the seat beside me. Claire, with a hand on the swell of her belly, eased back into the one right next to him.

"He said it should be around five or six hours—but every case is different." I rubbed the back of my neck. The muscles there were tighter than bow strings. Actually, every muscle in my body could successfully apply for the status.

"Who's Mac?" Claire's gold gaze flashed with curiosity as she wrapped a hand around her husband's.

"My cousin," Kil supplied. "The neurosurgeon working on Fletch."

"Your cousin is a neurosurgeon?" Her finely sculpted brows shot up into her hairline but dropped in resignation. "And why did that even surprise me for a second?" Bafflement took over on a new frown. "But have I met him? Was he at the wedding? Like I remember anything from that production. What a blur."

Killian's features tightened too—enough to ensure at least Claire and I picked up on it. "We're not...close." His tone was clipped and brusque.

"Oh?" She looked at him, her face finishing the open question.

Kil just sighed. "We don't...normally speak. I don't want to get into it right now, Fairy. The story's long and boring, and no one really wants to hear it." The man glanced at her, clearly knowing that wouldn't be enough to satisfy his wife.

"Ah. So, you'll tell me later, then. Good." She never actually waited for his reply.

Killian chuckled softly. "Damn. You're spending too much time with my sister. Margaux's brass balls are rubbing off on you." He dragged Claire closer and kissed her forehead. She eyed him with mischief but smiled with the clarity of love. The two of them were a walking, talking commercial for perseverance, and everyone lucky enough to be in their presence knew it.

I was in the middle of that contemplation when Claire turned to me, taking my free hand into hers. "So, what can we do for you, Drake? Anything at all? Have you eaten?"

"I'm not very hungry." The tone was harsher than I intended, but she only smiled warmly. Guess the woman had my number by this point. I was thankful when she moved on to Talia. She needed the attention and affection of her friends right now.

"What about you, sweetie?"

Talia looked up. "I'm good. Really, it's all right."

"No," I interjected. "It's not." The comprehension slammed, hard and ruthless, that we'd been at the hospital for close to ten hours now, and Tolly hadn't had so much as a glass of water. I was furious with myself. I could mandate my body into survival mode. She didn't have the same advantage.

"You need to eat something." I didn't leave any room for argument.

"I do but you don't?"

Apparently, I had left room. Either that or her courageous-kitten thing got an injection of boldness when her girl posse was together. But when I hit her with a new glare, more direct this time, I heard Taylor suck in her breath.

"Shit, Talia. Just listen to him. You need to eat something, girl. If you don't, you may need medical attention."

"I would never hurt her," I snapped. "Ever." I was tired and testy, my fuse shorter than normal—but when Taylor cringed from me, I felt like an even bigger ass.

"Joking, Chief," she placated. "Settle down." She swiveled to Talia again. "Let us take you downstairs. Have a bite to eat? A little walk, change of scenery? It'll do you some good."

"You're right," Talia answered her friend but looked at me. "Will you come with me?" she entreated. "You need to eat as much as I do, even if we aren't hungry. When Fletch wakes up, he's going to need us. We won't be much good to him if we don't take care of ourselves."

"Go ahead, man." Killian held up his cell. "We'll text or call if Mac comes in, and you can hustle back up here."

An hour passed while we ate the most mediocre burgers Chicago had to offer, though if it had been the finest cut of steak in the city, I wouldn't have tasted it, either. My thoughts were all over the place, like sticky notes in a windstorm.

Every message was important, but I couldn't pin any one of them down. Though Tolly and I were too stressed for much conversation, I knew I would've been utterly lost without her by my side.

"He can't die." And that was what I picked to speak for the first time in thirty minutes?

"He's not going to."

Her confident tone did nothing to alleviate my cresting panic.

"I wish I were more like you." It was just a hoarse whisper, but I meant every syllable. To the depths of my soul.

She almost choked on her drink before setting it down to focus completely on me. As she responded, she intertwined our fingers again. Her stare, compelling mine to stay locked with hers, undoubtedly confronted the adoration of my heart.

"Why would you say that?" she demanded. "You are amazing—for so many reasons. But right now, you're amazing because of the friend you are to Fletcher, even though he's not even here to see it. You didn't back down to those horrible snotty parents of his, standing your ground when they tried to force us out of all this. Because of you, we're still sitting here, involved and connected, instead of waiting at home for a phone call—that, let's be honest, might not have ever been made."

I closed my eyes and drew in a long breath, soaking my raw senses with the medicine of her words. "I appreciate all of that. Thank you. But you..." I opened my gaze, taking in the miracle of her classic Russian features. "You just do everything with...a certain grace. I guess that says it. No, it doesn't. I don't know how to word what I'm feeling." I rubbed at the pain in my chest, but it didn't help. "I'd be lost without you, Tolly. Right now—and forever. I just..."

"Just what?" she prompted.

"I just can't imagine my life without you and Fletcher now. Last year, when I thought leaving was the best for everyone? That absence... It was overwhelming. It was awful. I can barely breathe remembering the isolation of it."

"Ssshhh. Stop this." She rubbed my forearm with her soft hand, trying to soothe away the desperation crawling beneath my skin. But the bizarre apprehension wouldn't let me go. So much here was beyond our control. My best friend—my brother—was upstairs having his skull drilled open. His family's new diplomacy was just a thin veneer. I couldn't escape the feeling we were headed for another chasm, and God only knew what lay in wait at the bottom this time.

"I never want to feel like that again." My grate was a paltry defense, but it helped to vocalize the intention.

"I know." Her assurance bolstered me too.

"I mean it," I emphasized. "I'll do whatever I have to so I never have to—"

The phone in my back pocket vibrated. An incoming text.

"It's time," I said, reading the brief words from Killian. "They've moved him to recovery, and Mac will be out in a few minutes to tell everyone how it went."

Talia had already tossed our half-eaten meals and taken the trays to the return window. I scooped her hand into mine. Without another word, we jogged back up to the trauma surgical unit, joining our friends in the waiting area.

"Has he come in?" I asked at once.

"Not yet." Killian snorted. "Just like the arrogant ass to have us all panting like dogs for his arrival."

And there was a subject I'd be calling the guy out on, as soon as the shit storm of my own life settled. Kil, who'd more than earned his nickname as the Enigma of Magnificent Mile, was uncharacteristically vocal about his ill-will toward his cousin. For now, I was happy to let Claire take care of the reprimanding.

"Would you stop?" she scolded. "He's your family."

"Barely."

"You are really going to tell me all about this later."

"Later." His echo doubled as a dominant directive. There was the Kil we knew and loved.

"Oh, I won't forget." Claire arched both brows, scoring a point right back. "But now, we're here for Drake, Talia, and Fletcher."

"You're absolutely right, Fairy." He kissed her forehead, turning them into such an adorable portrait, I ached. Damn. If I were in a better mental place, I'd be taking notes to use the moment later as ammunition. Instead, looking on from the edge of my emotional chasm, I watched with envy at the way he and his beautifully pregnant wife fed off each other. The hole in my chest sucked in air, growing even wider.

Mac came in like a hurricane. His eyes, so blue even a dude had to notice, were full of frenetic energy. His hair, despite its short style, stuck out in all kinds of places. It'd been slicked back earlier, but the style was long gone now. I noticed that his height came mostly from long legs, still encased in the bright-blue scrubs we'd seen earlier, though his scrub shirt had been replaced by a plain white T-shirt. The tee was pristine and fresh, contrasting sharply to the rest of his clothes, including the typical white doctor's coat with his nametag over the outer pocket.

He paused in front of Richard and Francine, waiting for the rest of us to gather around before diving in on the debrief.

"Okay. Things went really well—as well as we could hope for in this situation. He'll be in recovery for an hour or two. Since we'll keep him heavily sedated for the next couple of days, what we need to see now are consistent vitals. Even with the ventilator in place, things can get a little rough after such an intense surgery, so we'll wait until he's stable to move him over to the neuro ICU. There, he'll have round-the-clock care and monitoring."

He paused, not looking up from his file for even a glance at our faces—though I sensed he already heard our unspoken questions. The most important one anyway.

"Once he's in ICU, you'll be able to sit with him for short periods of time, one at a time. That's the rule at this place. If the ward is quiet, sometimes they'll allow two, but that's at the nurses' discretion, and I wouldn't advise you cross any of them."

Only then did the man's head lift, finally noticing what a huge audience he had. He blinked as if emerging from a dark tunnel into the sun, or even an addict coming off a high. He'd been in some sort of frenzy when first arriving, and now the buzz was subsiding. I had no idea what I witnessed, but having the power to save or end another person's life had to mess with a guy's psyche.

"So," he finally said, almost stammering his way through the single syllable. "Can I—uhhh—answer any questions?" He looked to the Fords first, then to Talia and me, finally noticing Killian, Claire and Taylor stood there too. He frowned at Killian, passed right over Claire, and then settled on Taylor.

Hard.

Something changed in his demeanor again. "I'm sorry," he bit out. "You are?" Under his breath, he mumbled, "It's like a fucking circus in here today."

Kil and I restrained mutual groans—parting shots for the man's balls. I'd been in enough meetings with Taylor to predict the reaction she wasted no time in issuing.

"Circus?" She shot it out with a hitch of her hip. "So, what does that make you? A clown?"

"That's Doctor Clown, and again, you are?" His retort came without skipping a beat.

"Taylor. My name is Taylor Mathews. And these are some of the finest people I've ever known, so I'm not sure where your attitude is coming from. If you hadn't just saved my best friend's bae, I'd kick you in the shins. Or places higher."

His eyes blazed, the blue intensified by disbelief. But the next second, an enormous grin spread across his face. He rocked back on a heel, raking an assessing stare over her feisty stance.

"Taylor." He dropped the smirk as he echoed it, looking like he'd tasted something unpleasant. "Who names a girl Taylor?"

"My mother is fucked-up in—oh I don't know—twenty ways from Sunday. Naming her daughter Taylor was probably one of the most normal things she ever did. Not that it's your business, Dr. Clown."

Claire and Talia joined Kil and me at biting back the snickers now—especially as the firecracker didn't give poor Mac a second of breathing room. Sauntering forward, she tapped his name tag two times in succession. "Maclain Stone. How come we've never heard about you?"

Mac stiffened. His unease after the post-op high was just an appetizer for his tension now. "Direct your inquiry to that asshole, ma'am." He jabbed a thumb Killian's way. "Not everyone can breathe the special air at the top of the food chain, you know."

"Okay." Taylor extended both syllables, filling the terse silence he'd dropped. "I have no idea what that all means—but regardless, thanks are owed to both of you." After he and Kil gave her nothing but confused snorts for that, she finished, "Thank you, Doctor, for dropping everything in your day to help our friend. And thank you, Killian, for making this all happen."

"Oh, this is fantastic." Mac groaned it out when Taylor sealed her gratitude by hugging Killian. "I just worked magic in there for five hours, saving your friend's head from blowing up like a watermelon with rubber bands around it, and you're hugging him?"

Taylor planted a new pose where she stood—five clear feet away from the doctor. "Rubber bands? Really? That's where you just went? Someone is watching way too much YouTube." She pretended to laugh. She also pretended to ignore Mac's reaction. None of us were buying either move.

"I'm done here," Mac muttered. "Unless anyone else besides this one"—he pointed hard at Taylor—"has any questions?"

Silence. A long, speechless pause.

Everyone but Mac and Taylor—yeah, including Francine and Dick—played a fast round of what-the-fuck? Frisbee. What had just happened? I wasn't sure the doc and the firecracker would take their chemistry to blows or tear each other's clothes off.

Finally, Francine broke up the fun. Clearing her throat with nasal emphasis, she asked, "Doctor, how long will you keep him sedated?"

"Uhhh..." Mac just kept staring at Taylor.

I glanced to Kil, who was likely my mirror in the dumbfounded department. The man had gone Millennium Falcon in the woman's tractor beam. Taylor gave as good as she got, staring right back, her stiff little spine straight as an arrow, making the most of her five-foot-two-inch frame.

"Dr. Stone?" Richard called out his name. "Dr. Stone?"

With a grunt, Killian finally stomped forward. He got into Mac's grill, openly gritting his teeth. "These people are asking you questions about their son, Maclain. Can you circle back to fucking earth for a minute and get your head in the game?"

Taylor turned bright red and fled the room. At once, I watched conflict tear across Talia's face. Her duty as a friend dictated going after Taylor, but she'd miss hearing Mac's answers about Fletcher. Thank fuck for Claire, who hurried out of the door behind Taylor.

I caught Mac midsentence when turning back to his conversation with Francine.

"—about four to seven days? It's different for every patient. We'll monitor him very closely now. The next twenty-four hours will tell us a lot about how this recovery will go."

"Very well." Francine pivoted from Mac to her husband. "I'm going to step out and call Sasha. She's worried sick at home, but I told her to just stay there. We already have enough of a crowd milling around here."

Neither Talia nor I missed the bitch's parting jab. I reached for Talia, letting her settle against my chest with a weighted sigh. Long minutes later, she tugged away a little. Fresh tears shone in her eyes, but she fought them with a valiant effort. Her chin wobbled; her throat was taut.

"He's going to be okay, baby." I swiped the drops escaping

her eyes anyway. "You heard the doctor."

"I know," she whispered. "I know. These are tears of relief." She tried for a smile, but it barely scratched the surface of her normal joy. "I think they are, at least."

"Want to know what I think?"

"Of course."

"I think we should go home."

I was ready for the panicked whip of her head, as well as the urgent plea across her face. She wasn't going to accede without a fight.

"No. No. I want to stay. Drake, please. We need to stay."

"We also need sleep. And showers. And some decent food. We have to stay strong, Tolly—for him."

Her shoulders drooped. "I-I know you're right. But what if something happens? What if he needs us, and we aren't here? Maybe we can go in shifts. You go rest, I'll stay here, and then we can trade. That way—"

I interrupted her the most effective way I knew. With a strict kiss. "I'm not accepting no on this. You're near hysterics because you're hungry and exhausted, and I've only made a suggestion. How will you be able to handle it if a real crisis happens? Fletch is stable for now. Let's use the time to fortify ourselves."

She dug in like a child resisting a nap. "I am fortified."

"God damn it, Tolly." I muttered it while dragging a vicious hand down my face. "Don't make me be the bad guy. I'm responsible for taking care of you, above anything else."

"Above Fletcher?"

"That's not fair."

"Sorry." She pulled at the front of my shirt, extending a new pout. Her adorable one. Yeah, the look that unraveled me every time. "I really don't want to go."

"I understand that." Yep. Every time. "So let's compromise."

"I already suggested one of those."

"Yours wasn't acceptable." I kissed her again, simply because I couldn't resist. That fucking pout. "We will wait until they bring him up to the neuro ICU—and if we can visit with him quickly, we will. After that, we're going home for some rest. Deal?"

Her irresistible pout turned into her irresistible smile. "Deal."

She wrapped her arms around my waist and laid her head on my chest. I exhaled into her hair, wishing we were at home.

At home—with Fletch.

Damn. I wished it more than anything in the world.

Finally, I broke our embrace. Gently, I tilted her chin up. "I'm going to go tell Dick and Frannie we'd like to see him ASAP and then we're heading out. If they know our plan, they'll likely be more amenable to us seeing him."

"Good thinking," she murmured.

"Do you want to go find the girls?"

"Yeah." She reached for the ceiling, stretching the muscles in her lower back. "I'd better see what's going on with Taylor. I've never seen her act like that. Okay, maybe I have, but that was some crazy sass, even for her."

I twisted a sardonic smirk. "I'm weirdly gratified to hear that."

"Well, I'm just confused. Did those two have serious sparks, or was that just my imagination?"

"Wasn't your imagination," I affirmed. "But knowing Killian, he's already torn after Mac and threatened him within an inch of his life if he jumps on any part of that."

She nodded. "The only thing weirder than the energy with Mac and Taylor is the energy with Mac and Killian."

"Go find her." I bussed the tip of her nose in encouragement. "She probably could use her friends. And you could too."

"I love you." She wrapped one more hug around my waist, ensuring my liver and kidneys were mashed into a casserole from the pressure, before she walked out of the door. I kept meaning to ask her if she'd gotten the Spidey connection back with Fletch, but I didn't want to bring it up if the answer was no.

Fate had given me all the challenges I could handle at the moment. I couldn't bear her heartbreak too.

CHAPTER SEVEN

Fletcher

"Baby...don't cry."

Why won't she look at me?

"Tolly, don't cry. Please, you're breaking my heart. Baby?"

I don't understand why she won't look at me. Her eyes are red and puffy. Her sniffles are interjected by occasional hiccups. I need to comfort her. Christ, I need to hold her. It feels like forever since she was in my arms...when I'd wrapped myself around her in the shadows of the night and had fallen asleep breathing against her skin...

What happened after that?

Why can't I remember?

But more importantly...why won't she look when I call her name?

"Natalia."

It works for Drake, but not for me. Why? Why?

"Please don't leave me. Don't leave us. You have to fight, Fletcher."

Her voice... It breaks me. This grief... I've never heard it from her before.

"I'm not leaving you. I will never leave you—ever. Why are

you saying this? What's wrong, love? Please tell me so I can fix it. Just let me hold you."

But when I try to lift my arms, something holds me down. What the hell? What's wrong?

My arms aren't working the way they should. I try again... Nothing.

She doesn't look at my face. She's fascinated with my hand, clutching it like a lifeline. But I can't feel her tentative, almost cautious, fingers.

"I was so scared. I was so scared this morning when you left for work without saying goodbye to Drake and me. You never do that. Damn it, why did you do that, Fletcher?"

Something is so off with this whole scene. I can hear her voice, anguish and sorrow gutting me as I process each word, but I have no idea what she's talking about. She's not making sense.

"Talia, please. Oh, baby, please stop. I'm so confused. You need to tell me what has you this upset."

She grips my hand harder. I can see the strain in her forearm. But I still don't feel her warm skin on mine. Is this a dream? But it feels so real. Her agony is so damn real. She eviscerates me where I stand.

But I'm not standing.

I don't feel the floor beneath my feet.

I'm...prone. Lying next to her but not next to her. She's hunched in on herself, over my hand, clutching as if I'll float away if she lets go.

"I need you. I love you more than anything, Fletcher. I

need you to come back, wake up, and tell me you will never do something like this again."

A liquid laugh breaks through.

"Drake says he's going to kill you. I'd like to see him try. You're a force of nature, Fletcher Ford. You're our force of nature. And Mac says you'll be okay, but you have to fight. Do it, Fletcher...please. Fight your way back to us. Fight for us."

I will. I will. Don't cry. Don't cry.
Who's Mac?
She doesn't answer. She fades away.
Come back. Come back!
The scream blasts through my head but nowhere else.
Tired. I'm so tired all the time. I hear people near me again, in and out, but none of the voices draw me out from the fog like Talia's and Drake's. I need them. I need them...
This time it's him. My best friend. My brother. The only other man on earth I'd willingly give my life for. I remember the day we met. He'd walked into the aquatic center at the club like he owned the place. Dark hair. So thick. I'd wondered aloud if it would shed water like the feathers on a duck's ass. Gained him a similar nickname for years.

"Dude, this shit has to end. You need to stop being a lazy slob and wake the fuck up."

Thanks, Mr. Eloquent. I love you too. But what the hell was with everyone telling me to wake up? Can you tell me something better, like where Tolly went?

For the most part, I don't feel like I'm sleeping. It's more like...quicksand. And it's kind of nice. It's easier to drift off, slowly settling into the muck, than focus on his voice. No. His nagging. But the asshole has other plans, apparently.

"Talia needs you, damn it. She needs us, together, like we promised. You do remember that, don't you? How we swore to take care of her?"

What do you think? Stop looking at me like I'm in a coma. Of course I remember. I'll never forget.

"Now you're falling down on the job, dude. Come back to us, God damn you. Wake up, Fletcher. Look at me!"

And your duck butt hair? Bring Tolly in, and I may think about it.

"I know you can hear me, you big fuck. And you need a haircut. Honestly, I had to stop the nurses from braiding it for you the other day."

Nurses? I don't know any nurses. I don't think I do. Are those the voices I block out when I'm sinking deeper? They're annoying. They say a lot of stuff I don't understand, so I drift off to sleep when I hear them. Easier that way.
Talia.
Yesssss.
She's back. I smell her jasmine shampoo, her lavender soap, her incredible skin. God, I want to touch her. I miss that skin so much. Smooth as peaches, entrancing as apricots. So sweet.

With a huge effort, I focus on her voice. This is worth the effort.

"Remember when the three of us spent the day in Old Town? You loved that Wyatt Earp used to hang there. Drake bought that stupid parrot hat. We ordered that gallon-sized margarita and drank it from three straws. You remember? Look at the pictures I saved from that day, baby. Open your eyes and look at them, Fletcher. Open your eyes and look at my phone. Remember with me, laugh with me. Please, baby...oh, please let me see your beautiful blue eyes again. I miss you so much. And Drake too... We don't know how to live without you. The condo is a mausoleum right now. We miss your smart-mouth comments, and I miss being in your arms. Wake up for me...please. Try. Try."

Tolly. Damn it. Stop crying. I'll try. I'm trying...
What the hell am I trying?
I'm still so confused.

"Baby, come back to me!"

But I'm right here. Damn it, Talia.

"I miss you. I miss feeling you in my head. If you just wake up, I know you'll be there again. Please come back..."

I haven't gone anywhere. Baby, I'm right here.
I'm...
Right...
Here...

But I'm not. I sink again. It's too much...all her tears. Her sadness, somehow because of me...

Why?

The next time I come to the surface, she's gone. Mom sits here instead. She's quiet. An occasional sigh, a dab to the corner of her eye with a starched white handkerchief. She holds my hand. Strokes the skin on the back of my knuckles. But still, not a word. I'm fascinated. The woman never shows emotion, but here she sits.

Crying.

For me.

"I know you're cross with me, with us, right now."

"Cross." Oh, Mom. I think you're the only person alive still using that word. Just saying.

"But you need to set all that aside and come back to us, Fletcher Frances. Darling, come home. We've set up the best care possible for you to recover at home with us. But you need to wake up first. We can't take you home if you don't wake up. Once you do, everything will be better, I promise."

I almost laugh out loud. I want to. Fuck, how I want to.

I have a home, Francine—and it's not with you.

Vehemently, I pull my hand away from hers. Her startled face tells me I may have actually done what I wanted this time.

"Oh, my God. Fletcher? Fletcher! Can you hear me? Open your eyes now. Look at me!

"Nurse? Nurse? Get in here. Hurry. He moved. He moved.

Get Dr. Stone at once."

Well, shit.

Killian has these fools convinced he's a doctor? Now I've heard it all. A new laugh bubbles up my throat and turns into fire instead. Scratchy dry fire.

"Oh, my God. You're awake. Finally!"

She beams at me with—what? What's she feeling? Pride? Now I know where I'm at. The fucking Twilight Zone.

"Well, look at you, son. My son. I knew you'd hear me. You want to leave here as much as we want you home. Thank you, Jesus."

She looks to the heavens, hands clasped in front of her chin. So fucking ridiculous. She used to say she was agnostic.

"Our prayers have been answered!"

She leans in and mauls me in a hug. Her perfume smells like cinnamon that's steeped for too long. I can't move. I just watch with cloudy eyes. Despite the clouds, the light in the room is blinding. It hurts. Bad.

Mom straightens again, thank fuck, beaming like she just singlehandedly cured cancer.

"I knew you'd come back to me!"

The quicksand rises over my consciousness once more.

Pulling so hard, not to be denied. I fight it with everything I have, because Francine needs—needs—to be told who I really climbed this high for.

"Tal-Talia. Draa-aake."

Her jaw hits the floor—nearly literally. It's priceless.
And worth it.
I let the quicksand take me again. Now, that I know I can beat it, I'll save my energy for the only two people I want to talk to.

CHAPTER EIGHT

Talia

The condo wasn't the same without Fletcher. He breathed a certain life into every crevice of the place, proved with crystal clarity over the week since the accident. Right now, it was a house, not a home. Without him, it was just living space.

Taylor and Claire stopped by every morning to bring me a breakfast sandwich and a huge cup of coffee, though I repeatedly told them we had food and I was capable of taking care of myself and Drake.

In one ear and out the other.

The doorman called up right at eight thirty, announcing their daily arrival. When I opened the door, they were midstream in an intense debate.

"They did what?" Taylor accused over her shoulder before kissing my cheek and then cutting right off the foyer, toward the kitchen.

"I'm serious!" Claire exclaimed while waddling past me as well. "That's what Kil said."

"But that's ridiculous."

"Didn't say it made sense."

"What adults behave that way?" Taylor hiked her eyebrows toward her hairline as she slid into a seat at the counter, on the dining room side.

Before Claire claimed a chair as well, she patted Taylor's hand, maternal vibe in full swing. "Ohhhh, you really have been living under a rock, sweetie, haven't you?"

"What on earth has you two hens ruffled so early in the morning?" I asked incredulously—though tacked on a smile. To be honest, it was nice to have a distraction from my own worries, if only for a few minutes.

Claire laughed while pulling the drinks and sandwiches out of the cardboard carrier. "Well, I'm trying to explain to our sweet southern belle how the Stone family dynamic works, dysfunctional parts included." She finished with a mock-pitiful glance in Taylor's direction.

"Ohhhh, boy." I seconded her chuckle. "Good luck with that. I'm not sure I still understand it all." I popped the lid off my coffee and took a big whiff of the steam. Heaven.

"It's definitely a tangled web." Claire grimaced, the high chair obviously disagreeing with her and the baby, prompting her to plop down onto the sofa instead.

"Have you heard from the hospital this morning?" Taylor gave me a hopeful glance.

"No—which I'm taking as a good sign." I blew on the hot liquid, cradling the cardboard cup with both hands. It was already a warm day in the Windy City, but I'd had a chill since climbing out of bed this morning. Who was I kidding? I'd had a chill since last week. Half the sunlight of my world was still trapped in a bed at Chicago Memorial. "I was just about to call but was waiting until after the shift change. The nurses are so busy right after they come on."

"Ah." Taylor took a hungry bite of her sandwich. "Good thinking," she remarked after chewing.

As she ate a second bite, I set the cup down and eyed her

with determination. "Have you heard from the hospital, or rather someone who works at the hospital, this morning?" Maybe a little sisterly teasing would get Taylor to open up about "the throwdown that would not be forgotten" in the waiting room with Mac last week—and the unmistakable friction every time she'd crossed paths with Dr. Hotpants since.

A sheepish look flashed across her face. Two seconds and it was gone, as she dived back at the sandwich with a defensive blush. "I don't know what you're talking about."

"Oh, nice try." I smiled so she would know the ribbing was in good spirit.

"Well," she huffed, "if you mean that Neanderthal surgeon who saved your man's life...why the hell would he call me?"

"Oh, Taylor." Claire tossed her head back on a playful groan. "Ohhh, Tay, Tay, honey."

"It's all right, sugar." I assumed the hand-patting duties— except this time, Taylor yanked back like I'd branded instead of consoled her.

"Cut it out," she snapped. "All that's missing from you guys is a 'bless your heart.'"

"Easy, missy." Claire pushed off the couch and hurried back over, engulfing Taylor from behind at a slant due to her adorable bump. "We're teasing. Someone's a little touchy, hmmm?"

I winked my approval at Claire. As Killian had so astutely pointed out, she'd definitely borrowed some lady balls from Margaux lately. I couldn't believe I actually missed that woman, but it was true. Falling in love with Michael had been the magic spell for her, revealing a woman of heart and passion beneath her bitch-on-wheels act.

"Still teasing?" Taylor leaned out and cocked her head to

the side, side-eyeing Claire as if to say bring it on."

"Okay, ladies, please." I held up one hand, touching middle finger to thumb in the universal Zen position. "Give peace a chance. I already have enough on my plate, so refereeing two of my best friends is not the greatest way to align my morning chakra." As they gawked at each other and then me, I shrugged. I had to step in before they were wrestling on the floor like Drake and Fletcher. "Don't make me call Margaux, because I will."

Claire sucked in so forcibly she choked a little. "You wouldn't." She leaned an elbow on the counter. "Can we back things up to the real point?" She leveled a new scrutiny at Taylor. "You honestly can't tell me you didn't feel the spark between you and Killian's cousin?"

"Spark? Ha!" That was like calling the Grand Canyon a little hole in the ground.

Claire quelled me with a glance. "Everyone else in the room sure recognized it."

"Well, then, you're all a bunch of crazy fools." Grimacing as if her stomach hurt, Taylor wrapped up the rest of her breakfast, dumped it into the bag, and then rolled the top down to seal it shut. "That man holds no interest to me. None. Whatsoever."

I ducked my head. Sometimes the only way to mask a face-splitting smirk was with a chug of coffee. Didn't stop me from muttering, "The lady doth protest too much, methinks."

Claire and I giggled in unison, but Taylor found no humor in my Shakespearean foray. "Taylor," I chided. "You know I'm just joking. Fix your face, girlfriend—but do know this. The ju-ju with you and Dr. Clown was seriously palpable."

When Taylor flung her glower from me to Claire, our little

preggo nodded sagely. "You two could've been the emergency power generator for the whole wing."

"And you can't be angry with us for wanting something good for you."

Taylor whacked a hand atop her leftovers bag. "What makes you think I don't have 'good' right now? Sheez, you guys. I'm happy and busy—"

"With work and little else," I cut in. "You never go on dates, and the only time you go out is when one of us drags you."

I let all that hang in the air, but Claire picked up the ball and ran with it.

"You are beautiful, smart, clever, and funny." She wrapped an arm around Taylor's shoulders. "You have so much to offer a man, yet you're never interested in the ones constantly panting after—" Her self-interruption came with a perfect O of her lips. "Oh. Wait a second. Are you a lesbian?"

I wanted to swoop up my phone and capture the next few beats on film. The perfect circle of Claire's lips. The wild reaction shot on Taylor's face, brows leaping and eyes bugging. Priceless.

"No! I'm not a lesbian—"

"Not that there's anything wrong with that, honey. If that's what you like, then that's what you like. Everyone deserves to love and be loved. This is a no-judgment zone."

"Good to know." Now Taylor got her turn to laugh. "Except that you're being ridiculous." And to mete a little pap-pap across Claire's hand. "For the record, I like boys, Claire. Men. Good old-fashioned dick." She chuckled again, shaking her head. "Maybe the experts are on to something. Maybe hormones do make pregnant ladies crazy."

All three of us giggled over that one. "Shit," Claire groused. "It's probably the truth. But do you blame me? I mean, I look like the Goodyear Blimp here!"

"Shut. Up." I wadded one of the paper breakfast napkins and lobbed it at her. "You're gorgeous, and I'm not the only one who thinks so. The enigma himself can't keep his damn eyes off you."

"Psssshh," she rebutted. "Seriously, look at my feet. It's nine in the morning, and they already like Barney Rubble's. If this keeps up, I'll be wearing Vans with my business suits."

"Well, you'd rock the look," I piped in.

"Thank you. You guys are the best." Claire huffed up to one of the stools, leaning back enough to rest folded hands on her big tummy.

With the balance of the universe restored, at least in here, I stepped back, phone in hand. "I'm going to go call the hospital and see how Fletcher's night went, and then I'll need to head over there. Drake had some client appointments this morning, so I'm point on Fletch Watch. I'll be right back."

I went into our bedroom for privacy. I wouldn't mind if the girls heard the conversation, but over the past few days I'd been getting more morose after the nurse cheerfully reported he'd had "a great night with no changes." Now, I was even feeling foolish for the tears. The accident hadn't killed him. He was technically still here, and every member of the medical team viewed his steady status as the best news—but every day that clicked by in which he ended the day as still as he'd begun...

They got harder and harder.

Heavier and heavier.

Time's special weights around my ankles, dragging me into dark waters I couldn't tread.

"Chicago Memorial Neuro ICU."

"Good morning, Maya." I recognized the nurse by her subtle Calypso accent. "This is Talia Perizkova."

"Talia." The woman threaded exotic warmth through my name. "Yes, yes. Fletcher's girl."

My smile spread from ear to ear. She gave me the dopey look whenever I sat at his bedside. "You need to wake up, Mr. Ford, so your pretty girl can see your smile." Her sweetness always warmed my heart.

"How was his night?" I took a calming breath, steeling myself for the usual.

"Well, my dear..." She lilted it into a purposeful pause. "Today is the day you get to ask him for yourself."

I dropped to the unmade bed. My heart hit my stomach at the same crashing speed, only to bounce up and lodge in my throat. "I'm...sorry. Wh-What did you say?"

"He's awake."

She answered so matter-of-factly, I thought I'd misunderstood her. I took a long second to replay the miraculous words, only to shake my head, unwilling to believe them.

"I'm sorry," I repeated. "I actually thought you said—"

"I did."

"You...what?"

"Your man has regained consciousness."

Tremors overtook me from head to toe. "Oh. My. God."

Her confused hum filled the line. "You...did not know this?"

"No. Shit. No. If I did, I'd already be down there." I had to call Drake. I couldn't wait to call Drake.

"He is still very groggy but talking to his parents right

now. Ms. Perizkova..." She replaced the hum with an irked huff. "Mr. and Mrs. Ford said they had called you and Mr. Newland. I truly thought you already knew, or I would have called you myself."

"It's all right, Maya." I threw all the joy of my heart into the reply. Not even the stabbing pain of Francine's and Richard's assholery could drown my elation. "I understand—and I'll be there shortly. I'll call Mr. Newland now. Thank you! Thank you so much!"

With my phone pressed to my ear, ringing through to Drake's cell, I raced out into the living room so the girls really could hear my conversation.

"Hey, baby." His deep timbre was so damn hot. For the first time in a week, I closed my eyes and actually allowed myself to think it. His sexy baritone took away the last of my reserve.

"Drake." So much of my relief and joy poured into it, he responded at once. I listened to tire rubber against road and sincerely hoped he'd hit the brakes someplace safe.

"Is he awake?"

I nodded through tears, thickening and rolling as Claire and Taylor screamed. Remembering he couldn't see that, I plowed on. "Yes. Yes. I called to get the morning report, and Maya said he's alert. I'm heading there now. Can you meet me?"

"An army of hellcats couldn't keep me away. Why don't I pick you up? I'm leaving my last appointment now." The Range Rover's engine could be heard as he accelerated.

"I'd like that. Yes."

"I'll text you when I'm downstairs."

"I'll already be waiting."

"Better plan. You always have them."

"I love you, Drake."

"I love you more, baby."

As soon as I set down my phone, my girlfriends swarmed me in celebratory hugs—and yes, buckets of tears all around. "Thank God. Thank God he's okay."

"Whoa. Killian really owes his cousin now." Though Claire said it beneath her breath, Taylor and I heard her clearly. The result was a dorky three-way laugh—ended first by Taylor, who was still way too unnerved by the subject of Mac for anyone to dismiss. I imagined we'd receive a temperature reading on the two of them sooner than later—but right now, the most important update of the day still chimed in my head like celebration bells.

Despite the bells, I pulled back and extended both hands. Flattened them on the air, putting a visual to the calm I forced back into my heartbeat. Okay, calm down. To my friends, I said, "Let's just wait and learn about his condition when I get there. They keep telling us he may have a long road to recovery. It's important we don't lose sight of that."

"Ohhhh, no." Taylor swept an arm in the air, snapping her fingers at the peak. "We need to celebrate, girl. Rejoice in every single milestone as they come. Every achievement is worthy of a party!"

I joined Claire in indulging her with laughs. The woman's optimism was always so infectious, blooming in every inch of every room she entered—but this time, just beneath her verve, I detected a strange energy. It sneaked into her blue-gray eyes, giving her a far-off look for several moments. Her body was still here, but I was certain her mind had suddenly jumped far beyond my living room.

"Hey." I touched her arm, bringing her back to the present. "You okay?"

She jolted, gazing at my hand as if she didn't recognize it. The next moment, she was back to recovering with her trademark no-fucks-given grin.

Nice try, girl.

Her veneer was becoming more and more transparent. I showed her I knew that by narrowing my eyes, undaunted by her upturned paddle of a hand.

"Don't."

"Don't what?" I went full throttle on feigning innocence, but I wasn't the only one punching through masks today.

"Don't go there," she accused. "I see it on your face, sister, and I'm not pickin' up what you're throwin' down. This is all about you right now. You and that sexy god of a man who's waiting for you. Men," she corrected with a mischievous wink.

I threw up my arms. "Fine. This slides for now because I can't even think straight—but we will revisit 'you' eventually."

Her eyes adopted a mock-pissy mien. "Did you really just air quote at me?"

I folded my arms and sashayed my head. "I totally did."

"Air quote at you?" Claire finally chimed in. "Is that like 'caps-lock text shout' at someone?"

"Pretty much."

"Well, hell." She giggled. "Guess you've earned the right to it this week, girl."

"Week?" I returned. "What about the last year?" I rolled my eyes and went for new air quotes. "'Life with Strongly Opinionated Men.' I could write a survivor's manual."

Claire bumped the giggle to a full laugh. "Oh, is that what you call them? Strongly opinionated? Oh, my God. I need to write that down, use it on Kil." Her eyes danced with burnished flecks. "It'll probably earn me some sort of evil punishment."

Under normal circumstances, Taylor and I would be all over that little tidbit like white on rice, but nothing was normal about today—as I was reminded by the alert ding of my phone.

"Drake's downstairs." My voice wavered with excitement and joy.

As we walked to the elevator, Claire quickly dialed Killian. "Hey, Chicago. No, I'm fine. Great news, though—Fletcher's awake. Yes, really. I'm still at Talia's, but Drake's here to take her to the hospital. Yes. Yes, that's fine. Okay, we'll wait for the car here and then we can meet up with them at the hospital? No, you're right. Yes. Okay. Yes, I've had breakfast." A quick pause as he fired another question. "Yes, I've taken my vitamins." Pause. "Yes, she's kicking like crazy this morning." Another. "Yes, I love you too. Okay, bye."

On the elevator landing, Taylor and I watched from our end of the conversation, our jaws completely slack.

"What?" Claire's huge sienna eyes added to her soft maternal innocence.

"Unbelievable." Taylor uttered it to me more than her.

"Right?" I volleyed.

"What?" Claire demanded.

Taylor shook her head, her blonde waves crowding her face. "He loves you so much. It makes my heart hurt just witnessing it." She rubbed the center of her chest, a pained look on her face. "No, really. It hurts."

Claire brushed a toe over the marble floor. "Well, you'll be out of your agony soon. Kil's just in papa-bear protective mode right now."

"Bullshit." I disguised the word by pretending to sneeze.

"Huh?"

There were a couple of quarters in my coat pocket. I grabbed her hand, turned it over, and smacked the change into her palm. "Here. For the clue you need to buy. Because that man loves you that much."

She looked away, shy at first, before lifting her head with a wry laugh. "Yeah, fine, okay—I'm the luckiest girl on the planet."

We formed a tight group hug in the middle of the elevator car, circled around Claire and her belly. When the door slid open, we were just disengaging, sniffly noses and teary eyes all around.

Standing right in front of the lift was my dark beast of a boyfriend—who stopped dead in his tracks when realizing he was less than six feet away from three overly emotional women. If he could've escaped, through any egress possible, he likely would have.

His midnight eyes were wary, trying to gauge our next move. Claire and Taylor, having already hugged me goodbye, turned at once for him. When they jointly moved in, whispering their excitement about Fletcher's breakthrough, he visibly relaxed. He attributed the emotional display to our recent news, which I guess was on the "approved emotional instigator" list.

As soon as the girls cleared out, Drake strode straight for me. He wrapped me close in his massive arms, kissing my hair, my forehead, my nose—before consuming my mouth in a searing kiss.

Wow.

"This is the best day already, baby."

I nodded, stroking the powerful jut of his jaw. Just like

that, I was on the verge of losing it again. So many emotions collided, having built up over the last seven days. Hope. Despair. Desperation. Reflection. Frustration.

And now...

Gratitude.

"Let's go see our guy."

The drive to the hospital seemed eternal. Traffic was heavy as people set out for early lunches in the gorgeous sunshine, adding to the existing congestion of the bustling downtown corridor. My anticipation added to my impatience. I held off telling Drake about Francine and Richard neglecting to call us with the news. Today was a day for celebrating, just as Taylor had decreed. Besides, I carried no illusions about the journey ahead and knew Drake was on the same page. We had a long road ahead of us, and an uphill battle wasn't the right way to start.

By the time we reached Fletcher's room, the pound of my heart shook my whole body. My pulse throbbed in my ears. This was more nerve-racking than the first kiss I'd shared with these two, so long ago in Vegas. It was more daunting than the first time we'd made love, on that same trip.

When we approached the nurses' station, Maya came out from behind the desk. She warmly hugged me and then Drake.

"He has been asking for you two nonstop," she declared with a smile. "And your timing is perfect. His parent just left for lunch."

"Thank fuck," Drake gritted.

I calmed him by squeezing his hand.

"You can both go in together if you promise not to get him too agitated," Maya offered.

I let go of Drake to grasp her hand in appreciation.

"Thank you," I whispered.

She lifted a finger. "Now I must ask one request."

"Of course." Though I wasn't sure we could truly deliver. If she asked us to wait even five more minutes to see Fletch, my heart would likely burst from my chest and race into his room anyway.

"If he is sleeping, please let him. I think the Fords might have worn him out during their time."

Her face was sorrowful by the end of her statement, sparking my curiosity. Why did I get the impression there was more to what she was saying?

I have to stop with the second-guessing.

Right now, nothing mattered more than seeing him. I needed to gaze into his beautiful blue eyes. To behold his wide, wicked smile.

Finally, finally, Drake took my hand. We paced quietly as we went into Fletcher's room. I still wasn't feeling his hum in my head but was convinced it would return any moment now. He was still "groggy," as Maya had described it. That had to be the explanation. He'd just woken up from a coma, for heaven's sake.

We approached cautiously. The curtain was drawn, blocking his bed from view to anyone entering or walking by. I had no idea what to expect. I was so nervous. Still so damn scared.

As soon as I saw him, all my breath left me.

He was propped higher in his bed than before, and the horrible ventilator tube had been removed. The room was strangely quiet without the low hum of that machine. The lights were dimmed, so the room's main illumination came from a swath of sun streaming through a part in the curtains.

That beam stretched over the bottom of the bed, right across Fletcher's feet. It probably made him uncomfortably warm. I'd have to fix that.

As if he sensed us here, his eyes fluttered open.

Screw breathing at all.

I rushed to him. Drake mirrored me, doing the same on the opposite side. Fletcher was unnaturally still. Slowly, he gazed at me and then Drake. Back to me.

Then heaven gave me my miracle.

A small smile spread across his dry, cracked lips. I sobbed. Just that action was clearly exhausting for him. He was still so banged up. It had only been a week since that truck had turned his car into a modern art piece.

"Hey, you." My voice was so quiet, lost somewhere between my heart and my mouth.

"Tolly." His rasp barely had volume. It was the most beautiful sound I'd ever heard.

"Hi, baby." I grabbed his hand, pressing my lips to the bruises on his knuckles. Just as swiftly, I lowered it. My action had hurt him. I could see that even without our bond in the deep creases across his forehead. "Sorry," I whispered. "I'm just so happy."

"Brother."

As soon as Drake said it, in a whisper as shaky as mine, Fletcher's eyes darted to him. Drake reached down, covering the pale hand on the sheets with his seemingly larger, tanner one.

"Fucker." There was a lot more confidence in that bite. Drake even added a sarcastic snort. "You gave us quite a scare, you know."

Fletcher's grin spread. Miracle number three. "Oh, here

we go."

"Damn straight, here we go." There was nothing but affection in Drake's drawl. Miracle number four. Their banter was back, and I had the oceans of tears in my eyes to prove it. A bright drop even slid down Drake's cheek before he dashed it away.

"I've never been so happy to see your beautiful eyes in my entire life." I said it to give Drake a second for self-composure—but also because it was true. I leaned in, running my fingers through Fletcher's thick golden hair, pushing it away from his forehead. "Wow. You really need a haircut now, Mr. Ford."

"I love it when you call me that, Ms. Perizkova."

I coyly pursed my lips. "I know."

His face tightened again. Alarm shot through me, until I observed the difference with this grimace. It was confusion, not pain.

"How long have I been like this?" His words were slow, but he was putting them in the right order. Mac had warned us that might not be the case when he woke up.

"A week," I supplied. "The longest one of my life. Of all our lives. Oh, my God, I still can't believe this. I'm so thankful you came back. Thank you for coming back!"

I didn't want to cry. I wanted to be brave and strong like Drake had been, but the tears came and fell, unbridled and uninhibited.

"I'm so sorry!" I said.

Drake answered first. "Why are you apologizing, Tolly?"

"I didn't want to waste time with all this boo-hooing—but I can't help it. I'm so happy." I looked between the two of them. "So damn happy."

"Then there's nothing to apologize for."

Drake slanted over, lifting my free hand to his lips just as I'd just done with Fletch. His lips were firm and warm on my knuckles, and his dark eyes burned into me. His pupils had turned nearly black, igniting instant fires in my bloodstream—and my heart.

We broke apart as Fletcher let out a pained sound. The spell of Fletcher's gaze was shattered, blaring guilt through every pore of my body. What the hell had we been thinking? This wasn't the place or time for getting hot and bothered.

I yanked my hand in closer, feeling like a kid sneaking a sip of her mom's diet soda—and getting caught. With my defenses down, my psyche clicked into its default mode of hypercrazy caregiver.

"Are you in pain, baby? Can I get you anything for it? Maya's right at the nurses' station. I can just go run and get her. Are you hungry? I'll bet you want some real food right about now. A shower too. Maybe they'll let us get you a shower."

"Natalia." Drake's commanding voice sliced into my frenzy. "Settle down. We weren't doing anything wrong."

I jerked my bugged-out eyes in Drake's direction. "What?"

"You're acting like a teenager who just got caught sneaking in after curfew. Stop. We're happy our partner is back with us. That's all. Why are you freaking out?"

"I'mnotfreakingout."

Fletcher burst into a chuckle. The reaction made him sink deeper into his pillows. He closed his eyes again, but a broad smile now adorned his perfect angel's mouth.

Under any other circumstance, I'd smack the arrogant bastard. Instead, I suddenly witnessed my insanity of actions through his calm aura—and I laughed too.

And it felt so damn good.

I really had been ludicrous. Drake and I had barely even kissed over the last week. Nothing felt remotely right without Fletcher, especially being intimate. I had nothing to feel guilty about.

Today wasn't for guilt. Or anger. Or blame. Or sadness. Or pettiness.

Today was about celebration.

And right here, right now, I had an invitation to the best party on earth.

CHAPTER NINE

Fletcher

"I can do it."

The snarl wasn't my first intention, but I couldn't take it back now. Drake would get over it, of that I was sure. Probably one of the few assurances about my life at the moment.

"Just lean on me." He boomeranged the bite back at me as soon as we got out of the Range Rover in front of our building. "Stop being stubborn and let me help you."

I should've been reveling in this moment. I was finally free from the medical prison that dinged, beeped, and alarmed at me every hour of the day. I wouldn't be sleeping on a plastic mattress tonight. I'd be eating home-cooked meals again.

And, oh, yeah...I was alive.

But I couldn't escape the moroseness. It slammed harder as I studied the exhaustion lining my brother's face. Drake was bone tired, and I was a lot of the reason for it.

But not all.

Even superheroes had to get some rest. Not that this one would ever admit it.

"Fuck you," I muttered, though it lacked the bite of real anger. Hell, maybe the reasonable touch would actually get through to him. "All I've been doing is letting people help. I need to start doing things for myself and not waiting for someone to come rescue me."

"Fletcher—"

"Tolly. Don't."

She sighed heavily. "Please, just listen to Drake. It's only been a week since you opened your eyes and started breathing on your own. There's no need to rush your recovery. You remember what Mac said? One step at a time?"

"Fuck him too."

"There's something you and Killian will finally agree on." Drake paused, hands on his denim-covered hips, and laughed. His eyes, nearly matching his charcoal sweater, glinted in the afternoon sun.

"And probably Taylor too—but for other reasons."

I shot her a puzzled glance at that, but she was busy checking out the large bag of supplies the hospital had sent home with us. I swung my sights back to Drake, who only shrugged.

I released a tired breath myself. Early afternoon, and it had already been quite a day. I hadn't expected my discharge to be as emotional as it was. Drake and Talia had forged tight friendships with my regular nurses while I'd been "out," as we'd come around to calling it. Holding a bedside vigil was a trying experience, so there were lots of tears, hugs, and choked-up well-wishes that had been both awesome and awful for me to watch. My life had been in the hands of these people for two weeks. I owed them everything.

Mom and Dad had come for the departure as well. Neither would ever shed a tear in public—gasp, the horror—so they'd stood in tight silence while Talia had hugged and thanked every person who'd participated in my recovery. Yeah, even the orderlies and hospital volunteers. Drake and I had accompanied her, beaming as she'd promised to come back and visit them all. She'd even discreetly exchanged phone numbers with her favorite, and therefore mine, the sweet Maya. Talia was beautiful and brave and generous, and I was so damn proud to be by her side.

That was all the good stuff.

I just still had to reconcile myself to the hard stuff.

The really hard stuff.

There were big holes in my memory of the events leading up to and including the accident. I clearly recollected the night before. I'd been pissed at my family and then myself, foolishly taking it out on Drake and Talia the next morning. I'd left home without saying goodbye to either of them, but that was where things went blank. I was told I'd been broadsided by a delivery truck, an accident totaling my beloved B6. I couldn't talk about how much I'd miss that car, knowing I'd get lectured about the miracle of being alive—and I was thankful, especially when Drake and Talia had finally arrived.

When they'd walked back into my world again, that afternoon last week...

Fuck.

I'd never forget that moment, ever. All the joy, relief, exultation, and gratitude would be indelible parts of me. And more. So much more. My body and mind had been swimming against the strongest current in a vast, dark sea. I kept swimming but got nowhere. I'd been drowning—until suddenly, the tide changed and I could make it to the shore...and there they were, waiting like angels. My anchors. My safety. The two people I loved more than anyone else.

The two people who'd then driven me insane with their pep talks, rah-rah inspiration—yeah, even Drake had been "bouncy"—and can-do crap about how I'd be back to myself in no time. "Just a little physical therapy" and I'd be "good as new."

A little PT? In no time?

A week had passed, and I still couldn't take a piss without someone helping me. The right side of my body had its own agenda most of the time, and my fatigue after even the simplest tasks was maddening beyond measure.

Just like new?

My ass.

I'd had a chance to talk with Mac before they'd all came in this morning. I'd requested the early meeting with the doc, needing to hear the unvarnished truth about my recovery. Part of me also wanted to assess the man when Killian wasn't around, to try to glimpse why he and Kil had declared themselves the new Batman and Joker—but, yeah, mostly it was about me. I couldn't take the sunshine everyone kept blowing up my ass. From Drake and Tolly to every care and service provider on the hospital's staff, I'd had enough of the "let's-go-team" to last three lifetimes. I knew they cared, but I just needed someone to level with me, man to man.

"Am I seriously ever going to walk again? Run? Play water polo? Fuck my girlfriend? Just tell me the truth, Doc. I can't take this rainbow and unicorn crap any longer."

He'd laughed, but the humor never reached his eyes. Far from it. Which was god damned terrifying.

"Put yourself in my place, man. I just want to know what I'm up against. I can handle it. Just shoot straight with me."

Mac had sat on the edge of my bed, fiddling with the shiny Tag watch on his wrist before leveling his gaze with mine. I'd asked for this but hadn't been certain I wanted it anymore. Too late by then. When he'd spoken, his tone had been different than before.

Different—but not morose.

Simply speaking to me as a friend, instead of a medical professional.

"Yeah, Fletch. Of course you will. But exactly when? Well, that'll be up to you. You've had a serious head injury, dude. You're looking at some hard rebuilding in your immediate future. But if you stay the course, there is no medical reason to prevent you from returning to a full, natural life—in every aspect."

I'd nodded, hoping my deep gratitude showed on my face, because words weren't possible. He'd seemed to read the message. Mac himself was usually a man of few words, and on most days, I'd fully appreciated it. Talia had been talking enough for three people since I'd pushed back into reality. It was how she handled anxiety, but it was making me tense and angry.

Everything was making me tense and angry.

I hated it.

But was helpless to tame it.

Pushing that giant snowball harder up the self-control hill.

Things that I typically had patience for suddenly lit my fuse—with its super-short wick. Just last night, when I hadn't been able to get the last mouthful of corn off my dinner plate with my fork, I'd flipped the dinner tray table like the infant I felt most of the time. My own body had abandoned me. Nothing worked the way it should anymore.

Snowball. Hill.

"Okay, man. On three, we're going from the car to the

wheelchair right there. Ready?"

"For fuck's sake, D."

He ignored my outburst, hauling my half-useless body into the waiting wheelchair.

Awesome. My very own wheelchair.

"Soooooo, we've scheduled a home health nurse to come in and give us a hand for the first couple of weeks. I think you'll like him. Maya helped me interview a couple candidates, and Marcus was the best fit." Talia chattered away while Drake maneuvered the wheelchair. When I didn't respond, she started backpedaling. "Of course, if you don't like something about him, or you just don't get along or whatever, we'll have the agency send us someone else to try. No problem. They've been very helpful. They want us to be happy, so if you don't—"

"Tolly. Please. He's going to love the guy. Who wouldn't love him?"

If I thought Drake had been her biggest fan before, it was nothing compared to his new dynamic with her. They worked in nearly flawless sync with each other. Anticipated needs before they were spoken. Divided up tasks like well-oiled gears. Practically finished each other's sentences.

Exactly how she and I had once been.

"I know, right?" Her eyes sparkled—literally—when she gazed at him. She dropped back a step to bump celebratory shoulders with him too. Awwww, so cute. "And did you hear him saying he could help with meals too?"

"That'll be a big help." I guessed his damn eyes were sparkling too.

Talia stayed by his side as he pushed me into the building. Thankfully, none of the other residents were hanging about. Talia scooted in front of me and pressed the Call button.

She leaned down to be level with my face, tenderly kissing my lips. "I'm so glad you're home. It hasn't been the same here without you." Unshed tears pooled in her incredible sable eyes.

"Hey." I reached out with my "good" hand and touched her cheek. "No more crying, okay?"

"But they're happy tears now." She turned her lips into my palm. "I'm just so thankful. So grateful that this is the moment we're sharing right now."

"That doesn't even make sense." I scowled.

The elevator doors opened. Drake swung me around so he could back the chair into the car.

"Of course it makes sense." Again, she donned her rose-colored glasses. "Believe me, they prepared us for a lot of possible ends to this story, mister. This is the best one by far."

I didn't relinquish my glower. Likely made me look like a teenage asshole, but just the thought of pretending otherwise felt as though I were standing at the base of Everest right now. "Sorry, baby, but I don't see how me being a burden pain in the ass for an undefined amount of time could ever be viewed as a positive thing." I'd meant it during my conversation with Mac. I was done with the sunshine and sparkles.

As had already become customary, they both went to silent mode. When they couldn't toss another rainbow kitten at my blatant facts, they just shut their mouths—and maybe that was for the best. Eventually they'd get tired of playing nurse. I was simply the only one willing to say it so far.

Two weeks passed in much the same way. We all developed a routine—sort of—which ate away at more of my hope each day. Bright spot? Marcus ended up being a pretty cool guy. He looked better suited for action movies than nursing but had no interest in show biz and simply enjoyed taking care of his clients. Most importantly, he knew when to lay off the peppy horseshit just before I lost my cool, as well as sensing when I needed to be left alone. Best of all, he had a way of taking care of my daily living needs while leaving my dignity intact.

For the most part.

Physical therapy was the worst hour of every day. I hated it. No. What was a word worse than hate? My once athletic, capable body betrayed me at almost every turn. The exercises the therapist put me through were elementary and boring, and I was humiliated at my inability to complete even those.

On the "super lucky" days, my mother, father, or sister came to visit. Their forced civility to Drake and Talia never stopped making my skin crawl. My fuse didn't run short during their stays—the rope just burned and then blew. Drake and Talia deserved to be canonized for the monster they inherited in me after those hours, but it was impossible to pretend I felt otherwise. Over and over, I replayed the night we'd all but been thrown out of the precious anniversary celebration—the starting spark to my rage, leading to my disgusting treatment of Tolly in bed that night and then my horrific bender afterward and the morning I'd fled my own home like a shamed puppy.

Because of them. Because of their pretentious, ridiculous airs. Everyone in this fucking town knew Dick and Frannie Ford were imposters, so why was I the only one forced to tolerate them? If friends were the family one chose, what were the family you yearned to unchoose? Life had no box to check for that one. Fucker.

By the third week, my attitude had taken a total shit. I was miserably disappointed with my progress. When I went for the follow-up appointment with Mac, he was positive and animated, firing off all good news. I just couldn't see it. All I saw was where I was currently and where I used to be.

Mac urged me to get busy again, in careful increments. But work held no interest for me. Things were starting to pile up at FFE, things needing my personal attention. I didn't give a shit about any of it.

But none of that was the worst of it.

I began watching Drake and Talia when they thought I was resting. I listened to their whispered words of love and passion, followed by heated touches and kisses, and knew they suffered because of me. They were holding off on making love until I could participate.

Talia was clear about her viewpoint. She refused to be with Drake and not me. We had never made love to her separately. She was adamant that practice wouldn't start now. She'd stated, with yet more tears, that she never wanted to experience one of us without the other. She'd backed it up with all the new-age crap like balance and harmony and completion and karma, but I'd wheeled away—literally—before the diatribe was done. She overwhelmed me with babble because she didn't know what else to do.

Because none of us did.

I forced myself to consider how badly my brother must be aching. Drake had to be ready to explode right now. It had been five fucking weeks since the accident.

The string of thought brought me to a singular conclusion. It was time to take one for the team.

They had to find some relief. I hadn't had a single moment of arousal since the accident, especially with my mental link with Tolly still snapped. To be honest, I wondered if things would ever work again. Everything else on my body seemed to have its own agenda—why would my dick be any different?

But damn it, I needed this too. I needed to feel something other than misery. I needed to touch Talia's skin. All her skin. To watch the warmth of her spirit flare into fire and bask in the heat of her awakened sexuality. I needed to be her lover in at least a few ways, if not all. If that meant I was just their voyeur, then that was what I'd settle for. Lying beside them, encouraging where I could, had to be better than constantly snarling at them.

Timing would be everything with my proposition. I considered talking to Drake about it first but knew deep down he wouldn't go for my idea. His savior routine was getting harder and harder to swallow every day. I didn't want to resent my best friend, but I was starting to—another solid supporting argument for this plan. If we didn't turn the man's balls back to a normal color soon, I'd deck him in his perfect Adonis face. I wasn't sure it wouldn't happen anyhow.

No anger. Not now. Push it down, man.

The dinner dishes were cleared and the drapes drawn until morning. Our typical routine dictated we'd all watch a movie or do something together before turning in for the night. Since coming home I'd slept in my old room because all the supplies and equipment Marcus used were in there. Drake sacked out on the sofa most nights, and Talia was all alone in the big bed that had once been our heaven.

Here went nothing.

"I want to sleep in our bed tonight." I squared my shoulders against the back of the couch as I announced it, completely meeting their upturned gapes. "Yes, with both of you," I addressed to the question on both faces. "I'm tired of waking up alone every morning."

My timing for the comment was odd, to them at least,

but my intention had been to catch them off-guard. I'd purposely waited until Tolly started fast-forwarding through a commercial break on the recorded series she'd made us watch. Somewhere between "Got Milk" and the Aflac goose, I blurted it out.

"Ohhhh kaaaaay." She darted her eyes to Drake, taking a fortifying gulp of air. "But...ummm..."

"But what?" My tone was full of a lot of things, but anger and hesitation weren't any of them. I was calm. Even solemn. And determined.

"Well, are you sure that's a good idea? I mean, is there anything you need from your room in the night? Marcus has everything set up so nicely..."

"The only thing I need is you." I had to breathe in as desperation broke through my composure. Talia's features, softening as I spoke, didn't help. "Yeah, both of you. I'm-I'm so fucked-up, you guys. I can't get my head on straight, and I think it's because there's something missing. My body isn't fully cooperating because my fucking head isn't. And a huge part of my head...is us."

Drake sat up straighter. "I hear what you're saying, man."

"Good," I rebutted and then filled in his pause. "But...?"

"But I'm worried about you." Savior Man was trying, in his surprisingly awkward way, to remind me of my shortcomings. His gaze beseeched mine. "Are you ready for all that?"

"There's no harm in just sleeping together." I was ready with the argument, having already scripted out their reactions in my mind. So far, they'd both followed the play to the letter. "Just lying in our bed, side by side by side, closing our eyes like we used to do. When we wake up, our girl is the first thing we see. How can you deny me that?"

"I'm not denying you anything. I just think we should talk to Mac first."

"You want me to talk to my neurosurgeon about the bed I sleep in?" Yep. Right on the scenario. Drake would try to approach this from every angle. An X-ray of his head would show a million gears turning right now, but in the end, there was no viable argument to us "just sleeping together."

Of course, my motives weren't entirely innocent—and Drake detected that too. He saw how I'd already banked on them being unable to resist each other, once we were all horizontal. Why assume otherwise? Since the beginning, whenever we climbed into bed together, instincts just took over. Even innocuous afternoon "catnaps" hadn't been immune. It was just the energy of us...

I had to hope against hope it would happen this time too.

Talia clicked the TV off and set the remote on the end table. She looked at me and then Drake, her dark eyes smoldering. "I would love nothing more than to sleep between my two loves. I've missed the nearness of you both, and I think it's a great step forward." She punctuated that with a raised finger. "But we're sleeping only. Nothing more. Got it?"

"Got it." I smiled.

Drake didn't.

"Why don't you go get ready for bed then, baby?" He stoked the glower, aimed strictly at me, while issuing it. "We'll be in right after I lock up."

"Perfect." She practically floated past us, happily proceeding down the hall toward our room.

Our room.

It would be that way again tonight. Thank fuck.

As soon as the door clicked shut behind her, Drake bolted

to his feet.

"Dude."

"Don't." I had that at the ready too. The guy was still hitting every cue I'd written. "Not now. There's no harm in sleeping in the same bed. You were just listening to Tolly, weren't you? She's been missing us too."

He clapped his hands slowly. "Congratulations, Sherlock. What magnificent deduction."

I kept my posture rigid. This time, the savior didn't get to prevail. "Why are you fighting this?"

"Because I'm calling you on your shit, asshole. You and I both know damn well what happens when we get into bed with that woman. It's been the very same since Vegas, and it'll be no different tonight." He wheeled around, openly exposing his clenched fists—and the bulge beneath his crotch. "You'd better be damn sure about this, on both levels."

"'Both levels'?" I almost pulled a Tolly and air quoted at him. "What? You feel more comfortable about this if we put it in gamer boy speak?"

"Coy isn't attractive on you, Fletch." His nostrils flared on a brutal exhalation. "One, you'd better be fucking sure you can physically handle this shit. And two, you'd better have a damn good backup plan for when this hare-brained one falls apart." He spun back toward the kitchen, hands clamping across the back of his head. "You sure about this, Fletch? Are you willing to disappoint not only her but yourself?"

Fury vise-gripped my chest. I didn't know if I loved him or hated him right now. Probably both. Maybe neither. "Fuck me, Newland." A chuff burst out. "When did you become such a pansy? Seriously. How is sleeping in my own bed—my real bed—going to bring on the apocalypse?"

He dropped his arms. "So, this is how we're playing it? Denial until the end?" He flung one of those arms, as if tossing breadcrumbs for pigeons. "Fine. Okay, dick. But I'm going to be the other guy in that bed, and I won't be able to turn her away. Just getting that out there now. I know what my Achilles' heel is, and it's that woman and her pussy. You can't seriously tell me you believe this'll just be strictly sleeping."

With that, he stormed around the condo, making sure doors were locked and lights were turned out. During that part of his hissy, I pulled myself up to stand, leaning on the sofa arm for balance. I'd finally graduated to an old-lady walker the day before, but the contraption was just beyond my reach. I hated that thing with a passion, especially when realizing I'd have to let go of the furniture to get to it.

One step.

Twelve inches.

I got this.

I tried using momentum, pushing off the sofa and heaving all my weight toward the walker. Drake stood by, watching but not offering to help, knowing I needed to do it for myself—

Or just waiting to see me fall on my face.

Fucking Savior Boy. I'll show you.

I stepped out with my left foot, shifting my weight over the center of my body. The action landed me perfectly on the walker's hand grips. I huffed with relief as Drake lowered a reassuring hand on my back.

"That was awesome, dude. You really just did that."

"Yep. One whole step." I laughed wryly. "I'm on fire."

"Hey." His voice was gentle but forceful, demanding I look up and meet his stare—a contact I'd been avoiding for weeks. "I know this sucks, Fletch. I also get that I have no real idea what it's like for you right now, but I have had some experience with uphill battles and fighting the odds."

I clenched my jaw. Gripped the walker tighter. "Which is supposed to mean...what?"

"That you need to fucking stop this self-destructive shit," he gritted. "It's killing me to watch, and it's killing her too." He thumbed over his shoulder toward the bedroom. "We're on your side, Fletch. We want you to recover and be you again. We aren't the enemy here."

I tilted my head to the side a fraction, joining my bitten tongue to the self-control effort. No way could I spew what was in the forefront of my mind—that of all the supportive shit he'd just rambled, only one rang through my brain like a taunting refrain.

He'd said "we"—and meant only him and Talia.

We. You.

Them against me.

"Thank you, man. That means a lot."

Well, listen to that. I was getting to be a fantastic liar too. Chip off the Ford Family block, after all.

Drake narrowed his eyes. He scrutinized my face before taking in all my body language. Very little got past this guy, and most of the time I loved him for it. Relied on him for it. But now? I wanted to knee him in the balls and stroll off into the sunset.

Me and my walker.

"Let's go to bed." He fell in step behind me as I shuffled down the hall. I wouldn't even have to bother changing into pajamas. Flannel lounge pants and old concert tees had become my daily uniform. I did take a few minutes to use the restroom and brush my teeth, all accomplished with sloppy results, but heaven save their skins, Drake and Tolly stayed out of my way. There wasn't a single offer of help.

By the time I made it to the bed, a fine sheen of sweat moistened my brow.

"I'm just going to pull the covers back." Tolly's chatter was strangely comforting now. "How's that? You do the rest yourself. I'm just moving this heavy comforter. Take your time."

She bustled around, adjusting the bedding, and I was truly grateful. No way could I have handled the cover and my walker at the same time. My eggshell ego appreciated her nervous efficiency.

"Sit on the side of the bed, and I'll help you get settled." She moved my walker out of the way, and I complied with her request. When she came back and stood in front of me, I looked up into her stunning, freshly washed face. This was my favorite way of seeing her. No makeup, so clean and dewy and ready for bed. Perfect. Fucking perfect. I'd needed this so badly.

With some effort I reached for her, finally managing to wrap both arms around her waist. Although it took focused force, I tugged her between my legs. My head rested on her stomach, and for a moment, I simply listened to her breath moving in and out.

Fuck. Yes.

This.

The curves of her small form in my arms. The magic of her presence, wrapped up with mine. The feeling that I could protect her from the world...or give her the world if that was what she wanted.

When she pulled back, I didn't want to let go.

I fought to hang on, but my arm was still so damn weak.

She was able to easily disengage, though didn't go far. She bent over, dipping her head in and touching her soft lips to my forehead.

A breath in. A breath out.

Magic.

Her mouth sought my eyelids, my nose, both sides of my jaw—and at last my lips. I tilted my chin up, deepening the kiss...reveling in every incredible sensation of it. So long. Too long, since I'd drowned in her taste. I groaned as our tongues twirled with one another. For the first time in what felt like forever, my heartbeat quickened.

"I've missed you so much." She gazed deeply at me... looking into my soul. Though she lifted a serene smile, her coffee-colored eyes were still heavily hooded from our passion. "Let's get under the covers and drift off to sleep. The three of us. The way we're supposed to be."

She waited patiently while I pulled my legs into bed and settled against the pillows. With the same happy smile, she dragged the covers up to my waist. Her action made me smile. I didn't like covers all the way to my neck like she did, one of the thousands of little things she knew about me.

All the things she'd once known before I could ever speak them aloud.

My smile vanished.

I hated the chasm where our mental connection had once been—and was terrified it might not ever return. Had the accident killed it? Was that the price karma had demanded in exchange for my life? Wasn't like I could go to Mac with those queries. How do you ask a doctor questions like that? I had to settle for hoping it'd come back on its own.

Waiting.

Hoping.

Recovering.

The story of my damn life now.

Talia crossed around the foot of the bed and climbed in from the other side. Drake turned out the light and sandwiched her between us on the huge mattress. Because it wasn't as easy for me to move as it was for them, we were all piled onto the left, nearest to my side. I began freaking about the logistics— like a moron, I hadn't scripted out this detail—but all was solved the moment Talia nestled her beautiful face against my chest. When I wrapped my arm around her shoulders, pulling her closer still, she sighed with contentment.

I almost flung a gloating glance Drake's way. See, you bastard? We could sleep together without complicating things with sex. Drake just hadn't given us the credit we deserved.

When I looked past her, the gloat dissipated.

Drake was already burying his face into her long locks, breathing in deeply, his eyes closed in rapture. The guy looked like he was inhaling her essence into his very soul.

It only meant he liked the way she smelled.

I did too.

I pressed a kiss to the top of her head, breathing the same luscious scent. The jasmine in her hair. Her wildflower-scented body lotion.

Damn.

Damn, she smelled good.

We needed to connect in the worst way. More than this. So much more...

I felt the longing gather in the marrow of my bones. Why wasn't the rest of my body on board with the program? As Tolly burrowed tighter against me, my arousal spiraled. Her skin was smooth and flushed under my fingertips. Her breaths hitched and then quickened, turning into needy pants as I traced circles on the shell of her ear.

Things moved with surreal surety. We became dancers, flowing with instinct and arousal and awakening. Reconnecting to each other. Rediscovering ourselves...

Drake glided his hand up Talia's hip as he slid to his side and pressed up behind her. Talia sighed. Drake growled. I seconded the sound at once. God damn...yes.

She was so fucking sexy. Her little silk booty shorts and matching tank top showed off all the right things. The gorgeous V of her cleavage. Her heart-shaped ass. The silk set wasn't as hot as the lace ones in the same style, but I wasn't sure how much more torture I could endure before admitting to her what was physically happening to me.

Fuck.

The more correct phrase?

What was not happening to me.

What the hell? All the pieces were in place, but the last one wouldn't click in. Was it the medication I was taking for the muscle spasms? The antibiotics for the infection risk from the surgery? The pain killers that took the edge off my daily aches? They all had side effects I'd never bothered to research, but now it was a clear and present problem. I needed to face this shit. It had to be one of the medications. It wasn't a permanent result of the brain injury. I refused to accept that.

Until Mac's words echoed at me.

"But if you stay the course, there is no medical reason to prevent you from returning to a full, natural life—in every aspect."

Every aspect. Okay, I needed to refocus.

I also needed to ask for their help.

If Drake and Talia gave me some incentive...

Hell, they were the hottest thing I could think of to watch. Maybe they'd be my perfect kickstart...

With a determined grunt, I pushed Talia to her back. As she twisted backward, her legs untangled from mine. She was now settled between us. Drake stared at her flushed skin and aroused gaze and then instantly slid his eyes shut. Dude was likely praying for the strength to honor his vow against fucking her—and probably begged the Almighty to hold him back from clocking me at the same time. I'd just laid her out like a feast for him to devour. A few more taunts, and he would take the bait. I knew every single thing that made this guy tick—and was now determined to form an irresistible trail of breadcrumbs with them.

Without speaking, I moved my hand under Talia's tank. Swiftly, I dragged the fabric up and over her nipple, jutting inches from my best friend's mouth. His harsh exhalation brought goosebumps to her mocha flesh. Her areola darkened, puckering as it extended her berry-dark nipple even higher.

Drake swallowed. He licked his lips as though her breast was the finest candy on the planet. With quivering effort, he managed to tear his gaze up—directly at me. His eyes, nearly black with lust, squinted in fury. His lips, twisted and tense, mouthed just one word at me.

"Why?"

He was way-the-fuck turned on—and lethally pissed. His thoughts were practically branded across his prominent forehead. To him, this was betrayal in the worst possible way. I'd come in here knowing he refused to screw Tolly but was offering her to him like a piece of fruit between buddies.

Forbidden fruit.

I'd pay to never see that look on his face again. He was clearly suffering. Despite that, I wasn't sure I cared. Like the selfish, pathetic dick now was, I had to keep going. Had to know if I could ever bring Talia pleasure again, even if it meant using Drake as my tool. It wasn't fair, especially when I glided my hand over and exposed her other breast, but I was on a mission and wouldn't be deterred.

I met his furious stare with undaunted purpose. "Kiss her," I challenged.

"No," he snarled.

"Drake," Talia pleaded. In the same urgent manner, she flashed her gaze to me. "Fletcher. Please. Can't we—?"

"Kiss. Her."

"Why are you doing this?" He bared his gritted teeth just as I did. "Why the fuck are you doing this to me? I've given you all I have over the past five weeks. Everything."

"And you're making more of it than you should," I hissed. "Just kiss her. You want to, don't you? Look at this." I reached over, ruthlessly pinching her nipple. Her back arched, bringing her plump offering right to his lips.

"Ahhhh." Talia writhed between us. "That...feels...so..."

Her eyes shut slowly. Drake's gaze widened. He shifted, beginning to buck his hips. The kid in the candy store was quickly losing his willpower.

Damn you.

If his gaze was a physical object, I guessed at a lethal bullet or a poisoned spear.

I kicked up one side of my mouth. "Kiss her."

"Dear God," Talia begged. "Someone, please kiss me. Lick me. Bite me. Touch me. I don't care. I don't care. It's been so long." Her freshly painted nails dug into my arm, leaving little marks behind. "Too long. Too long."

Her eyes stayed shut, so she didn't fathom the war going on over her body. With our bond still shattered, she couldn't feel any of my anguish. My excitement. My frustration.

"Do it," I mouthed it to Drake. "She wants it."

His cobalt eyes were an abyss of pain, rage…arousal. But, as he'd clearly warned me, he wouldn't deny our girl pleasure. Ever.

He let out a coarse growl—right before covering her areola with his full mouth.

"Yes!" Talia cried.

He sucked on her with force. She'd have a bruise in the morning.

"Ohhhhh. Yessss. God, yes!" She threaded her fingers through his thick hair to hold him in place, but Drake didn't need encouragement. Once begun, he was a ravenous beast. A depleted battery. A dry drunk with a fresh bottle in sight. The need was palpable, an electricity in the air crackling with intensity.

He pushed up, gaining himself better access to her tits. Her tank top was a quick casualty of his pursuit, thrown over his shoulder and landing on the floor.

"My God, you're beautiful." He followed the declaration with a trail of kisses along the side of her breast, over her chest and neck, ending in a deep, smoldering conquest upon her lips. He smashed his way into her mouth, becoming her breath and giving her no quarter, while I watched in enraptured silence.

Tingling sensations lit up my flesh as the scent of her arousal filled the air. It swirled with her natural wildflower mystery to create heady magic.

I wanted to feel her.

And like the asshole I still was, I went in for what I wanted.

I readjusted my weight, turning fully toward her. I was on my side like Drake, so our bodies bracketed her stunning beauty. My blood pumped faster, creating a dull ache in the base of my skull. A momentary flash of concern washed in. Was I overdoing it?

Talia's high-pitched yelp brought me back to the moment. Drake had returned his mouth to her nipple. I guessed he'd just sunk his teeth into the tender bud. His grin was obscured by the swell of her breast, but he loved to bite as much as he loved to lick and kiss.

Maybe...I could do this. Participate...at least a little. If I stuck to simply feeling her skin...

And if I kept up with lies like that, my nose would grow like a little wooden boy's.

At least something would be growing.

I ejected the thought from my head by violently shaking it. I refocused on Talia's skin—one of my favorite things about our beautiful goddess. It was silken tan perfection. Fuck, yes...

I glided my hand to the flat plane of her belly, causing a slight tremor of her muscles there. Her eyes popped open wide. My touch had no doubt stunned her, since I'd been the observer up to that point. After her surprise, the woman appeared more than fine with the twist. A sweet smile spread across her graceful lips. She closed her eyes again, sinking deeper into her lusty haze.

"Thank you, Fletcher." Her voice was low and husky, sending shivers through my nervous system.

"No, baby, I should be thanking you." My murmur was reverent. "For your perfection."

I skated my hand from her belly to her strong thigh, reveling in the smoothness of her flesh. As my fingers neared their juncture, she instinctively spread them. So needy. So brave. Sexy as hell.

"Do you need something, baby?" I couldn't help but encourage her. I couldn't risk Drake bailing out at this point.

"Yes," she whispered. "Touch me."

"I am touching you. And you're the heaven for my tortured soul, Tolly. My personal savior." But when I got to the edge of her damp curls, I strayed. Directed my fingers back to her thigh, down to behind her knee, even around the sensitive top of her kneecap.

"Fletcher!"

"Hmmm?"

She arched up again. "Please!"

"So pretty when you beg." And my worthless cock just lay there. Slack and uninterested, though every other part of my body screamed to pay attention and give our girl what she needed.

I was losing hope.

Drake studiously ignored me. It was a full departure from his usual approach. He was normally like a hawk, noticing every muscle twitch and facial expression from us both, but now he only focused on Talia, as if I wasn't in the same bed with them.

It stabbed a new hole in my heart. That poor organ was Swiss cheese at this point, but this puncture hurt the worst. He'd move on without me if I couldn't get my shit back in the game—and I wouldn't blame him.

I slipped my hand back to her hip. Drawing figure eights with the tips of my fingers, I moved toward her center. Her breathing came in sexy-as-fuck little pants. As I roamed my fingers near her pussy, her fire heated me more...pulled me closer. If I swept over her clit, she'd likely go off at once. It had been too damn long for her. For all of us.

"Please," she moaned. "Please don't make me wait any longer. I'm burning up." She undulated her hips, battling to coax my fingers closer to her heat.

"Baby, ssshhhhh. Let us make you feel good."

"I do. I feel sooooo good already. Please, just—" She choked and bit her lower lip, as if editing her next words. Finally, she just huffed and went for it. "I need someone to fuck me. Please!"

Something in Drake snapped. He pushed my hand off Talia, replacing it with the entire length of his body. He wouldn't be denied any longer. Her begging, her actually uttering the words, had pushed him past his breaking point.

He hooked an arm under one of her legs, hiked it up so her thigh smashed her breast. In one fluid motion, he was inside her. Her quiet moan signaled he'd hit the right spot on the first stroke.

I watched in rapt wonder. Their passion was mesmerizing. Desire painted her face with shades of pink and rose, his in brown and black. Their bodies surged into each other, their rhythm a flawless sync. I would never tire of watching Tolly claim her pleasure—and fuck it, I was even happy for my brother, who took his satisfaction with bold, thrusting, angry abandon.

"Drake. Oh, my God. Yes. So good. Don't stop. Harder. Harder."

He said nothing in answer. A slick sheen of sweat glistened across his body. He buried his face into her neck, pumping with greater fury. His hips bucked and pushed and conquered and stabbed, setting a punishing pace. His cock sank deeper and deeper into her. Their thighs made sharp smacks. They were so crazy with pent-up need and emotion it was like watching animals in the wild.

The room started spinning. The air was hot and stuffy, perfumed with Talia's feminine arousal and Drake's masculine sweat. I closed my eyes, trying to rein myself in. Get your shit together.

But they were like savages beside me, now tearing through the jungle together...leaving me in the dust. I could've been in the living room watching reruns of Bones for all they noticed.

This joining would scar us all.

And it had been my dumb-shit idea in the first place.

I'd let my selfishness wound us. Again.

Just like the perfect Ford I'd become.

"Natalia." Drake's voice was nothing but a raw rasp. "Come for me."

She tossed back her hair. Dewy with her sweat, it snaked against the pillow. "I'm trying," she panted. "I'm trying!"

"Now, Natalia." He wasn't even a savage anymore. He was a madman, pounding into her so fiercely the entire bed slammed against the wall. "Come. Come. Come!"

"I'm...I'm almost—"

But then he roared, throwing his head back. Then growled, sliding his glistening cock out from her. He fisted the thing, pumping twice before emptying his load across her thighs and pussy.

I blinked. Stared at him for long moments, wondering what creature had really taken over the person I called my best friend.

I hadn't seen Drake take his own pleasure first since we pledged ourselves to Talia. No—longer.

And I thought I'd fucked shit up.

This was the most insane stuff I'd witnessed from him since our try-everything-once phase, picking up random females from an assortment of clubs and bars. He'd liked doing that barbaric marking thing back then too. He always said it was a turn-on, but I'd known better. When Drake spent himself inside a woman, part of his spirit went with it. Underneath the Captain Bad-Ass cape was a man looking for his someone, just like the rest of us. Climaxing like that turned the act into nothing but an act for him.

The asshole had just turned our woman into an act.

His head fell forward as he held himself above her. His face was still contorted. His neck muscles were tight. A tic throbbed in his jaw. He was already beating himself up, and I wasn't about to stop him.

He pushed up from the mattress. Left the bed in one ruthless sweep of motion. Strode into the bathroom, where he slammed the door with a loud bang. The lock was engaged—the click seemed deafening.

I prayed he'd turn on the shower. As soon as he did, I reached for the softly sobbing woman beside me.

"Baby," I crooned. "Oh, baby...please don't cry. He's not mad at you. This is shit between him and me." I forced enough strength into my weak arm to fold her close. It was a paltry stand-in for the way I used to crush her close, but I did it. I was holding her. I was here for her. As she snuggled closer, I murmured into her hair, "It's okay, love. It's going to be okay."

But it was another lie.

This wasn't okay.

We weren't okay.

I'd just used both of them for my own disgusting needs. Forced him to fuck her, though he'd begged me not to, to further my selfish quest for my missing manhood. What the fuck did that even mean anymore?

I'm not a worthy man for either of them.

Shitty thing was, I'd heard that refrain before. The night I'd downed a bottle of scotch and glared drunkenly at the skyline from the patio. The next morning, instead of facing them, I'd run from them.

I couldn't run this time.

Not from the mess my damn ego had created.

Not from the man I'd become—more worthless than my limp body portrayed.

I thought our love would lift me up from my hell. Instead I'd lassoed it and trapped it. Dragged the most beautiful thing in my life down into the darkness with me.

CHAPTER TEN

D r a k e

Fuck him.

Fuck me.

Actually, fuck everyone. And everything that went along with this fucked-up shit.

Fuck. Fuck. Fuck.

What had I just done? Because of him. For him. For that messed-up, screwed-up, jacked-up excuse of a brain beneath his god damn thick skull.

"Talia." Her name burned my throat, like a demon in hell praying to a saint. I had no right even pleading for her. The most innocent, perfect treasure I'd ever had the honor of loving, and I'd just treated her as though she was a random hook-up. Not even that. I at least made sure the hook-ups got theirs eventually.

I pounded a fist into the shower wall. Longed to bellow Fletch's name as I did—but that would be too easy. He was the easy blame but not the true one.

The true asshole here?

Me.

He hadn't cocked a gun to my head and forced me into the bedroom. I'd gone willingly, even after declaring I was fully onto his shit. I could've said no.

I should've said no.

I should've been stronger. Gotten out when I still could. From the moment he'd demanded I kiss her gorgeous breasts, I should've rolled the other way—and done exactly this. What would've been the difference?

The pelting ice on my back helped with that answer.

Twenty minutes.

Twenty stupid minutes.

At minute one, I'd still been completely clear. One of us still had to be strong, carrying the weight for all three of us. I'd been the obvious choice for the job. I'd gladly taken on the job.

At minute twenty, I had been a failure at the job.

The weak asshole who'd given in to the siren song of her body. Her urgent, erotic need. Her glorious, giving arousal.

She was my cocaine. I was her addict. I never once denied it. Would be happy to shout it from the top of the god damned Willis Tower.

Like an addict, I'd thrown everything away for my high.

I'd treated her as though she was a valueless stranger—and now would have to live with looking into her eyes, knowing I'd let her down. Knowing I'd taken her gift and nailed it to the wall like any other notch on my bedpost.

I cranked the shower from the extreme C to the extreme H.

I forced myself to take the liquid fire scalding over my back, but even that pain didn't erase the memory of what I'd done—the last sight I'd dared to take of her, with my load all over her thighs. I'd marked her pussy like a half-wild Neanderthal. Not that Fletch and I had never considered it—but we'd wanted it to be an orchestrated scene, planned well in advance with her ultimate pleasure in mind. That would've been hot as hell.

Hotter, actually. What guy didn't savor the idea of seeing his seed as a visual imprint of his ownership on his woman?

That—out there—had not been planned.

I'd been furious with Fletcher, and the revenge was as easy as openly staking my claim on my woman.

Our woman.

Not mine.

A fact I'd easily tossed out of the window, along with all the respect I carried for my best friend...my brother. God damn it, I'd never meant for any of it to happen like that—but he'd kept egging me on, tormenting me with her flesh. Offering her to me. I groaned, just remembering how he'd squeezed her nipple as if it had been a succulent fruit. I'd pleaded for release, knowing I'd be weak, but he'd bulldozed past my walls. Torn down any semblance of control I'd been clinging to.

Leading us right back here.

In the land of the impossible.

Without a god damned road map.

I washed my hair and face and then scrubbed at my skin with the puffy loofah thingy Talia kept hanging in the shower. The scratchy sensation felt good. I could do this a while and be set.

Maybe if I stayed in the bathroom long enough, they'd both be fast asleep when I emerged. Fletcher's pain medication usually took a half hour to start working, so at least he'd be out.

But he wasn't the one I dreaded seeing the most.

I dried myself with the clean white towel on the rack, using a corner to swipe at my hair before wrapping the towel around my waist. For a second, I stood and just stared at my reflection in the full mirror above the sinks. Where was the gaping hole in my chest? The one where my heart had once been? The rip marks from where it had been seized from my body?

"Wuss," I muttered. "Get your shit together. Pick up the pieces later."

Talia and Fletcher had to remain my first priority, even if I had just become the douche of our triad. Didn't change a thing. Last year, I'd sworn I'd never abandon them again. I'd meant it then, and I meant it now.

Quietly, I unlocked the door. Slowly, I pulled it open.

They were both asleep.

And had never taken my breath away more.

Talia lay against Fletcher's chest, her cheek nestled over his heart. Both his arms—even the weaker one—were wrapped solidly around her. They breathed in tandem, their shoulders rising and falling in the rhythm of deep slumber. They clung to each another as if their lives depended on it.

In so many ways, they did.

We all did.

Like it or loathe it—and there had been so many days filled with both lately—we had become a unit. To be a cohesive one, all of the component parts were needed. Talia and I had been so adrift when Fletcher hadn't been here, trudging through our daily routines with little mattering but his recovery. It had been the prime focus. It still was. Talia had taken an extended leave from her duties at Stone Global, and I was leaning so heavily on my office's team I expected them to stage a mutiny any day.

But where was the end?

When would we get back to normal life?

What if this is our new normal?

I had to let that thought drift away with the midnight clouds, skidding across the sky beyond the dark living room windows as I left the bedroom. If I started down that dismal road next to Fletcher, the three of us would never survive.

Not. Acceptable.

I had to be the strong one. The one to save us all. Dramatic? Definitely. But the truth? Probably more than anyone wanted to admit. And despite what I'd just done in there—maybe because of it—I was ready for the mantle now. Last year, I was the ass who'd torn us apart. This time, I'd be the force to piece us back together.

While my body was exhausted, my mind raced. I plodded into the kitchen to look for something to eat. Marcus was spoiling us with his amazing cooking. The big guy was more domestic than a lot of women I knew. My family would love him.

Thoughts of Wyoming opened up the hole in my chest again. I couldn't believe our trip back to the ranch had only been a couple of months ago. I touched base with someone there almost every day. Mom, Dad, and Lizzy had been nonstop supportive and worried as hell about Fletcher. He was like a son and brother to them. I ached for them like I had during the first week of Marine Boot Camp. I wished they were closer.

In the refrigerator, I found some enchiladas left over from last night's dinner. As I stuffed the plastic container into the microwave, Talia's birdsong voice came from behind me.

"Don't put that in there, silly. It'll melt."

I swung around. Instantly grinned at the sight of her angelic face glowing in the light from the open microwave. I pulled the container out. She was right about it, of course. My head was so not in the game, especially since she'd come in. She was still talking to me, thank fuck.

I set the food aside. Opened my arms for her. Immediately, she flung herself against my chest. And started trembling.

I held her, mute but not still, as she wept into my worn T-shirt. I gently stroked along her spine and tangled my fingers into her hair, the contact becoming the instruments of my comfort. I didn't blame her for a single shed tear. If I hadn't been programmed my entire life that men didn't cry, I'd be joining her in the weep-fest. The whole situation sucked, and we were all standing right in the middle of the shit pile wondering where to go from here.

Finally, I pulled back—but only far enough to slip a hand into hers. "Let's go sit down for a bit. I think we need to talk."

She gave a quick nod and followed me into the living room. I lowered into the sofa, and she followed but sat with way too much distance between us.

"Come here. Please." I patted the cushion beside me. "I want to feel you."

She scooted closer without hesitation. My heartbeat stuttered. Why had she sat so far away? Did she trust me anymore? Would she forgive me for the way I'd treated her?

"Natalia." I inhaled deeply. "I have an apology to make."

She immediately surged forward, an obvious protest on her lips. God, I loved this woman.

"No. Hear me out." I positioned her so her back rested against my chest. "I'll feel better if I just get it all out, okay?"

Amazing girl. I literally had to play off her compulsion to put my needs above her own. I hated using the subtle manipulation, but I'd spoken the truth. We needed to just deal with everything that had happened.

"I love you, Tolly. I love you more than my own life. You know that, right?"

"Of course I do." She ran the fingertips of one hand over my forearm. Steady strokes from my elbow to my wrist and then back. "And I love you."

"So you need to know...I'm sorry."

She stopped stroking. Just for a moment. "What the heck for?"

"Natalia."

"Drake." She bantered it back, imitating my ominous inflection.

"I was a total dick in the bedroom, and we both know it. Let me finish," I insisted, using an upheld hand when she jerked up and tried to twist around. Her pause was the break I needed, to measure how I'd phrase the difficult words to come next. "I knew what he was doing, baby," I finally uttered. "I knew what Fletch was doing, and how he'd set us up to do that—and I played right into his fucked-up plan."

A soft hum curled out of her. "His plan...meaning he assumed we hadn't been physical all this time and that we'd both be desperate."

"More or less, yes." I tucked my head in, kissing her temple. Amazing, insightful woman. "Then he started taunting me—using you as the bait. You didn't see it, but he knew I wouldn't be able to resist getting inside you...and feeling your heavenly pussy grip my cock again..." My direct words made her squirm, but I wasn't sure that was such a bad thing. After a second to shift my thoughts away from her cunt and back onto reality, I went on. "Well, you saw how long I lasted, even knowing exactly what he was up to."

She nodded and even let out a light laugh. "Oh, I was there for the party."

"But I was the party asshole."

She sat up now, turning to meet my gaze directly. "Drake. What the hell are—?"

"I was inconsiderate and thoughtless, Talia—and I never want to be that kind of lover with you, ever again." I brought her hands up to my lips and brushed both sets of knuckles with reverent kisses. "I'm sorry...so sorry for rutting on you like that. And I'm sorry for coming all over you the way I did. It was rude, disrespectful. I hope you can forgive me."

Her face crumpled with emotion I couldn't identify—though hope was strong as she pulled her hands free, lifting them to frame my face. "Oh, Drake," she rasped.

"I just...lost control. I was so lost in the moment yet so pissed off at him at the same time...some insane instinct took over. That sounds stupid, yeah?" I paused for a beat. "Instinct. Yeah, that's pretty fucking moronic." I forced out a laugh. "Let's try this. I was being a piggish guy, and I regret every single second of it."

I braced myself for a number of reactions from her.

What I got wasn't any of them.

She grinned at me. A wide, playful, adorable smile across her lush, incredible, kissable lips.

"Okay, what did I miss?" I crunched in my eyebrows. "Are you laughing at my apology? The way I'm squirming here, afraid you're really pissed?"

"I'm not laughing at all. Honest." She nuzzled into my neck before planting a warm kiss there. "I'm just ridiculously happy right now."

"What the hell?" She did laugh as I reared back to see her face. "How can you even say that?"

"Okay, look at things from my perspective for a minute. I was in the same bed you were tonight, Drake. Remember?" Impishly, she tapped a finger at my skull. "And seriously, I was never more desperate for physical satisfaction ever in my life."

I let a grin quirk a corner of my mouth. "You were soaking wet, baby."

She blushed. "And you were pretty magnificent too."

"Magnificent?" I gaped as if she'd grown horns—though they'd be really cute horns. "Excuse the hell out of me?"

"Okay, fine," she conceded. "Are you normally a more generous lover? Absolutely. But what does that say about me normally? I'm the selfish one usually. You and Fletcher always, always put my needs above your own, and I happily go along with it. So where was the harm in switching it up a little for once? Your needs were met before mine—so what? It's not going to be something that defines us, Drake—or at least I hope it won't. I'm not going to let it, and I hope you won't either."

For long moments, I couldn't speak. What would I say, anyway? What word could halfway plumb the depths of my gratitude for the gift of her words, as well as every truth she sincerely meant behind them? And where the living hell had this astonishing, amazing, giving, abundant woman even come from? And how was I such a lucky bastard to call her mine?

Ours.

Yes.

I had my answer. The words alone wouldn't do it. With that prompt, I swept around, lowering to both knees before the couch—and her. "Natalia Perizkova." Her hands slipped from my face but weren't dropped for long. I swept them back up and dragged them close over my heart. "You are a gift to be treasured above everything—everything—in my world. You are the most miraculous part of my life—and right here, right now, I vow to honor you, protect you, and keep you right here, for always." I flattened my hands over both of hers, locking them in place in the middle of my chest.

"Oh, my." Talia gulped. Her chin wobbled. I prepared to hold her through another burst of tears, but she recovered with humor instead, coquettishly batting her eyelashes. "Goodness. That was quite the poetry recital there, Mr. Newland."

I chuckled, savoring the view of the silver moonlight mixing in the chocolate depths of her eyes. I kept her hands wrapped in mine while resettling myself on the cushion next to her.

It was time to address the next issue. "Baby...we have to help Fletch."

Sober angles took over her face too. "I know," she offered, nodding solemnly.

"He's battling some serious internal shit." I huffed. "It's deeper and uglier than I thought. We really have to help him. I don't want to lose him for good."

"I know," she repeated. "Now more than ever. Even without feeling him here"—she touched her temple—"I sense he's really raw right now." She gazed intently into my face. "Has Mac mentioned anything to you about possible dysfunction—you know, sexually? I haven't had the courage to bring it up..."

"That so?" I drawled it with purposeful sarcasm.

She batted my shoulder before going on. "To be honest, I didn't think much about sex while he was in the hospital. But now..." She winced and shrugged. "I have no idea what to expect and am too weirded out to do any internet research on it."

"Fuck, no," I concurred. "Do that, and I guarantee you'll think he's got advanced-stage cancer, leprosy, the Bubonic plague, or some exotic combination of all three."

"And for all we know, what he's experiencing is totally normal. Like most of the other things he has going on, it'll just be a matter of time until he's back on track."

I let her words settle on the air while I glanced in the direction of the bedroom. I couldn't escape the feeling that we were betraying Fletch by having this conversation without him. But he was sleeping, and sleep meant healing.

"I never talked to Mac about it either," I finally offered. "Maybe I'll float the subject past Marcus in the morning, just to see if he has any insight. I can also set up a meeting with Mac on my own."

She squeezed my hand in silent gratitude. Her expression grew thoughtful. "Maya told me about a caregivers' support group at the hospital, specially geared toward caregivers of people with traumatic brain injuries. I'll find out when their next meeting is."

I nodded, ushering in a long pause of quiet between us. She lifted my arm and then scooted beneath it, cuddling into my side. Absentmindedly, I toyed with her hair. Softly, she rubbed circles into my sternum.

Together, we gazed out over the maze of Chicago city lights, appearing like pieces of a dream between the drifting fog clouds. A dream. How many times had I beseeched whatever god or gods there were to shout a cosmic "psyche!" and return the three of us to where we'd been five weeks ago?

Crazily, I no longer wanted that anymore. We were here now, and we'd survive now, end of story. And somehow, in some way, we'd be forged into something stronger. We'd been platinum before this. We'd be titanium after it.

"Those are good places to start," she murmured at last. "At least it feels like we're doing something now, instead of sitting on the sideline and watching him tear himself apart."

She lifted back up until I could see her eyes—her aching

heart on full display in them. "I'm worried about him, Drake."

"I know," I answered firmly. "But let's start with these things and go from there. It's possible he may need to talk to someone about the depression. Maybe his regular shrink needs a call too. I'll see if Mac approves of that guy or has someone better in mind. I have his name and number in my contacts."

"So we have a plan."

"Yep. But for now, let's go to bed. I'm exhausted, and I think I'll finally be getting a good night's sleep. For several reasons." I layered a salacious wink on the end of that, making her giggle as we walked hand in hand back to our bedroom.

★ ★ ★ ★

We weren't out of the woods yet.

It began the morning after that tumultuous night, when Fletcher refused to accept anyone's help in getting out of bed. He'd bellowed at Talia like the Beast ripping Belle a new one for touching his fucking rose—only that morning, he was no rose. Only Talia, with her whispered words and placations, had held me back from marching in there and showing the asshole some god damned thorns—called my fists.

The next week, bad turned to worse.

Most days, Fletch wouldn't come out of his room at all, even when Marcus threatened to double his plank time. He simply changed the side he was lying on and then pulled the covers up over his head. Again, only Talia saved his stubborn ass from me waltzing into his wallow hole, stripping the bedding from where he lay, and delivering a nice, heaping helping of Come to Jesus.

And Talia and me?

Once more, we prayed for the cosmic joke. To wake up from the disgusting dream. Watching someone we loved give up on their life was harder than watching them battle for their life. After the accident, things had been out of Fletcher's control. We'd relied on a lot of luck and a lot of fate. But this bullshit? Every speck of this was his doing, and it was driving me to the brink. Of what, I didn't know yet—but the madness definitely involved me kicking in his thick skull, no matter what ordeal it had just been through.

The plans Talia and I had formed after the disastrous sex experiment—as I'd fondly begun referring to it—were now as good as chicken scratches on pavement. Mr. Ford had other plans all together—and if the man was anything, it was stubborn. The trait that had served him well in business and in the pursuit of our girl was now dragging him down like a lead weight.

After dinner Friday night, when Talia emerged from his room carrying the dinner tray still loaded with his untouched meal, I finally lost my shit.

I slammed down the book I'd been pretending to read. The small iron sculpture on the coffee table did a nervous jig next to my novel. "That's it." My temper jumped from simmering to seething. "I've had enough of this crap."

"Drake." Tolly's shoulders sagged. Her voice was tired and defeated. "Just leave him be."

"And what good is that doing us?" I bellowed. "He won't eat. He won't do his home program. He's showering only after Marcus threatens bodily harm. Have you seen him? He looks like a fucking hobbit. That beard..." I shuddered. "When was the last time he showered? He probably has science experiments growing in his body cavities." I grimaced. Science wasn't my thing. The world turned. Things lived and changed. I couldn't stomach learning how.

"I-I don't know what else to do." Talia whispered it while sliding his tray to the kitchen counter. She pitched into a plaintive rasp while slumping over the sink. "I've tried everything..." She wiped her forehead with the back of a hand. "Maybe I'm just trying too hard..."

"You?" For lack of anything else to do, I perched both hands to my hips. "Why do you have to be 'trying' at all here?"

She pitched her gaze to the ceiling as if I hadn't spoken at all. Desperation dominated her face, as if the vibe in the whole condo was using her as its spirit animal. "Maybe if I go back to San Diego for a while, see my family... I don't know... Give you two some space?"

"The fuck?" I chose anger over panic, but the resolve lasted for those two syllables only. "Why would you even say that?" I stalked over, clearing the two steps up to the kitchen with one leap—only to stop short as comprehension struck right between my eyes.

Maybe she needed the break. She was just so damn sweet, she couldn't come right out and say it. She was probably racked with guilt about it too and was trying to diplomatically ease out from the burden. It made such complete sense...

Fuck.

Well, I wouldn't force her to stay. As long as she promised to come back.

"We don't need space, baby—but I understand if you do." It was one of the hardest things I'd ever had to say. "If you need to take some time for yourself, I get that. I was listening when we went to the caregivers' group on Wednesday. If we don't take care of ourselves, we won't be able to take care of him.

Go back to California if you need to. Marcus and I will handle things here."

I looked down. Jammed my hands into my pockets, trying to disguise how saying that had gutted me.

"Drake. I don't want to leave—"

Thank fuck.

"—but I don't know what to do if I stay." She came over to me, palming both sides of my face so I'd look at her. "I'm at the end of the only rope I have, baby. Everything I say or do only makes it worse."

I sighed. Gazed at her for a long moment. My astounding woman. Our girl with the boundless heart. "We all feel like that right now, love. It's not just you." My lips twisted. "It's that god damned man in there—"

"Sssshhh."

I nodded and kissed her palm. "You can't take any of this personally. But if you do go, you have to get the fuck back here after you've rested." I tried, and probably failed, not to sound like a needy bitch. But I could barely breathe when I thought of going a single day without her.

"I'm not leaving you." She pressed in that assurance by wrapping a hand up to my nape. "Either of you. I just want to help him—"

"And you are, baby—in your way. I know it."

She nervously wetted her lips. When her gaze skittered away, I had to bite back a captivated smile. I'd lay down a Benjamin she was going to start talking about dicks.

"Maybe, since the whole impotence thing set this off, he just needs to be around other guys, not me?"

Yep. Dicks. Only the subject wasn't a joke for her. She was nervous because she was scared, and she was scared because she loved the fuck out of the hobbit in the next room.

"Maybe he just...needs to talk it out and doesn't want to do that in front of me?" she ventured. "I don't know, Drake. I've run every possible scenario through my head at this point." Tears pooled and started streaming down her cheeks. She angrily swiped at them. "And for Christ's sake, I've cried more in the past three months than I have in my entire life. Enough!"

The woman rarely raised her voice—and when she did, it carried the wonky effect of turning me on. Not this time. I pulled her to my chest, holding her while she quietly sobbed out her frustration.

Again.

All I could do was gently rock her back and forth, words fucking failing me. I had said every one of them already.

And none of them were helping.

CHAPTER ELEVEN

Fletcher

Just when I thought I'd reached rock bottom, the chasm opened deeper.

Now, even a day later, I was still lost and scrambling for a clear path, any path, in that shitty blackness.

Just like every other night, Talia had come into my room to pick up my uneaten dinner. The food always looked amazing and smelled even better, but what did eating it turn me into? The fucking Shah of Persia? And what did that turn her into? My slave servant girl? I'd degraded her once like that already and didn't expect her to ever forgive me for it. But with every meal she brought in, all I felt was her absolution, her devotion, her steadfast love. She'd already forgiven me, and I hadn't even gotten to the apology.

I'd barely deserved her when I'd been a whole man.

I sure as hell didn't deserve her now.

Talia had come in for the tray but hadn't collected it at once. She'd glanced at the food but had left it all on the table, opting to sit on the foot of my bed—

And quietly cried her eyes out.

Shit.

It had to have been a test—or so I'd assumed, using wariness as a convenient mask for my shame. She'd had to be going for the whole guilt route, trying to coax me out from my hideaway. No dice. I'd refused to give in.

Until she'd wielded the announcement, shattering what little was left of my spirit.

"I...I wanted to be the one to tell you," she'd finally murmured after quietly blowing her nose. "I'm going back to San Diego on Friday morning. I've purchased a one-way ticket with the promise to Drake, and to you if it even matters, that I'll come back when you decide to be the man I love."

She'd paused, waiting for me to interject. Our bond still hadn't returned, but I hadn't needed that hocus-pocus to feel her hope, so palpable on the air—and how my silence had destroyed it.

"I know you're going through a lot right now, Fletcher. I get that—but I also can't be a part of it. I can no longer sit here and watch you self-destruct, taking everyone down with you." She'd patted my foot. My fucking foot and nothing else. "When you call and let me know you've finished this phase you're going through, I promise I will be on the next plane back to you and Drake—but for now, I think this is what's best." The bed had shifted when she'd stood, and her shaky breaths had piled atop the misery I'd already slathered in the air. "If you don't want to drag your backside out of hibernation for me, then at least, please, consider Drake. Fix it with him, Fletcher. Make it right with the man you've called brother for so long. He's hurting too—and no one can repair that but you."

If I hadn't already hated myself, that would have sealed the deal.

Still, I should've said something. Done something.

But what? What?

She'd carefully considered every damn one of those words.

Talia lived every moment of her life with her heart leading the charge, but if I'd let mine do the same in that moment, the bunkers of her soul would've been bombed into the next century by pain, disillusionment, grief, failure, frustration...

Impotence.

I had nothing worthwhile to give to her. I couldn't just leap out of bed and shout that I'd been healed, that she was right, that this was nothing but a selfish pity party fueled by a lifetime of feeling inadequate, crystallized in one humiliating night not so long ago—when even my cock wouldn't stand up for itself.

Worthless dream.

Pointless argument.

She was right to leave. So fucking right.

So I'd lain there with my eyes squeezed shut, listening to her gather up the dinner tray and quietly close the door behind her.

Then, something had broken inside.

Then something else.

And more, like a chain of C-4 charges on a dam, setting free the emotions in my carefully guarded reservoir.

I'd been breached.

The dam had cracked. Then leaked. Then burst wide open, crumbling beneath the weight of so many emotions stored on the other side.

Hot, horrible, unwelcome tears had filled my eyes, streamed down my cheeks, and wetted the hair grown so long I could easily qualify for a sizable man bun. I hated this. I needed this. I could no longer avoid this.

"Tolly," I'd croaked into my soaked pillow. "Tolly."

I had nothing to live for if she left us. Yeah, I had Drake, but there was a damn good chance his thoughts were the same as mine. With Talia gone, we'd be alive but not living. Going through the motions. Was it too late to even make things right with him anyway? He'd barely come near me for a week, though I couldn't blame him. The stunt I'd pulled with them in bed was unforgivable—and as my luck would have it, the whole thing had just seemed to bond him and Talia tighter.

That joke was really on me.

Add it to the bawl-fest tab.

I'd cried for so many things that night. For the love slipping through my fingers because I wasn't strong enough to hold on to it. For the gold-standard friendship I'd all but destroyed with my selfish behavior. Yeah, I'd even cried for my parents, who'd never give me their love without the price tag of their control.

And last of all, I'd cried for myself.

I'd never be the same man I had been before the accident. I had to stop pretending I was. The effort of it was exhausting. The truth was, my life had been unalterably changed. Some random asshole had plowed his truck into me one morning while I'd been making my way to work. It was fact, and I wouldn't wake up tomorrow morning to anything different. And yeah, I was angry about it. I wanted to jab a middle finger at God, or whoever the hell lived up there, and demand to know why. Why me? What had I done that was so wrong, that this was happening? How the hell was I supposed to deal with it now? I wasn't strong enough for a regular life, let alone one with so many obstacles.

I had fallen into a deep and exhausted sleep that night, wrung from finally letting the dam burst. Shit. Tears were really tiring. How many had I caused Tolly and Drake to lose in the last six weeks? Too many, of that I was damn sure.

When I woke up the following morning, I had a pounding headache. The entirety of Mission Beach had been flown in from California and dumped under my eyelids.

The thought started a chain reaction in my head.

Mission Beach.

San Diego.

Talia.

Talia!

"Whoa. Rough night, man?" Marcus sat in his usual spot beside my bed, looking up from his magazine when I stirred. That was another cool thing about the guy. His impressive magazine collection. Everything from Car and Driver and Top Gear to Esquire and GQ was in his stack. In his line of work, interesting reading material was probably necessary.

"So I really look as bad as I feel?" I responded to his query.

"Hate to say so, boss—but yeah." His caring smile overtook his entire face.

"Doesn't matter." My voice was rough and dry. I reached for the water glass on my nightstand and swiftly chugged the contents. Marcus's eyebrows jumped, but I didn't care. "Is Talia still here?"

His brows descended into a curious V. "Yep. She was out in the kitchen when I got here."

"She's leaving," I said matter-of-factly. "Going back to San Diego."

His eyebrows didn't pop back up. The surprise was on me this time. "Is that right?"

More bewilderment. Why wasn't he more shocked now? Outraged on my behalf?

"Yeah," I stated carefully. "That's right."

"So, what are you going to do?" He looked at me pointedly.

I stared back, angry and puzzled. "What the hell do you mean?"

"You just going to lie there and watch the best thing in your world walk out on you?" He carefully placed a bookmark into the magazine in his hands. Yeah, a bookmark in a magazine. Still wasn't as weird as his Mr. Miyagi approach to this shit. "Not that I blame her at this point, boss. You are one smelly fuck." He smirked as he got in his dig.

I wanted to laugh. He was a cool guy. But his words, piled on top of whatever the hell I'd broken through last night, hit home. Hard. For the first time in ten days, I seriously wanted to get out of bed.

"Okay. Point taken, asshole." I'd called him worse—way worse—during PT sessions. "Help me up. I don't want her to leave."

I sat up with gusto—and quickly learned the lesson about that move. The pain in my head shifted. I clutched at the side as if to hold the contents within.

"You okay?" Marcus prompted.

"Just a headache. I didn't sleep well."

"I'll get you some Motrin." He stood and headed to the medicine cabinet in the other bathroom. It hadn't escaped my notice that all medication was now kept outside this room and bathroom—away from the depressed patient.

"No time for that." I jabbed a finger out to stop him. There was no time to lose. "I need to stop her, man. I need to see Talia." I frantically looked around the room. Where was my robe? Fuck it, who cared? "Wait. Shit. What day is it?"

"Thursday."

"Thank God. Okay. She said she was leaving Friday." I slumped back into the pillows.

Marcus stomped back over. The Mr. Miyagi thing was oddly perfect for him, despite having a dozen tatts and at least seventy pounds of bulk on the original. "So that's it?" he leveled. "Are you really going to wait until Friday to try stopping her?"

"Of course not," I snapped. "I just need to think of a plan. A good one. As soon as my head clears." I slammed a hand to my forehead. "Damn, it feels so weird."

Something was happening, but I couldn't pinpoint what. The longer I lay there, the sadder I felt—but was strangely detached from the emotion at the same time. I thought I'd cried every shred of pain away last night, but my head hummed louder and louder with the shit. I took a deep breath, trying to gain clarity, but there was an overwhelming feeling of anguish inside me.

Then, like lightning, it hit me.

Talia.

A slow grin spread across my lips.

Talia.

She was back. Right where she belonged. Inside my head.

Our current was here—at least for me. She was here. She was here. I'd shrouded my mind in pain and misery for so long, adding extra layers with all the medications, that I'd shorted out the wires of our connection. Last night, I'd cleared out gunk. Rewired the control panel.

Could she feel it too? The answer mattered but didn't. I could feel her, and what I felt wasn't good. So much pain... more sadness than I had ever sensed from her heart. Could she really be so devastated?

I had to do something about it. Now.

I pulled myself up again, swinging my legs over the side of the bed. Once more, I clutched the base of my skull as pain radiated through my body. I now understood why the agony was so intense. It wasn't just mine. Her pain was consuming me too, even if it was secondhand. Only I could make it stop.

Because I am the cause of it.

My T-shirt clung to my body nearly on its own power. Damn thing smelled like the Bulls locker room. My hair stuck out in thirteen different directions. Finger combing wasn't going to help. Shit, I actually had tangles. A full beard covered my jaw and chin, the fast result of not shaving for two weeks.

Though I felt and looked homeless, I needed to find Talia. I'd apologize—and mean it—and then vow to spend the rest of my life making all this crap up to her. She didn't deserve to feel so hopeless, and knowing I'd caused all of her anguish moved my sorry feet, one in front of the other, to find her in the condo.

By the time I reached the kitchen, I was damn sure I'd faint. Panic at the thought of her catching an earlier flight motivated me deeper into the room.

"Where is she?" I barked when I saw Drake.

"Well, hello to you too, asshole." Yep. Pissed. Much more than I'd given him credit for.

"Drake."

He just stared at me.

"Where. Is. Talia?"

He set his coffee down so hard, the liquid splashed out over the counter. "Out. Said she wanted to take a walk along the lake one last time. You know she's really leaving tomorrow, don't you? She wasn't just trying to get your ass out of bed—though apparently, that did work."

"I know." I attempted to drag back my hair again. Christ. I'd likely have to cut out some of these knots. "I know, but—"

"But what? She's made up her mind."

I barely heard him. The hum in my brain got worse. "But she's...miserable," I said in a drifting murmur, trying to mentally reach her. Trying to find her...

"Duh, Poindexter." He swiped at the spilled coffee with an angry slash of a hand towel.

"No. Drake." I tapped my head and then my heart. "I feel her. She's sad. So sad. I..."

"It's back?" He quickly clued in to what I was talking about. The towel got sacked into the sink.

"Yeah."

"And can she feel you?" He rushed to where I stood by the breakfast bar.

"I don't know. It seems to be independent of each other. There's not a manual here. We just both have it." I shrugged. It was so hard to explain to other people.

"Damn. I will never understand—"

He was cut off by the doorbell—odd in and of itself, since one of the doormen always called up to announce a visitor. Maybe Talia had forgotten her key. Fuck, I could only hope...

Drake opened the door, and two of the most pregnant women I'd ever seen pushed their way inside. Claire Montgomery-Stone was here, this time with Margaux Asher in tow. Judging by their rough trudges and their fierce glowers, they were both in the middle of a contraction.

"Ladies. Good to see you." Drake kissed each one carefully on the cheek, trying not to gawk at the dual bellies taking up most of the room.

Margaux snorted at his tact. Like a lie of omission, it just highlighted "things" with brighter strokes. "We know, we know," Margaux huffed. "We look like beached whales. Newsflash—we feel like them too. This is the ugly stage, so keep your arms and feet inside the cart at all times. You never know what'll get taken off." Despite the grousing, she winked at Drake to finish off her opener.

Claire giggled while leaning back against a counter. "And I thought she was a handful before."

As Claire drawled the comment, I realized neither of them had noticed me on the other side of the breakfast bar yet. Maybe that was a good thing.

"So where's our sweet little bestie?" Margaux asked. "Did you leave her tied to the bed again?"

I almost gave up my presence with a snort. Few people on this planet could incite a blush on my brother's face. Margaux and her brass balls were VIP members of the club.

"Not this time." He kept it together long enough to score a comeback.

When his eyes shifted to me, theirs followed suit.

"Whoa." Claire's quiet comment slipped out before she slapped a hand over her mouth.

Margaux didn't possess the same filter. "What the fuck happened to you?" She eyed me once, head to toe, appearing lost between a grimace and a chortle. "Dude, the brain injury excuse will only take you so far." She waved a hand, demonstrating her point in one shitty but accurate gesture. "Unless you're floating possible Halloween costumes? Let me guess. Homeless zombie? Backwoods goat herder? Luke Skywalker on a bender?"

I lifted one side of my mouth in a sneer. "How that man of yours doesn't gag you, I will never understand."

The woman snickered. Margaux loved a good bounce back, no matter how crude.

"Right? That's what Killian says all the time too," Claire

chimed in, tossing out another giggle when Margaux began with the icy glances. "Earned the immunity idol against those dirty looks a long time ago, sister. Not going to work."

"Well, shit."

They both busted into giggles again. At the same time, I traded a don't-even-try-to-understand glance with Drake, tempting us both to add snickers to the girls' mix. No wonder Talia held these two so close to her heart. Their joy was infectious, despite how they were both carrying a whole extra human around in their bellies. None of it had slowed down their spirits or their wits.

Claire turned her caramel gaze to me. "Let's get serious for a second, Fletcher." She winced, tiptoeing into her next query. "Did—ummm—Mac tell you not to shower or something? Is that it?"

Drake cleared his throat from behind them. "It's...been a rough go around here, lately."

They turned in tandem, detecting the subtext of his tone. After observing the backup confirmation on his face, they rotated back toward me. Their movements were so in sync, I almost wondered if they'd rehearsed. Not that I was going to ask. The new glints in both their gazes were tough enough to take—but right now I'd stand up to an army of real zombies, if it meant getting through to Talia.

"Oooohhh." Claire drew it out for dramatic effect. "Waaaiit a minuuuute."

Margaux folded her arms. "We've seen this before, haven't we?"

"Absolutely." Claire nodded sagely.

"What the hell are you two talking about?" I couldn't resist their bait any longer.

"This." Claire's scrunched her nose. "This...look."

Margaux sniffed. "You're being generous, sister."

"Yes, well...Fletcher remembers too. He just doesn't want to admit he does."

I scowled. "I remember what?"

Claire's lips pursed. "The forty days and forty nights of Surfer Jesus Killian?"

Margaux burst out laughing. Even Drake's lips twitched.

"The hell?" I rejoined.

Claire raised both hands. "All right, all right. You didn't disappear completely off the grid. We'll give you points back for that."

"Haven't been living in gutters and hostels like he did, either," I defended.

"No points for that one," Margaux countered. "If the beastie smells the same..."

Claire flashed a perky smile. "Luckily, I came along and saved him from himself."

"And they all lived happily ever after." Margaux wiped her hands together as if to say "my work here is done."

"It wasn't quite that simple, but you get the point." Claire smiled to me and then Drake.

"And if her husband was here right now, he'd glow and preen and say how she lifted him up at his darkest moment and how the sun shoots out of her bum when she poops."

Drake laughed. Hell, even I laughed.

Claire just rolled her eyes. "Off topic much, girlfriend?"

"Right." Margaux jabbed a determined finger back at me. "You."

"Me?"

"You, mister." She walked over and propped a hip against

the bar. "What the fuck are you doing here?"

I blinked. Frowned. "I live here."

"Shut up. Follow my figurative, golden boy." She sliced out a flat hand, karate-chopping the air. "Be straight with us. Are you about to break her heart, Fletcher Ford? Because I don't think we can sit by and let that happen."

Margaux stepped back into the living room, peering around. "Where is our girl, by the way?"

"Out for a walk," Drake answered. "I suspect she'll be back any minute."

"Perfect." Claire smacked her hands together, channeling a WWE wrestler at show time—fascinating look for a woman nicknamed Fairy. "We can say this while she's not here."

She snapped her stare to me while finishing. When Margaux joined her own scrutiny to the mix, I instinctively straightened. And tensed. Yeah, here it came. The throwdown of the century from the most ruthless girl posse on the continent. But whatever they had to dish out, I could take.

I had to. I almost wanted to.

The sooner I could start paying my dues on this mile-long debt to Talia, the better.

"All right." I squared my shoulders. "I'm listening."

Margaux, now joining Claire, stood shoulder-to-shoulder with her friend. I almost wished for a zombie army instead.

"Simply put?" Margaux began. "You need to pull your head out of your really smelly ass, dude. The sooner the better."

Claire threw a shoulder forward. "You want to lose the best thing that ever happened to you? Keep this bit up. No woman wants to see her man down, especially when he brings it on himself. Take it from the voice of very vivid experience."

"You feeling us here, big guy?" Margaux matched her

friend's stance, driving in her ultimate point. They'd keep on coming if I didn't hand over an equally direct answer.

"Loud and clear," I gave back at once. "Thank you, ladies." I dashed out a two-fingered salute off my forehead, honoring them with a direct gaze to back up the implied respect. I had every intention of following their advice to the letter—as soon as Tolly and I got some privacy.

"A haircut probably wouldn't hurt, either." Claire tilted her head to the side, softening the borderline insult with her gentle tone.

Margaux wasn't so keen about pulling the punches. "And for fuck's sake, lose the beard. Not everyone can work the hipster vibe." She jerked her gaze at Drake. "Am I right?"

My brother simply raised both hands, wordlessly turning himself into Sweden on that one. After hitting him back with a generous pssshh, Margaux rubbed her round belly. "Mah little one's getting' hangry, gang."

"We just had breakfast." Claire rolled her eyes.

Margaux shrugged but finished it by walking over and yanking me into a crushing hug. Well, as "crushing" as things could get with a basketball-sized bulge between us. "We're leaving you to your mission, Grasshopper." She kissed me soundly on the cheek. "Make it epic, dipshit."

Claire followed right behind, giving me a quick wink and hug too.

After they both embraced Drake in similar ways, they left as swiftly as they'd arrived. He returned from walking them to the door with a dazed look across his face—bringing a wave of welcome relief. I wasn't the only one feeling like a two-funneled tornado had just touched down in the condo.

"I'm not gonna lie, man." I shook my head, leaning over

the breakfast bar again. "Those two scare me a little."

A smile jerked at my friend's lips. "Yeah, they're a handful."

His smirk disappeared just as quickly. Abruptly, without even looking at me, he turned on his heel to leave the room.

"Hey, D?" I called. "Can we talk a minute?"

I let him hear my contrition already. I had to mend our fence. Make things right, as Tolly had put it. I just hoped to hell he was ready too.

"She'll be back any second." Maybe he wasn't. If so, I'd have to accept that.

"I don't care if she hears what I have to say. The whole world can hear, for all I care."

I committed deeper to it, really praying he heard. For a second, I thought he'd hadn't. Or wouldn't. He took two steps back toward the office...

Before stopping, swearing beneath his breath, and then stomping into the living room. I waited as he plopped down on the sofa with a heavy sigh. Neither of us were looking forward to navigating this minefield—but sometimes doing the right thing didn't always mean doing the easy thing.

I left the walker behind, using various pieces of furniture to support my trek into the space before him. Carefully, I lowered into the easy chair closest to him. It was tempting to just dive right in, but I waited for my breath and my equilibrium to return, lending me a clear head for this. He deserved that much.

He deserved so much more from me.

This was where all that started.

"I owe you an apology, brother." When he didn't tense at our meaningful word, my resolve was fortified. "I mean a really big, monumental apology."

"True." He nodded but wouldn't meet my gaze. That had to be okay too.

"I probably don't have to list all the things I regret from the past couple of months."

Drake snorted. "Oh, no. Go right ahead. Don't let me stop you." His snark stemmed from anger—rage he had every right to. "I'd almost love to hear what you perceive as the problem around here."

I grunted out a laugh, more from nerves than anything. "You're really not going to make this easy on me, are you?"

"Do you deserve easy right now, Fletch?"

Massive exhale. A matching inhale, shoring my determination once more. "No, I don't. You're...you're right. I've been an ass. On so many levels."

"Soooo many." His interjection was clipped.

"I have to start with the morning of the accident—" I caught the sharp jerk of his brow and amended, "Yeah, all right. I'll start with the night before. The way I treated Tolly, when we were together then..." I let my head drop along with my shoulders. Slumped over my knees, supporting all my weight with my good arm. "It'll haunt me forever, but I can't undo it. Even if she decides to forgive me for that debacle, I will never forgive myself."

As I issued all that, Drake had started shaking his head. I understood he was peeved, but now he was just being a peeved ass, as well.

"Okay, what the hell is your problem?" I finally snarled.

He helped nothing with his bitter chuff. "You really think that's what you need to apologize for? After everything else that's been going on, that's what you pick as your worst offense?" He swiped a hand over his mouth, nostrils flaring a harsh breath over his fingers. "We're more fucked than I thought."

"Okay, stop." I flung up my weak hand. At least the fucker was good for something. "Let me finish, damn it. I was going in chronological order so I didn't miss anything."

"How sweet and organized of you."

I ignored that. "Trust me, I've had a lot of time to think about this. I've being doing nothing but loathing myself for the past six weeks."

"Caught that memo. We all did."

I was getting impatient with his attitude but quickly reminded myself I had no right to feel that way. I'd given up that right by being a complete ass for so long. I probably deserved worse treatment than he was dishing.

I took a deep breath and forged on. "Secondly, I need to apologize for the following morning. Leaving you guys without a goodbye was—"

"Shitty?" he filled in. "Immature?"

"Yeah." I scowled. "All the above. I really thought once I got out of the house and cleared my head, the night before would make more sense—that I'd see things the way you explained them to me. But we know what happened after that..."

That one hung in the air. We would all live with the memories of the accident for the rest of our lives.

I finally broke the silence with one determined word. "Drake."

"What?"

"I really want you to hear my next words. I mean them more than anything." I paused, waiting for him to look me in the eye. "I need to say...thank you."

When he just stared back, no hint of acknowledgment or

forgiveness on his face, I charged on. What the hell, right?

"Thank you, my friend, for everything you and Talia have done while I was in the hospital and since I've been home." I sat up straighter. It wasn't the most comfortable position, but he needed to hear and see the depths of my gratitude. "You've both put your lives on hold because of me. I know I haven't said it well enough, but I've seen it and been so damn grateful for it." I spread my hands, palms up, utterly offering my remorse up. "I'm not sure words are enough to express how grateful I am."

His countenance was still a sheer rock wall. Even his stare, normally shaded with dark-coffee textures, was stoic, static coal. He'd moved his hand to the side, resting his jaw against it like a modern-day Freud—only I was pretty damn sure the dude didn't want to hear about my childhood. "You know you're saying all this to the wrong person, man. Natalia's the one who needs to hear your speech, not me."

I scowled. "I owe all of this to you as much as her."

"Yeah? But we're tap dancing around the big ugly elephant in the room, aren't we?"

"I'm getting to that part." I took the most massive breath of this confrontation. He wanted to watch me fillet myself open and beg for his forgiveness? I was about to go for the gold.

"That night, in our bed, was fucked-up for so many reasons." I gritted my teeth as he simply nodded, forcing more words to my lips. The hardest words. "I was selfish and manipulative, and I know it caused irreparable damage to our friendship. I will regret that until my dying day. I never meant to hurt you or Tolly. I was so fixated on my own problems that the solution I concocted was beyond inconsiderate of everyone, including myself."

For the first time since I'd begun this groveling, Drake's face flared with real emotion. Just not the sentiments I was expecting. Not by a long shot.

"Really?" he spat. "You're making this all about you?" His bitterness seeped into every word. "Why am I not fucking surprised?"

I ground my jaw harder. I didn't need all that tooth enamel anyway. "Stop being a dick. You know how hard all this is for me. You know how fucked-up I am to begin with."

I knocked on my head with my fist, underlining my meaning. Drake caught the action before surging to his feet.

"Yeah, but guess what, my brother?" His voice, nearly trademark for him in pissed-off mode, was a lethal combination of calm and fury. "We've finally found the one person in the world who can make us whole—the light in every single day around here—but if you can't look beyond yourself when the shit gets heavy, you're going to lose her. We're going to lose her. And if that happens—if your stupid pity-party bullshit drives Talia away from us—I will never forgive you. Ever."

The front door opened and then shut. Talia entered, fresh from her walk.

Fuck me.

She was gorgeous.

Her cheeks were flushed from the exercise and the wind. Her hair was pulled back into a ponytail, making it easy to observe her eyes, still carrying flecks of sunshine and life.

The eyes that popped wide when she saw me standing there.

Yeah. I'd stood up.

For her.

So much of it would always be for her...even if she didn't

decide to forgive me.

Drake strode to her, kissed her lips passionately, and then pulled back to gaze into her eyes. With our bond plugged back in for me, I felt every drop of her desire for him. I also felt her aching love...and overwhelming anguish.

She was leaving—but didn't want to. Not any more than we wanted her to.

"Is Marcus still here?" she blurted.

"Yeah, he's probably cleaning up that cave of a bedroom." Drake kept his hands wrapped around hers as he answered. "He's on all day. What's going on?"

She held up her phone, almost seeming confused about it. "I got a text from Claire. She said she and Margaux came by to visit, but I was out. They're leaving today, and I'd really like to see them first. Once we all get back to California, life will take back over." The second she said the word "life," she looked lost. She'd put hers on hold so long for me she literally didn't know what the word meant anymore.

"They're leaving?" Drake queried. "Really?"

"Is that so shocking?" Her lips quirked.

"Frankly, yes," he groused. "Those two are enormous. I'm a little floored either of their husbands will allow them to fly like that."

"They'll be taking the Stone jet, baby." She patted his chest. "It's different than going commercial."

"No shit," he put in.

"This will be their last trip to Chicago before the babies come. Claire wanted to see Mrs. Stone before she brought her grandbaby into the world. She and Willa have grown close since Josiah passed, and Claire gets so sentimental sometimes." She smiled, thinking of her girlfriend. Drake acknowledged that with a gentle kiss to her forehead. Such a simple gesture, making her feel warm, loved, secure. I knew because I felt it all too.

I wanted that again. All of it—everything I watched between the two of them. The humor. The familiarity. The bond.

Everything I'd once shared with them too.

My heart ached with pain I'd never imagined. I'd caused so much damage to our relationship...a relationship I'd never be honored to know again. Right now, I felt more like the other furniture in the room. There. Available. But barely noticed.

"Are you ready now?" Drake's voice was tender and patient. "I'll drive you to meet them."

"Let me just freshen up, okay?"

Finally...she looked at me.

She stared for the longest beat, measuring her words carefully...issuing them formally. "It's good to see you out of bed, Fletcher."

I swallowed hard.

Furniture.

She turned, making her way back to our bedroom to get ready.

Ours?

Hers.

I had no idea what I expected her reaction to be, but that...
I didn't know what that was.

The guardedness, I could understand. I had hurt everyone more than necessary. A lot more. But her general disinterest really stung.

No. It fucking hurt.

I leaned my ass against the couch's arm to keep from

tipping over. I dropped my head into my hands. I'd just been kicked in the balls and punched in the gut at the same time. No. I'd prefer even that physical pain to this emotional jolt.

I'd royally fucked things up, and I still needed to apologize to her.

This was going to take a big plan.

Big.

Shortly after, Drake and Talia left for their visit. I looked around the empty condo, trying to soak up some "big idea" inspiration. I had to make amends with her, and I had to do it right. But where the hell to start?

Marcus appeared in the doorway. I wasn't sure how long he'd been standing there before I noticed him.

"Maybe you could start with a shower?" He looked at me with goofy hopefulness.

I stared back, amazed. How did he always know what I was thinking about?

"You need to make a serious show of commitment... right?"

I chuckled. "You're kind of a nosy dick, you know that?"

"Dude, I'm a home caregiver. That means I'm in people's homes. All the time. In their life's fabric. I've seen it all."

"Huh." I snorted. He had a good point. "So, Mr. Homebody, what's your take on my particular morass?"

"That you're making a mountain out of a molehill." He folded his sizable arms. His ink stretched tight over his forearms. "But from what I've seen, that is the Fletcher Ford way, yeah?"

"Know-it-all bastard," I retorted, mirroring his good-natured smile. When I didn't accent that by throwing anything, he took another step forward, hands now jabbed into the pockets of his scrubs.

"My advice, dude? Show her you're on the mend. In her mind, words are a dime a dozen from you right now. Show. Her."

We were quiet for a few minutes while I turned his suggestion over in my head. He was exactly right. Talia needed to see that I was serious. That I was ready to plug back in and do the work it would take to get us back on track.

To get myself back on track.

"Can you help me?"

"That's why they pay me the big bucks, my friend." He smiled again, this time extending his arm out to support me before we headed toward my room. I was taking the first steps on the journey home, and nothing had felt more right in a long damn time.

CHAPTER TWELVE

Talia

The afternoon with Claire and Margaux was exactly what my heart needed. There were defining moments in all our lives, and I was on the cusp of one my most vivid ones.

Leaving Chicago would be hardest thing I'd ever done—but I was backed into a corner with Fletcher's refusal to pull himself out of his funk—or whatever the hell he was calling it. I couldn't care anymore. I was so damn tired of caring. I'd always love him—but right now, I just didn't like him very much.

I had hoped my leaving would stir him to action. His cameo in the living room was a great sign—but not enough by half. He had to realize that he had work to do. Hard, emotional work but necessary if we had any hope of coming through this whole ordeal on the other side.

Drake dropped me off at the apartment where Killian and Claire stayed when they were in town. It was nothing like the one he had sublet to me last year, when I'd relocated to clear the emotional cobwebs from Gavin's abuse, but it was still amazing and posh, a new unit in the glamorous Aqua skyscraper. Only the best for the Stones.

Briefly, I wondered where Mac lived in the city. I had a feeling we'd all soon get the whole story behind his feud with Killian, but devoting any more brain space to the subject was too much. I had to focus on straightening out my own worries right now.

Killian and Drake ducked out for a game of one-on-one basketball in the Shore Club while I visited with the girls. We ended up staying longer than I expected, because when the mamas drifted off for their afternoon "disco-naps," I crashed right alongside them. We slept for hours, only waking up to the sound of the men coming home.

While I was completely refreshed from the sleep, I was sad but weirdly relieved we'd spent most of the time sleeping. I wanted to remember this time happily, not crying again over the issues with Fletcher. I wasn't even sure it was necessary, since Claire and Margaux had now seen him with their own eyes. Sometimes pictures were worth a thousand words—and in this case, Fletch's deterioration formed quite a picture. Though not much more could be said after that, I was heartened when Claire shared some stories from her darker days with Killian. If true love had brought the two of them back to the light, I held out hope it could happen for us too.

True love.

Was it strong enough for the three of us now?

I wanted it to be. Desperately.

I loved Fletcher and Drake with every fiber of my being. My life wouldn't be complete without them—both of them. I'd made peace with that tidbit last year when Drake had walked out on us.

But one thing was for certain. If we recovered from this mess with Fletcher—when we recovered—we were due for some effing great times. We. Were. Due. We'd served our cosmic sentence for whatever the universe thought we'd done wrong, and it was going to be our time to shine. It had to be.

I just had to keep believing.

Hoping, with just a shred of my soul...

I couldn't take another trial like this.

The drive home was quiet. My remaining hours in Chicago were close to single digits, and the weight of that awareness pressed down on both Drake and me. A significant part of me wished I hadn't issued the ultimatum to Fletcher, but my heart knew it was the right thing to have done.

"Want to get some take-out?" Drake broke the silence with small talk.

"Marcus probably left something for us. He's been so good to us. What a gem."

"You're probably right. And the guy can really cook. Almost as good as my mom."

I smiled when he mentioned his family. They'd been so kind to me when we'd visited and in the weeks since the accident. His mom had even offered to come and stay to help with Fletcher, but Drake and I agreed the condo would get claustrophobic if we stretched the headcount much more. We barely had any privacy now with Marcus there all the time, but the trade-off was worth it. At least for the time being. Now that I was leaving, Drake would really need the help and possibly the company.

Probably the company. Right now, he and Fletcher were tenants at the same address. If it were possible, my heart ached more for their broken friendship than our shattered relationship.

We stepped off the elevator about thirty minutes later and made our way toward the condo's front door. But Drake didn't unlock it. Suddenly, he whirled. Stabbed his hand behind my neck, compelling me closer to him. His firm lips pressed down on mine, bestowing the most tender, loving kiss he'd given me in some time. Though he didn't demand entrance into my mouth, I gave it to him. I opened willingly, even greedily. I needed his taste, his strength, his essence...the surety of knowing that despite the hell I was about to plunge us all into, he still believed in heaven.

Because I still did. With my entire heart and soul...

When we finally parted, I looked up into his gorgeous midnight eyes. They were glassy with unshed tears. Another piece of my heart splintered away.

"Baby." His voice was a hoarse whisper, thick with so much pain, too much longing. "Please. Please don't leave me."

"Drake." I spoke it against his lips, lifting a hand to commit the shape of his face to memory once more. As if I'd ever forget. "Don't make it harder than it already is. You know why I have to do this. I'm trying to save us..."

"I want to kill him. Honestly. I want to beat the living fuck out of him right now." Misery became anger as his temper flared.

"Ssssshhhh. He's your brother. He needs you right now. You need to be patient with him." I softened my voice, trying to soothe him like I would a spooked animal.

"I know. I know." He nodded, exposing his clenched teeth. "But I'd much rather take it out of his hide."

We were silent for long minutes. His rage bottomed out, leaving room for the despair to return. "I hate having to wrap my mind around this. I fucking hate the thought of waking up and not finding you bustling around the house. I can't imagine going to bed at night and not smelling that flowery lotion you always use." His voice cracked. The crimps in his forehead became dark furrows. "I can't imagine my life without you,

Talia. It's killing me..." A lone tear got away from him. It glowed with reflected light from the wall sconce, the brilliance stabbing all the way down to my soul.

"I'll come back the moment you call me." I ran my fingertips along his cheek. "I promise. This isn't the end of us. I'm trying to give us back a beginning."

"I understand it all. I do. But it sucks. Hard."

I kissed him again, not needing to debate about opening for him again. He conquered without asking this time, pressing me into the doorframe with his beautiful body. We gasped into each other when his erection pulsed against me, an evil tease of passion we wouldn't be sating now.

"Fuck." He dragged away, anguish washing his face in a ghostly white.

"It's going to be okay," I breathed out.

"I want to believe that."

"Then do."

A funny half grin took over his lips, as if he inwardly muttered "what will I do with you?" I shrugged impishly in return.

He kissed the back of my hand and opened the door.

I walked in.

And stopped at once.

"Errrr...Drake?"

"Yeah, ba—" He scuffed to a halt next to me. "Huh?"

Something was different in here.

No.

A lot of things.

The lights were out in the kitchen and living area, though at least a hundred small candles illuminated the room in a warm glow. I glanced again at Drake. His disbelieving stare confirmed this wasn't his doing.

Something smelled amazing in the kitchen. I took a few more steps in that direction, to find more candles down the middle of the dining room table. Drake, Fletcher, and I hadn't eaten a meal there in months, but now it held three perfectly placed settings, crystal water glasses, and matching champagne flutes. The tablecloth was pressed. Brocade napkins were stylishly tucked into hammered copper rings in the center of each plate.

The hair on the back of my neck suddenly stood at attention. An ineffable current pulsed in the room. Smooth jazz hummed in the background, but that wasn't it. The music was barely audible past that buzzing in my ears. What the heck was that? It was familiar but different, like the smooth jazz version of "24k Magic" playing through the speakers, only better. So much better.

My senses became hyperaware. All the pistons of my psyche seemed to be firing at once...an awakening of sorts. Stepping into bright sunshine. Bursting out of an ocean wave. Waking up from a bad dream...

My nerves fizzed like bubbles working through my bloodstream as something shifted in the doorway.

Not something.

Someone.

Drake and I swung to the right to find Fletcher standing between the doorjambs.

I nearly swallowed my tongue.

He was magnificent. Clean. Shaven. Hair cut much shorter than he'd ever worn. A smile graced his lips, confident and hopeful. His body, bordering on skinny because of all his muscle loss, was given extra volume with a pristine white button-front shirt tucked into dark navy slacks. He wore dress shoes to match.

My tongue was still missing. My breath joined it, catching in my throat. My head spun in giddy excitement.

He was back.

Really back.

I knew it in every drop of my blood. In every nerve ending I possessed. In the space of my mind no longer shrouded in shadows. It was filled with his brilliance. It vibrated with all of him. I was so happy. No. Wait. That was his happiness. I felt every one of his emotions again, as sure as my own.

My eyes widened. My heart exploded.

"Welcome home." He stood as tall and proud as he had before the accident. He had to lean slightly against the doorframe for balance, but he was so stunning, all I saw was his perfection.

"I hope you guys haven't had dinner. We have something special to celebrate tonight." He lifted his sexy smile, melting my heart and panties in one fell swoop. I hadn't seen that cocky, self-assured look on his face in so long, I'd underestimated its effect on my body. My entire body...

Next to me, Drake shifted. I looked in time to catch his curt nod of acquiescence. If Fletcher was extending an olive branch, he was on board for grabbing on together.

We walked into the dining room. Drake pulled out a chair from the circular table, waiting for me to sit. When I had, he instantly scooted me closer. Fletcher claimed the seat to my right, closest to the kitchen. Drake sat so he could face the openness of the room. He almost always chose that position, a habit I'd learn to love about him. Always my strong protector. Fletcher was my romancing rogue, always choosing to sit with his back to the room in order to give us both his full attention.

Two men. So different, with so many idiosyncrasies inherent to their basic natures—but that was why their friendship worked. Why the three of us worked too.

Their bond was still strong. I knew that for fact, since I could feel Fletcher's half of it in my soul again. Drake wouldn't stay mad forever, especially if Fletcher's change of attitude stuck.

Fletcher poured champagne in my glass and then did the same to Drake's. I passed the glasses to him so he wouldn't have to stand. It was one thing for him to clean up physically and emotionally—dear God, we could only hope—but his body would take more time heal, and we all had to be patient with the process.

He grabbed a second bottle from the table and filled his glass with sparkling water. "None for me with the meds I'm taking. But we can work around the small details, right?" He gave me a quick wink and then hoisted his glass in the air, waiting for Drake and me to follow suit.

"I'd like to make a toast." He paused to gaze meaningfully at both of us. "To our anniversary."

He pushed his toward the center so we could all clink brims. Drake and I reciprocated but didn't sip when Fletch did. We threw puzzled glances to each other and then back to him.

"Our anniversary?" I couldn't help but ask.

"Yep." He smiled. "This is the first day of the new us. Our brand-new start, which means putting all the crap behind us—and only looking toward tomorrow. I'm so damn happy to be here with both of you that I want to toast today—and every day that follows."

With that, he dropped the smile, exposing his raw nerves. I felt every damn one of them—and loved him more for being brave enough to show them to us. He didn't falter, even then. He just waited, pensive, glancing back and forth to both of us. I could only respond with a smile so wide it hurt. And yes... maybe a few more tears. I had dreamed of this moment so many times, and it was finally upon us. It was finally, really, happening.

"To beginnings." I tapped my glass to Fletcher's once again. Let the tears slip down my face as Drake copied me.

"To beginnings." He smiled at Fletcher as he uttered this time—and clearly meant it.

I was two seconds away from slamming my glass down and mauling the hell out of Fletcher, when he spoke earnestly again. "I'd like to make one more toast, if you'll allow me?"

How could I deny him? I couldn't count the moments when I'd despaired of that spark ever returning to his eyes. Now that it was back, I'd let him recite the Gettysburg Address as a toast if he wanted.

"I'd like to make a toast to the bond we share. The bond I share with you, my beautiful, smart, stubborn queen—and the bond I share with you, meathead, bastard, asshole...brother. My brother in every sense of the word. My best friend in this lifetime. In any lifetime."

Silence fell over the room, but it wasn't an uncomfortable pause. Just the opposite. It was a moment—our moment—to absorb what Fletcher had just said. To soak up the magic of our new beginning. To reaffirm the infinity of our perfect bond.

It was fitting that Fletcher finally spoke into the stillness. Tears filled his eyes, flowed down his cheeks, and wavered his voice. "I love the two of you so much. I've been an unbearable ass, and I've done nothing to deserve the happiness you both bring me. Nothing. I'm so deeply sorry for the pain and sadness I've brought into our home, but I want us to be us again. To be whole, to be happy. Please say you'll forgive me."

I pushed my chair back so fast it tumbled over backward, crashing to the hardwood floor. It could've fallen into a passage to hell for all I cared. I'd been there, done that, had the T-shirt. I never looked back as I flung myself into Fletcher's arms, all but crawling into his seat with him.

"Please don't leave me." His words mashed against my lips as I kissed him. "Please don't leave us tomorrow either, Tolly. I won't be able to watch you go."

"Let's talk about that later. I think this one wants to say something too." I moved out of Fletcher's embrace, sensing Drake still looming after he righted my chair. He stepped over, offering his hand to Fletch for a manly shake. Fletcher took it but pulled himself to stand with the assistance of his best friend and wrapped him into a tight, grunting hug. It was the very first time I'd ever seen him accept help without cussing or growling.

New beginnings.

"Are we good, man?" I heard him choke out.

Drake backed away, nodded quickly, and then hauled Fletcher back in, doing the whole back-clapping thing this time. "Yeah, fucker. We're good."

"Who wants dinner?" Marcus appeared from the shadows at the perfect time to serve us dinner.

"Smells amazing," Drake commented. "Lasagna?" He pumped a fist when Marcus lowered the dish, the cheese and sauce still bubbling along the top. "Yessss."

"Marcus," I chided. "You don't have to wait on us."

"It's my pleasure, young lady. It's the least I can do." He truly had a servant's heart.

"You've already done so much." Warmth filled my voice.

"Thank you, friend." Fletcher stopped his caregiver with a touch to his arm. "Seriously, thank you. For everything. You've put up with so much shit from me. You deserve a raise at the bare minimum."

Marcus gently chuckled. "Well, you can tell my boss that."

"Speaking of that..." Drake waited for Fletch to lower all the way back into his chair and then stated, "I had a thought today."

Fletcher snorted. "One more than you usually have."

Drake arced a graceful middle finger at Fletcher but kept addressing the burly caregiver. "You can take some time with this, man—and I'm going rogue here, because I haven't talked to them about it yet—but how would you like to leave the agency you're with and work for us directly? You could live here in my old suite at the back of the condo, and we'll work out a schedule so you could still have personal time. Talia and I have jobs we need to get back to, and it's uncertain how long Fletcher is going to require help. You've proven your worth around the kitchen, that's for sure, and maybe if you did some other household shit, it would be a win all around."

I was tempted to knock over my chair again. As it was, I bopped up both hands, shimmying in place with excitement. "My name is Talia Perizkova, and I approve of this message."

"My name is Fletcher Ford, and I do too."

I giggled and swooned in the same sweep of a moment. I'd missed my charming blond prince and his mischievous one-liners. In that luxurious shirt and that sharp new haircut, he looked more delicious than the lasagna. "Seriously"—

back to business. I could start thinking of dessert later—"it's an excellent idea, Drake. With Claire and Margaux going on maternity leave any second, I need to plug back in at work in a big way." The possibility of getting back to the office every day excited me. Now, I could do it guilt-free, knowing Fletcher was in good hands.

"Yeah, that's what got the wheels turning," Drake explained. "Kil and I discussed it this afternoon at the gym. They need a contingency plan, and up until Fletcher's accident, you were a huge part of that plan."

Marcus grabbed the bottle of champagne from the center of the table and held it up in a toast. "Then I want to make a toast to our new beginning too!" We all laughed and clinked our glasses to the bottle he held, just before he put the thing to his lips, winked, and then put it back on the table. "Still on duty, after all."

"Okay, hold the phone—or that bottle, whichever's closest." I shot up a hand, interrupting the boisterous celebration. "I need to address one thing about this plan."

The men sobered into silence, waiting for me to continue.

"Marcus, I'm not sure you're aware of what's going on here, with the three of us." In one swoop of motion, I included Drake, Fletch, and me. "Although things have been different than they normally are, and we've tried to be appropriate when you're around, you need to know a few things if you're going to live here." I met his gaze, trying to convey the gravity of what I was about to say. "You realize I'm in a relationship with both these men, right? We aren't some strange Three's Company reboot. I love them both. We share one bed. We share one love. In every form of the word."

For a second, Marcus just blinked at me. He looked

bewildered, but I didn't know how to be any plainer without using clinical terms, and that sure as hell wasn't going to happen.

"Uhhhh..." He threw that questioning stare to Drake and Fletcher. "Does she always stress the small stuff like this?"

The sellouts responded in unison—all too quickly, I might add. "Always."

I smacked them simultaneously, one with my left hand and the other with my right, but they barely noticed. It was time for Marcus's famous lasagna, which we invited him to enjoy with us. We ate our meal with gusto, excitedly talking about plans for the days to come—though I had the distinct feeling I wouldn't have to worry about accepting a second helping of lasagna. Orgasms burned sixty to a hundred calories apiece. But while I looked forward to that new beginning in our life, this one was worth reveling in. Life had been breathed back into our world, and it made me delirious with happiness.

Finally, we all pushed back from the table with smiles on our faces and contentment in our hearts. And for Fletcher and me, a connection burning brighter than ever.

I stepped over to snuggle into his lap again. With a long sigh, I pressed my forehead to his.

"Do you feel it too?" I whispered.

"I feel a lot of things right now." Again, he unleashed his rapscallion grin. As he lifted his hands around my waist, he took a sliding detour across my ass.

"It's back," I persisted. "I can hear you again."

"I know," he murmured. "I was waiting until you said something."

"Why?" I was genuinely puzzled.

"Well, what if it wasn't back for you? How crappy would

that have been? You might not have noticed, but my ego's been a bit fragile lately." He smirked again, letting me know the self-deprecation would end there.

"You're right. But you know what? I don't think our bond was ever really broken."

"No?"

"No. Maybe bent a little or buried. But there was no broken bond—for any of us. We just needed time. Sometimes relationships need that. We got a giant kick in our ass to make us realize it, but now we all know what really matters, what's most important in our world." I finished my speech with a kiss to his noble nose.

"I love your optimism. I could use some of it at times." His blue eyes danced, lighter than I had seen them in weeks, though traces of frustration lingered in the Caribbean depths too. He already knew, and accepted, that happy didn't cancel hard. Happy just made hard a word we could live with.

I kissed him soundly, so damn proud of him. As I pulled back, I waggled my brows. "Well, stick with me, kid, and I'll show you the way."

"You have yourself a deal, missy." He swiveled his hips, digging his erection into my ass.

"So naughty," I whispered playfully. "Between you and him, a girl doesn't stand a—"

My eyes nearly popped out of my head. I gaped at him. He smirked back.

"Mr. Ford?"

He ground up into me again. "Ms. Perizkova?"

"I do believe there is a...matter...rising between us." I bit my lip. He felt so good. Damn, this boy was ready to go.

"I do think you may be on to something." His irises

deepened, conveying a sole intent.

Beautiful, irresistible man.

I stretched and feigned a yawn, dramatically trying to reel Drake into our conversation. "Well, would you look at the time? I think I'll turn in now."

"Yeah, pretty tired here too. Drake? You coming?"

Drake was already on his feet, having heard every word of our conversation.

"If I'm lucky?" He rubbed the bulge in his jeans, groaning with the contact from his own hand.

"I love you both so much," I sighed.

Drake scooped me off Fletcher's lap, soundly setting me on my feet. "Go get ready for bed, Tolly. And make it sexy, little girl. We have an anniversary to celebrate!" He swiftly smacked my ass before turning me in the direction of our room. Another swat, and I scurried down the hallway to change.

They wanted sexy, huh?

Challenge accepted.

CHAPTER THIRTEEN

Drake

Marcus left with a promise to give our offer some serious consideration. We would have his answer by Monday. I let him have the weekend off, figuring Fletch and I would be spending a lot of time making our woman scream in every octave available to the human voice and maybe that wouldn't be a good first weekend for him in our employ, despite his beyond-cool attitude about our alternative relationship.

If I had my way, there'd be a lot more than screaming involved as well. Shit like moaning, clawing, gasping, and plenty of carb loading in between. Thank fuck for Marcus and his lasagna.

Fletcher was already settled into our bed, thanks to one last favor from his caregiver. Talia was hiding out in the bathroom, hopefully following my instructions to the letter. I turned out the last light, set the security alarm on the panel in the hallway, and walked into our room.

And stopped dead in my tracks.

Fuck me.

Jesus, Mary, and Joseph.

And all the saints.

I'd be sure to confess taking the Lord's name in vain next time I went into a confessional. That, and having impure thoughts. Oh, and premarital sex. And possibly coveting thy best friend's woman.

Screw the last one. Because I planned on doing a lot more to this woman, dressed so gorgeously in the specific ensemble I'd requested, than coveting. Besides, Fletcher was already grinning like a loon, so that canceled out the sin. My Catholic grandmother had to be rolling over in her grave. Sorry, Grams... not.

"Jesus fucking Christ, woman."

I wanted to be more poetic. I really did. But something about the sight before me, with the lingerie perfectly complementing her creamy skin, stripped me of coherent thought. Basic human intelligence fled as all the blood in my body rushed to one pulsing location.

Between my thighs.

Fletcher reclined against a stack of pillows in the middle of our bed. His hand already moved back and forth over the sheet covering his cock. He was loving and hating that boner at the same time. I couldn't blame him. It was past time to get this show on the road.

"Perfection. My God, you are perfection." I moved closer to touch her but stopped. A quick plan coalesced in my mind. By its culmination, the woman would know how much we treasured her.

God knew, we'd sucked the big one lately in showing her.

I walked backward until my knees hit the bed. Whipped my shirt over my head and tossed it to the floor. Except for the two seconds of the shirt's fly-by, I forcefully held her gaze.

When she took a step toward me, heeding the command she saw in my stare, I held up my index finger. "No. Stay there."

She'd be obeying me tonight. Just not in any of the ways

she thought.

She swallowed so hard I could see her throat undulate from where I stood. She already knew something would be different, just not exactly what. Her slight uneasiness was my king-size aphrodisiac. This was going to be so much fun.

She gulped again, bringing on a quick mental image. I saw her swallowing my cock down her throat, just about like that.

Fuck.

I shucked my jeans and boxers in one efficient action. They joined the pile started by my T-shirt, topped off by my socks.

I moved to the bed. Stacked up the remaining pillows so I could lie exactly like Fletcher. I quickly pulled the sheet over my lap, mirroring everything about his position. We were exactly the same—no longer the one who could or couldn't. Equals from the start.

As it should be.

"Turn around," I quietly ordered Tolly. When she just stood, frozen to the spot she was on, I raised an expectant eyebrow. "It hasn't been that long, baby. You shouldn't have forgotten your manners." I kept my voice flat and demanding— in the tone that turned her pussy into an aroused puddle.

Her nostrils flared with an inhalation of fortifying air. Without any more hesitation, she pivoted on the balls of her feet. That extra touch stretched her leg muscles, enhancing the long line of each limb.

"She's killing me. Literally. Death. Right here." Fletcher spoke directly to me.

"I feel you, man. Look at this outfit." I switched from my conversational tone with him back to the Dominant authority she responded to. "Spread your legs a bit, baby. Perfect."

Now, we could see just a sliver of open space between her thighs, accentuating the glorious swell of her ass cheeks. She wore the palest pink, or maybe it was peach—I couldn't fucking tell the difference—butterfly-shaped lace panties. Each ass cheek was barely covered by a butterfly's wing, stretching up to meet the band of satin fabric connecting the front to the back. The bra matched in style, lace cups providing a peek-a-boo view of her dusky nipples through the lightly colored lace.

"Turn back and face us."

Though she heeded my demand, her face conveyed sheer confidence...feminine power. She knew exactly what her body did to our resolve. The longer we stared at her form, the hotter we'd be by the time we touched her.

"Come closer." I waited as she moved, swaying her hips with the two steps she advanced. "Stop there."

"Dying." Fletcher's graveled husk broke the air.

"Right? You can see her pussy through that lace."

Another rough swallow from our girl. She was still uncomfortable when we talked about her sex. From experience, I knew it also turned her on beyond measure.

Fletcher sat up higher, ensuring he got the best angle. "No kidding. I can see it too. My mouth is watering. It's been way too long."

I tilted a "Hey, bro" glance at him, as if we simply discussed water polo strategies or the blueprints I'd brought home from the office. "We could fix that."

"I'm not so sure. I'll come in the sheets the minute I smell her."

"Then I can fuck her while you watch." Not a bad idea at all. I could take one for the team. It was dirty job, but...

"No," Fletcher insisted. "Not tonight. I need to be inside

all that." He pointed back to Talia like she was an object instead of a living, breathing, thinking person. But that was also part of my game. Sometimes the woman started thinking so hard, even at times like this—hell, especially at times like this—Fletch and I swore we could hear the gears in her mind turning.

"You guys." She extended the final hiss, clearly getting irked.

"Did anyone ask you to comment right now?" I arched a new brow, as if I were disappointed.

"No."

"No what?" We didn't go for the yes-Sir-no-Sir protocol, but I always expected her to express herself fully.

"No. I'm sorry," she finally answered.

"Come closer. Right here." I held my hand out for her to take. When she was in the spot I indicated, I dropped her hand. The loss of contact made her shoulders sag.

"Turn around again so we can see your perfect ass." She obliged at once. God damn, she had a delectable rear. "Now put your hands on your knees and bend forward."

"Drake!" She leveled a glare over her shoulder that would castrate a weaker man. It made my dick swell to painful intensity, almost rendering it impossible to keep my features neutral while cocking my head, challenging her to cross me again.

A few beats passed. Slowly, she complied. I sat forward and ran my index finger down her spine, ending at the waistband of those naughty, sexy panties. I did it again. A third time. I loved watching the goosebumps spread across her back and thighs.

"You like this? You enjoy it when I touch you?" My tone was antagonistic—again very much on purpose. I knew she trusted me—hell, probably saw right through me—but very clearly, the woman loved my ruthless boss veneer.

"Yes."

And there was the proof. Her shaky, breathy, oh-God-what-will-you-demand-next tone.

"Yes, what?" I barked it, just to keep her on her toes. It was a cruel game but so, so much fun. She loved this. Her pussy lips were convulsing against the crotch of those heavenly panties.

"Yes. I like it when you touch me." She sighed and hung her head until her chin touched her chest.

"Reach back and slowly pull your panties down." Fuck. Yes. "Stop there."

The magnificence before me...dear, sweet, bloody hell. I was tempted to scoop up my phone and snap some memories to keep, for our eyes only. Taut thighs. That incredible ass, cupped by those peachy lace panties...

"Christ. I'm going to explode over here. Stop tormenting all of us." Fletcher's voice was tinged with fresh pain.

"It's called the slow burn, my friend. Makes the fire even hotter when it ignites." My tone was still matter-of-fact. Just two guys, having a normal convo up in here.

"Except it's been months of burning for me, man." As if he needed to remind me.

"Talia. Pull up your panties before you kill Fletcher."

She looked back over her shoulder, thumbs tucked in the band of her sinful undies, not sure if I was calling the whole thing off or just changing tactics.

"Do it!"

My sharp dictate made her jump. When she settled, she huffed again and then complied. This, right here. It was the best part of her participation when I fucked around with her this way. When she pushed back, just a little, it fired every fucking cylinder of lust in my body. She always yielded in the end, but the tiny bit of rebellion always made my dick surge.

Just like it did now.

For a second, I glanced to the tent I pitched under the sheet. I'd avoided touching myself, afraid Fletcher wasn't the only one about to come apart, but that resolve might have to be changed. Fast.

"Climb up on the bed and straddle Fletcher's face." I motioned to my buddy and his strained scowl.

She shot me another glare.

Silly girl.

"What? Are you the shy thing again now?" I rolled my eyes dramatically. Her pussy had been on that man's face more times than I could count. Ordering her to do it simply added another element of forbiddance. An element she loved.

Fletcher's eyes were riveted on her as she walked around the foot of the bed, approaching him from the other side. She looked over to me, only to find my impassive stare. Not sure how much longer I'd be keeping that up, either.

She climbed onto the mattress, gracefully hitching one thigh over his groin before resting back on her heels.

"Do you need an anatomy lesson, young lady?" I pointed directly at Fletcher's mug, now lowered to the mattress after I pulled the pillows out from underneath him. "All aboard, baby. Now." I swung my eyes to Talia to punctuate the command.

She didn't huff this time. With her chest pumping, her lips parted, and her thighs flexing, she raised her knees and then scooted up his body. Inch by inch she wriggled into position, until she hovered just over his mouth and nose.

"My God, is this a sight. I don't know how much more I

can take, if I'm being honest." I reached under the sheet, finally stroking my swollen cock.

"This was all your idea, dickhead," Fletcher gritted back from between Talia's thighs.

"Says the poor guy with the world's most delectable pussy an inch from his tongue. What are you waiting for, dumb shit? Get in there."

With a deep groan, Fletcher pushed his face up into her cunt. His groan turned into a growl. He was separated from the heaven only by the thin lace fabric. He inhaled deeply, reveling in her luscious, musky smell, before nuzzling into the center of her arousal with his nose.

A low moan curled out from deep in Talia's throat.

"That's a good girl. Let him hear your pleasure, baby. Don't ever hold that back from us. Now, pull your panties to the side. Show us your naked clit."

My cock jumped when she reached down and jerked the lace to the side. Her tan fingers, the peachy fabric, and Fletcher's wet tongue were all jammed into the space between her legs. It was so fucking hot, I had to pinch the head of my dick to stop the threatening orgasm. Eventually I would convince her to let me video one of our nights together—or at the very least, get some pictures. For now, this exact frame would be preserved in my memory forever.

"You are so fucking sexy, Talia." My voice was deep and throaty, rumbling through my chest. "Let him take you with his mouth."

Her chest rose and fell with more violent breaths. Her nipples jutted through the butterfly wings, so hard and erect... perfection.

Fletcher ate at her with ravenous enthusiasm. She was in

the perfect position too. His bum arm and leg weren't even a problem. He could reach all he needed to.

Something shiny caught my eye on the nightstand. When I realized what it was, I had another brilliant idea. I snatched the scissors up without either of them noticing me. They were lost now, giving and taking a hot, steady flow of pure desire.

"I love these panties, baby." I caressed her ass again, enjoying the tactile feel of her silky skin and the scratchy lace coming together. "But, sadly, we'll have to get a replacement pair."

It took her a few seconds to register what I said, but she snapped a panicked look toward her hip just as I slid the metal scissors under the fabric and sliced through it.

"Drake!" she shouted.

"Sorry?"

"Not sorry," Fletcher added in a mumble from between her thighs.

I quickly kneeled up and then scrambled across Fletcher's legs to the other side of the bed. There, I gave the other connecting waistband the same treatment. I pulled the ruined pair of underwear from between her legs and threw them to the ground.

"Now, your hands are free for other things." I waggled my eyebrows at her suggestively when she looked at me over her shoulder, making her burst out in laughter.

"Fuck, I love that sound." I closed my eyes and smiled, letting the feeling wash over me. True happiness for the first time in months. We were all finally home again. I wanted to hold on to this sensation forever.

"I need to fuck you, Tolly." Fletcher snarled it while trying to move her down his body. "Please. God damn. I can't take it anymore."

Talia eagerly shifted, clearly loving that idea. Since I still stood at the end of the bed, I grabbed the flat sheet with one hand and yanked it all the way down to the footboard.

Like a magician's act, Fletcher's hard cock appeared from under the material. Talia's smile widened when she saw how aroused he was. It went without saying that we were all relieved to have survived the impotence phase with few battle scars. If that had gone on much longer, I wasn't sure even I could restore Fletch's manhood for him.

My friend reached down and gripped his cock, stroking the full length a few times while we watched. "I need you so badly, baby. Now. Please."

"You don't have to say it again, my love. I need you too. More than you'll ever know."

She held herself over his shaft while he gripped at the base, steadying the angle. "This is going to be the quickest, most embarrassing fuck of our lives. I promise it won't be like this again."

His apology cut through my lust. "Dick," I jibed. "Don't apologize for making love to our woman. It harshes the mood, you know?" I tried to keep my voice level. Anger could cut the ju-ju just as quickly.

He laughed but quickly sobered. "I'm so fucking hot, it's going to be like my freshman year all over again."

"I don't even want to know what you're talking about right now. Just do it already. Fuck me, Fletcher!"

I went for a full belly laugh, throwing my head back. Her bossiness came at the strangest times, and I wouldn't have it any other way.

My mirth went running as soon as she slid fully down on

Fletcher's cock.

"Fuck!" Fletcher took a turn at the tossed-back head gesture. "Shit. Yesssss. So good." His eyes closed tight and his neck strained taut, a mixture of agony and euphoria defining his entire body.

"Been there, man. Now, just relax and fuck her."

I tried to talk him in off the ledge, but his balls were beyond blue, and our woman did have the most amazing cunt on the planet. Fletcher held her hips with both hands, though he caressed with his left hand while he dug in with his right, sure to leave bruises with its intensity. It provided enough stability to encourage Talia to rise up again and then slide back down with a wicked but graceful pace.

She was so beautiful.

She was so breathtaking.

She was so ours.

I watched them fuck like the shameless voyeur I was, stroking my cock in time with her movements, imagining I was the one inside her. I had to stop short after about the third stroke, since the images in my head became all too real.

"Talia, fuck." Fletcher's thighs constricted. His feet dragged into the mattress, fighting to hold off the release his body demanded. "Baby, slow down. I can't hold on much longer. You feel so good. Too good. Shit!"

I stepped around, wanting to see the answering look on her face. She was flushed and panting, the pillows of her lips parted. Her eyes were brushed with a glaze of gorgeous desire.

I reached up, palming the back of her skull. "Look at you. Our fiery goddess. You love his cock in your cunt, don't you, Tolly?"

"Yes." She gave me the answer without hesitation or

shame. She'd try to be coy about it until the day she died, but this woman was built for passion, desire, and fire. "Yes, I do. I love it. I love his cock. It feels so good. So hard and full. Oh, Fletcher, you feel so good!"

"Oh Goooodddd. Fuck!" One last lunge, and Fletch froze on an upward stroke, his shout signaling his first orgasm in too damn long.

God damn.

I had to move in to satisfy my own needs. I thought I could be the martyr tonight, but now I had no interest in that role.

At.

All.

I strode to the other side of the bed. The second I got there, crooked my finger at Talia. Her eyes were ablaze. After quickly kissing Fletcher, she crawled on all fours toward me.

Perfect.

"Turn around. I want to see your wicked ass, baby. Besides, I want you to get Fletcher back in the game while I fuck you." I pushed her head down, forcing her face right into his lap. She'd know what to do from there. Something about a woman sucking your cock after it's been inside her pussy was a dirty, dirty turn-on. I knew the exact taste she'd experience when she took him inside her mouth.

I slid into her soaked cunt without hesitation, issuing her next command as soon as I was fully seated. "Taste yourself on his cock."

Tolly paused for a second, debating if that was really something she wanted to be a part of, and then went for it with aplomb. Our amazing, unafraid girl.

"Fuck!" Fletcher yelped when her mouth covered his crown. Yeah, he'd be sensitive at first, but that was all part of the enjoyment. The heightened sensation would have him rebooting in no time. Dude had a quick reset time to begin with, but her hot mouth and his dry spell would probably cut the usual in half.

In the meantime, there was her ass. Her ass.

I was helpless against the temptation of both silken globes, raised so perfectly to my thrusts. I need to claim it deeper...

Without announcing anything, I wet my index finger. With my other hand, I spread her flesh a little wider...and then sank my digit at least an inch inside her tight asshole.

Immediately, she tensed.

"Don't even think about shutting me out, girl," I gritted. "Not. Now."

She moaned around Fletcher's semi-erect cock. It sounded enough like a wordless protest that I smacked her buttock with ample force to bloom a red handprint.

"Relax," I mandated. "You love it when we get in your ass too. I'm not buying the whimpering."

I leaned over her butt crack to let a strand of saliva drip from my mouth to the center of her cheeks. With the new "lube," I probed deeper into her hole, twisting my hand with each stroke. Every time my finger plunged, the walls of her cunt closed in tighter on my cock.

Fuck. Shit. Fuck. Shit.

My God. She'd be the death of me.

The hot, satisfied, ridiculously happy death of me.

The muscles in her shoulders relaxed, sending that message all the way down the slope of her back. She trembled, raising her ass higher to me in offering. Who was I to deny the woman what she craved?

I added a second finger to my assault on her ass. Began

fucking her there in time to the rhythm of my cock in her pussy. She wouldn't be the death of me. She'd already found a way to kill me and was now my sweet, searing angel, welcoming me to heaven. I could only wish.

All too soon, the muscles of her channel fluttered. They gripped me tighter and tighter, telling me of her impending climax. She lifted her mouth off Fletcher, needing to release an urgent moan. That was just fine. I needed all her attention now. If he needed to get off again, he'd damn well wait until I did.

"You ready to come for me, baby?" I gritted it, my breaths shallow with need. That was what happened when hearts worked on other things, like pumping gallons of blood into a demanding dick.

"Yes. God, yes!"

"I can feel you clamping down on me." I pulled out of her ass, grabbing her hips instead. With my fingers, I clenched into her flesh, steadying her so I could pound my cock deeper. Jesus, thank you for this angel.

I pumped and pumped and pumped, clinging to the edge of sanity. Hovering on the precipice of a release that had already grown wings, ready to fucking fly.

"Drake. God! I'm coming. Oh, my God. Yes! Yes! So good. Sooooo..."

I shoved her shoulders flat to the mattress. Angled her body so I could stab down into her, nailing her deep with my stiff, aching rod. Her pussy took it. All of it. Vibrated with incredible little flutters, milking the heat out of my balls and up my shaft...

Until I exploded too.

"Fuck! Yes. God damn it, woman. Fuck."

I drove a few more times into her slick pussy before literally collapsing to my knees on the floor beside the bed. I leaned my head on the edge of the mattress. It helped with stopping the room from spinning while I caught my breath.

I seriously wondered if I really had died—because never in my life had I experienced an orgasm as intense as that. And by that point, I'd had a lot of them.

I finally struggled back up onto the bed—well, half of me—though my senses still dog-paddled in the vast ocean of postcoital bliss. Fletcher was already propped against the headboard with Talia snuggled into his side. I flashed them a loopy smirk, and they both laughed. Best damn sound in the world.

"Dude," he muttered, rolling his head and frowning at the frat-boy sprawl of my body. "You okay?"

"Yeah, yeah," I mumbled and then jabbed a finger at Tolly in mock-accusation. "I'm going to kiss you senseless, once I can feel my face again." As she giggled, I groaned. "That was the best fucking load I've ever blown. Fuck." Again, not so poetic but all I could do with a numb face.

Finally, I heaved the entirety of my spent body back up and then slid over so Talia was sandwiched between us. My eyes were closing on their own, the sleep deprivation I'd been suffering since Fletcher's accident finally having its way with me.

"I love you. I love you both so much." Talia's sweet whisper wrapped me in warmth.

"I love you, Talia Perizkova. With all my heart." Fletcher was the first to respond.

"I love yoooouu...mmmnnn."

And the curtain fell for the night.

Show's over, folks. Elvis has left the building.
Don't forget to tip your waitress.

EPILOGUE

Fletcher

"Don't you find it odd that in celebrating the social and economic achievements of the American workforce, we all take the day off from work?"

"Nah, man. That's all you." Drake smiled while giving me a side eye, ensuring I knew he was playing. It was Labor Day weekend, and life was literally the best it had ever been.

"Are you nervous?" Butterflies kick-boxed in my stomach as we buttoned our matching white shirts. Seriously. They were in there with their little mouth guards and gloves, throwing roundhouse kicks and upper cuts at the expense of my entire digestive system.

"Not even a little bit. Wait...are you?" Halfway through buttoning his cuff, he met my eyes in the mirror.

"No. Excited but not nervous. I can't wait to see her."

"Yeah. Do you need help with the cuff?"

"Nope. I got this. Therapy, dude." I thumped my chest. "Good as new. Maybe better. We've come a long way, my friend."

"Yeah, man. We sure as fuck have."

His somber but tender words ushered us both into a reflective silence.

"I still think she should be taking one of our last names,

though." Tradition was tradition, right?

"She beat us fair and square." Drake's dark eyes sparkled with laughter as he brought up our three-way rock, paper, scissors match.

"Pfffft. Who chooses paper? Like ever?"

He threw his head back, laughing with unbridled sincerity. It made me smile even wider than I had been.

All our friends were gathered in the spacious backyard of our new San Diego home. After the fallout with my parents and the car accident that had upturned our entire world, our decision about where we'd permanently settle had been decided once and for all. Drake and I had made some contingency plans with our businesses and put the necessary wheels into motion to establish West Coast branches. The transition had worked out well for Killian and SGC, so we were confident we could make a go of it too. There were still some gummed-up cogs in both our corporate machines, but we actually enjoyed the new challenges in our daily routines.

The most glorious reward for our sacrifice waited for us every night in our bed, where all the stresses of the day disappeared. Talia, with her love and humor and sexy-as-fuck devotion, made all the efforts worth it. She was joyous to settle back into California life, where she could be close to her big family and the job she loved.

Today, we celebrated the culmination of all those drastic changes...

As well as a new beginning.

Our life together, as fully committed partners to each other.

Just a few minutes now...

I still couldn't believe we were here and going to do this.

She was waiting too—waiting to declare our unique and perfect love in front of our closest friends, colleagues, and family. Yeah, there were some significant faces missing from the crowd. For many, our relationship continued to be too unconventional for them to celebrate, and we took that in stride. In the end, love was love was love, and all that mattered was making our woman deliriously happy—and she'd made it very clear that this would be a huge way of doing that. What girl didn't want to be a bride, walking down the aisle with love in her eyes?

She'd surprised the hell out of both us one night during the summer with the idea...with her proposal. We had been outside on the patio, enjoying the cool ocean air after a sweltering afternoon, and she'd blurted she'd been wanting to ask us an "important question," but had no idea how to express it in the right words. She'd sat between us, then handed us each one side of a pair of earbuds.

As soon as she'd hit Play on her smart pad, Bruno Mars's great voice had filled my ear. He'd sung to us about what a beautiful night it was, followed by the shocker,

Hey, baby, I think I want to marry you...

By the time our jaws had lifted from the deck, she'd produced two identical platinum wedding bands. And when the chorus hit—don't say no no no no no, just say yeah yeah yeah yeah yeah—we had both been grinning so wide, we likely had looked deranged. Hard to pinpoint the exact sequence of events after that, but we'd ended up in a sweaty naked pile right on the living room floor.

Thankfully, Marcus had gone out that night.

As I slipped on the jacket to my traditional tux, I looked at my best friend, who did the same. "I'm not sure I believed this would ever happen for us."

"Pretty crazy, right?"

"Beyond." We'd gone from legendary bachelors to two over-the-moon-happy grooms.

Drake's parents and sister sat in the front row of white wooden chairs set up on the lawn. They'd flown in a few days before, and Talia had kicked into nonstop tour guide-mode, showing them all the visitor trappings of her hometown.

Drake and I were hitting our limit of abstinence after the second night of houseguests, but once he'd reminded me about the "slow burn," we'd started planning our wedding night instead of focusing on our frustration.

I fiddled with my bowtie for another minute and finally sent a help-me-with-this-shit look to Drake. I'd never been good at these damn things even before the accident. How Mr. Marine mastered the task was beyond me. I was supposed to be the one with all the finesse.

After my accident, Drake had proved he was the master at a lot of things I'd never given him credit for. I owed him my life, now more than ever. He'd not only held his shit together when I'd been unable but had given Talia the strength and stability she needed too. I always said I'd lay my life down for him without a second thought, but he'd proved the sentiment went both ways by putting his on hold for me.

Physically, I was back in pre-accident shape. All the muscle weakness had been conquered during intense physical therapy and, as soon as my energy returned, some casual water polo matches. We'd already joined a team in San Diego, ribbing Killian that he was too pussy-whipped to join us. Of course, that had prompted him to immediately sign the membership contract too.

The Stones sat right behind Drake's parents. Killian

beamed from the end, right beside his stunning bride and baby mama. Claire cooed at the swaddled pink bundle in her arms. Beside her, Margaux Asher and Michael Pearson sat with a fussy pink bundle of their own. Bets were already being placed on how long until that little princess was stomping her foot in demand. The apple didn't fall far from the tree, after all.

"All right, you two. It's time. We ready?" Marcus ducked his head into the guest suite, where we were getting ready. Shortly after we'd gotten engaged to Talia, we'd sat down with him to float the idea of him moving to the West Coast with us. Barely two seconds had gone by before he'd readily agreed. Southern California was hard to turn down.

Talia's father had relented and would give her away. Our relationship still wasn't something her parents bragged about to their friends, but in the end, their daughter's happiness mattered more than their stubborn ideals.

I couldn't wait to see her walk down the aisle to us. I'd been dreaming about it since the moment she'd set this crazy ball into motion with that damn song.

"Let's do this." Drake's drill of a rally cry shook me from my daydream.

We took our places in front of the crowd. This was it.

All the smiles and eyes were on us—until the first few chords of the romantic Russian orchestral song were played. While this ceremony was initially for us, some traditional things had been added to pacify Tolly's parents.

And there she was.

The crowd turned in unison to watch as Talia Maria Perizkova appeared on her father's arm at the far end of the rose-petal-covered path.

Stunning.

More than that.

She took my breath away.

She wore a white dress, of course, but that was where the similarity to any other wedding dress I'd seen ended. It looked ethereal, flowing from her arms in a gauzy, sheer fabric. The front dipped down in a deep V between her breasts and then gathered at the waist. The back was exactly the same, making me want to find a wrap to cover her with so every man in attendance wasn't gawking at the perfection of her skin.

She looked like a goddess

She looked like an angel.

It really seemed as if she floated across the lawn to stand with my best friend and me. We were the luckiest men alive.

Vows were exchanged, tears shed by the three of us as well as most of the guests. Everyone there knew what kind of players Drake and I had truly been before we'd met Talia—well, except her family, and what they didn't know wouldn't hurt them in this case. The Perizkovas did sense the hell I'd put us through with the accident.

But most importantly, everyone knew how much this amazing woman had completely changed our world.

Had changed us.

We had given Talia a pear-shaped diamond ring, selected with help from Margaux, Claire, and Taylor. When it was time to kiss our bride, we were both ready to throw her over our shoulder, get the fuck out of here, and find somewhere for a private celebration of our own—but we were good. At least for now. We shared a meal, drinks, and laughter with our friends and family, letting everyone bestow their well-wishes upon us. I felt like the king of the world dancing with Talia for the first time as one of her husbands. We spun her back and forth between us, basking in her radiant glow.

Celebrating our love.

Knowing she was our one.

The one who made us whole.

The bond who'd keep us glued together for all time.

She would forever inspire us to be the best men we could be—for ourselves, for one another, but most importantly, for our beautiful Natalia.

Continue Secrets of Stone with Book Eight

No White Knight

Available Now
Keep reading for an excerpt!

EXCERPT FROM
NO WHITE KNIGHT

BOOK EIGHT IN THE
SECRETS OF STONE SERIES

CHAPTER ONE

Mac

"Okay, ladies—single ladies, that is—it's time for the bouquet toss!"

The DJ might as well have shouted "Last call" during spring break in Cabo. I smirked at the comparison—which wasn't a far stretch—as the dance floor, otherwise known as a bunch of flat wood squares fitted together across the private San Diego estate's back lawn, was packed with female lemmings hoping to catch the coveted ball of flowers about to be tossed by the glowing bride. Giggles, doe eyes, slutty dresses, and sky-high heels abounded.

I was tempted to sneer again.

Until the little throng seemed to part for her.

Her.

The tiny blonde I hadn't torn my eyes away from for the last six hours.

Damn her.

I would've been tempted to say it out loud, if I wasn't so consumed with thinking about fucking her.

Luckily, I only knew a handful of the wedding guests, or someone would've noticed my stalker moves as I navigated the party's perimeter, darting in and out of Mission-style archways and their terra-cotta shadows, angling for a better view of the dance floor. Not that I gave a rat's ass what they all thought, anyway. The only element keeping me around at this point in the party was her, the woman who'd consumed my attention from the second I'd spotted her earlier, while the wedding party had mingled with guests before the bride and grooms exchanged their vows.

Ohhh, yes. Bride and grooms—and the three of them still glowed with happiness now, after openly exchanging rings of commitment to their unusual style of love. And I'm the big expert of love all of a sudden? I did, however, know a thing or two about unusual—and that description was getting a workout today when it came to describing that stunning little number and her stranglehold on my dick.

What is this bullshit? The thrill of the hunt? There was nothing thrilling about this muck-fest. As far as I could tell, she hadn't realized I was at the wedding, let alone near this hilltop or even breathing on the same planet. Funnily, three women out on that dressed-up plywood with her had already tapped their numbers into my cell phone. Just as fast, I'd erased all three. They were invisible to me, even now.

She was it.

The quest. The prey. The big-game kill in a tiny, sassy-as-fuck body.

Damn her.

I still couldn't stop staring at her.

Taylor Mathews. Well, at least I knew her name. We'd met somewhere in the last few months, though I couldn't pinpoint the exact day and time. That shit was for people who had time to burn, and I wasn't one of them. The clock just wasn't that important to me. Things happened either before or after I operated on a patient.

Before or after I'd changed a life.

I had performed such a feat—emergency brain surgery—on the fairer of the grooms, Fletcher Ford. Taylor Mathews had been at Talia's side throughout the entire ordeal, but not just "sitting by" her friend. She'd fought valiantly for Talia, even standing up to me when she had to. Not a lot of men had that courage, let alone women. And from what I could glean from overheard conversations, Taylor had even remained in Chicago for most of Ford's recovery too.

So is she Talia Ford now? Or Talia Newland? That was the last name of the other groom, his dark head tossed back in laughter while watching their woman prepare to chuck her bouquet.

Maybe she'll just go for the trendy and hyphenate it at Ford-Newland. Keeping the peace, and all that. Can't be easy, since they're both such stubborn bastards—not that I noticed much of anything about them beyond the surface facts. Not concerned with the color of their fucking underwear.

Now, Taylor Mathews? I care about her underwear. Even better, about ripping it right off her.

My hypersensitive mind, ping-ponging from subject to subject with its regular fury, had suddenly bounced me into the danger zone. Trouble was, I didn't want to leave—especially as that blond spitfire strutted to the head of the pack on the dance floor like she owned every splinter in those wooden planks. Just the sight of her shifted me into overdrive, a very dangerous gear for me. I hadn't had anything more than a quick fuck in two years.

But Taylor Mathews was an engine class all her own.

She drew me, even now. Spoke to me without words. Awakened something inside, calling to base urges on levels I hadn't experienced in a long time. Who am I kidding? That I hadn't experienced ever. My throat burned as if I'd just chugged gasoline, rather than the craft beer in my death grip. My bloodstream was churning pure rocket fuel. And my cock?

Right now, I was really trying to ignore that bastard. Like he was agreeing to that bullshit. Every chance he could take, the message got pushed at me like a telegram stamped Urgent. It had been like that for hours, the primal yearning to make myself a part of her, becoming a fantasy fueling the better part of my thoughts for the entire afternoon. I could even pinpoint the exact second they'd begun. I'd been watching her from a strategic vantage point, one of the tables set off from the rest of the wedding bustle, placed for guests needing a reprieve from the Labor Day weekend sun—so while I was cloaked in shadows, she wasn't. Like I said, abso-fucking-lutely-perfect—until some young hipster jackass tried making a play for her. The douche nozzle couldn't scrape together two brain cells long enough to read Taylor's body language, mistaking her surface small talk for a prelude to the winning touchdown. He kept babbling until she faked a buzz on her phone and then a nonexistent text before her "apology" about being needed for some last-minute wedding emergency. I'd grinned from ear to ear as she bounded from the idiot faster than a gazelle spooked by a lion.

But goddamn, did I want to be her lion.

The commotion of the crowd roused me back to the unfolding "fun" on the dance floor. I refocused in time to watch the bride, escorted by both her proud grooms, flash a conspiratorial wink at Taylor, who nodded like a quarterback about to get the key snap of the game. The crowd oooed and ahhhed as Talia posed between her men, who leaned in from the sides to press tender kisses on her cheeks, freezing that way as the photographer captured their bliss on film.

After that, it was game on.

Talia flashed the group of women one more teasing look—

Before turning and tossing the ball of flowers directly to Taylor.

Pass complete. I chuckled along with the crowd as the little blonde tucked the prize to her chest, preparing to run for the proverbial end zone if needed. After a quick look around to confirm nobody was going to dare fight her for the prize, Taylor relaxed and straightened, her composure returning to regal queen status. Her face was the most fascinating part of the transformation, especially the telling glimmer in her eyes. I wondered if anyone else saw it besides me...how the reigning sovereign only existed on the outside. Inside she was still an imposter, no matter how court-worthy her jewelry or dress.

And what a dress it was. The material, some combination of firm but silky, was spun into the palest blue I'd ever seen, matching the cloudless Southern California sky at the spot where it met the horizon along the Pacific. Her china-doll skin looked even milkier next to the fabric, and I longed to run my fingers across her collarbones, where the skin seemed even thinner. The heart-shaped bodice hugged her frame, and the fabric ended just above her knees, making me wonder if they tasted as good as they looked.

Fuck.

I wanted to taste more than her knees.

A lot more.

Just like that, lust and need climbed on their mental motorbikes, churning my mind into a goddamned festival of filth. I thought of grabbing that woman by the hand then and there and hauling her away someplace private inside the house. Parking her sweet ass on a table, a dresser, a bed, anywhere, so I could hike up that gorgeous blue silk-satin-stiff whatever and then yank her panties off so fast, she'd gasp and writhe—urging her wet pussy up toward my waiting mouth. Then I'd taste her. Drown in her. Suck down every drop of her until she had no choice but to come for me, preparing her sweet cunt for the stretch of my aching cock...

"Holy shit." My harsh mutter interrupted my fantasies just in time. I shifted balance to get my dick back under some kind of control.

For fuck's sake. I didn't even know that much about her. All right, she was gorgeous. No. Stunning. She had an energy, perhaps even an edge, that made a man want to find an excuse for lingering in her vicinity—or, if he was a ballsy hipster, even trying to impress her enough to surrender a phone number. But she needed to eat more, judging by her bone-thin frame— though even her figure, what I could see of it, turned me on. She looked delicate and acted fierce. When that temper of hers was piqued, the cutest fucking Southern drawl set in too. She did it every time. Believe me, I knew. I swear, just the sight of me set off a dozen of the woman's hot buttons. Don't get me started on our conversations, if that was what they could be called.

Every. Single. One. Of. Them.

My dick started twitching again. Then throbbing. Just remembering her comebacks and insults, always infused with sass and sarcasm and passion, had actually forced my hand at having to follow and contribute to a conversation. What the hell? I didn't "converse" with people. I talked, people listened, orders were followed. End of story...

Until Taylor Mathews had started rewriting my narrative.

The woman would not be taken advantage of, that was for damn sure.

Not ever.

"Okaaaayyyyy, bachelors!" The DJ's shout hauled my attention back. "It's your time to shine now. Get on out to the dance floor so we can see who catches the garter from the grooms." He motioned toward Taylor with exaggerated enthusiasm. "That lucky fella gets to slide that thing up this beautiful belle's leg!"

Wait.

What?

In half a second, I forgot all about the ham's hokey phrasing, homing in on the implication of what he'd just said instead.

My hands. On her leg. Up her leg.

Far up her leg.

The crimson flush on the woman's face gave away how the concept had hit her brain like shock paddles. She'd definitely forgotten how this stupid ritual worked when making such a pro catch of the bouquet.

Well, isn't this going to be interesting?

The recognition instantly jolted my mind and body to autopilot—though it was my personal version of it, usually saved for the times a patient was split open for me on the operating table. The intensity was the universe's glaring reminder of how my knowledge and skill were the only things saving this person's life. Though the stakes were different now, they felt just as important—just as key to validating I had a purpose on this planet beyond mere existence.

Whatever.

Cosmic dribble aside, I was certain of one key thing. While this was a hell of a lot more complicated than brain surgery, I refused to accept failure.

Whatever.

That meant some key prep work. I hustled onto the dance floor, driven and determined, though kicking myself for not having my camera at the ready to capture the look on Taylor's face as I did. Our gazes locked for a few seconds, and I inserted half a smirk in place of stopping and admitting those blue depths nearly drowned me like the midnight wave they resembled, before she averted first. That didn't hide the little twitches at the corners of her mouth, making me guess at what incited them. Was she dealing with nervousness? Happiness? Excitement? Or covering up a case of sheer dread?

She gave me no time for further deciphering. The next moment, her emotions were schooled again behind a mask of gorgeous detachment. She stared with impressive blankness into the mob of guys collecting around me.

Fuck.

I had to catch that goddamned thing.

Which meant high-alert tactics were officially in order.

With a fast sweep, I wheeled in on the center of the crowd and indicated to them all that I needed a tight huddle. With arms hooked around the guys to either side of me, I leaned in and assumed instant quarterback mode. Thank fuck everyone seemed copacetic about the new pecking order.

"All right, fuckers, listen up. The blonde with the bouquet? She doesn't know it yet, but she's mine."

The guy to the right of me, flashing tatted muscles and a huge grin, nodded. "Prime choice, dude."

"Good. Because I'm going to catch that garter or will beat down the fucker who does."

"We're behind you, buddy."

I thanked the guy with a solid smack to the back while circling my stare back around the group. "Everyone else good?"

While the rest of the group didn't do much but grunt and stare, I sensed the overall receipt of my message, especially when I straightened and clapped my hands, breaking the huddle.

Round One handled.

Now for Round Two—represented by the groom selected to perform the garter-tossing duties, a sublime and smiling Fletcher Ford. Or maybe his shit-eating grin was because his own hands had just been underneath his woman's filmy white dress, reaching for the treasure up her own thigh—"treasure" being open to interpretation. Were the woman's panties now tucked in his pocket along with the garter? Or maybe he and Newland had ordered their bride not to wear anything down there today. I snorted. I didn't know those two that well, but instinct told me they were the kind of kinky bastards to do just that.

My kind of kinky bastards.

The thought made it easier for me to motion Ford over. I wasn't comfortable with the buddy-buddy rah-rah act just for the hell of it, but right now I was a man on a mission, and he strode over as if sensing just that. At my motion to lean in closer, he complied.

It was time to talk like men.

"Dr. Stone."

"Mr. Ford."

"Now that we've gotten that out of the way..."

I barely gave his sarcastic chuckle a look. Humor often seemed a waste of time to me, and this was definitely one of those occasions. "Down and dirty? I catch the garter, all right?"

"Uhhhh." Another snicker, this time more arrogant. "All right. I can't make promises..."

I rammed his shoulder with mine. Hard. More wasted time on sarcasm. "You can, and you will," I dictated from between locked teeth. "You owe me."

"That I do." He was sober now. Properly so. Probably had something to do with staring into the face of the doctor who'd made it possible for him to be alive for his wedding day at all.

"So this'll happen?" I pressed. His answering grin, which could've lit the whole San Diego skyline, came as proper confirmation.

I watched as he jogged back over to Drake, letting him in on the plan too, before swinging my attention back to the other side of the dance floor—and the adorable little blonde now comprehending how thoroughly her fate was sealed.

She gaped, eyes wide and mouth wider. In return I smirked, but just a little. She volleyed by tightening her features into a glare, realizing exactly what I was up to. I returned the shot by waggling my eyebrows, letting my lips broaden into an arrogant, evil smile.

That's right, spitfire.

I'm coming for you.

If I had my way, she'd be coming for me by the end of the night. At once, at least twenty scenarios bloomed in my mind. All the sinful, filthy things I could do to quench the blue flames raging in her gorgeous eyes.

Rope, tape, cuffs, zip ties...

"Three...two...one!"

At that, Fletcher tossed the garter over his shoulder...

This story continues in
No White Knight: *Secrets of Stone Book Eight!*

ALSO BY ANGEL PAYNE

**For a full list of Angel's other titles,
visit her at AngelPayne.com**

ABOUT ANGEL PAYNE

USA Today bestselling romance author Angel Payne loves to focus on high-heat romance starring memorable alpha men and the women who love them. She has numerous book series to her credit, including the popular Honor Bound series, the Secrets of Stone series (with Victoria Blue), the Cimarron series, the Temptation Court series, the Suited for Sin series, and the Lords of Sin historicals, as well as several standalone titles.

Angel is a native Southern Californian, leading to her love of being in the outdoors, where she often reads and writes. She still lives in Southern California with her soul-mate husband and beautiful daughter, to whom she is a proud cosplay/culture con mom. Her passions also include whisky tasting, shoe shopping, and travel.

Visit her at AngelPayne.com

ABOUT VICTORIA BLUE

International bestselling author Victoria Blue lives in her own portion of the galaxy known as Southern California. There, she finds the love and life–sustaining power of one amazing sun, two unique and awe-inspiring planets, and four indifferent yet comforting moons. Life is fantastic and challenging and every day brings new adventures to be discovered. She looks forward to seeing what's next!

Visit her at VictoriaBlue.com